Stuart Neville

STOLEN SOULS

Harvill *Secker*

LONDON

Published by Harvill Secker 2011

2 4 6 8 10 9 7 5 3 1

Addresses for companies within The Random House Group Limited can be found at:
www.randomhouse.co.uk/offices.htm

The Random House Group Limited Reg. No. 954009

A CIP catalogue record for this book is available from the British Library

ISBN 9781846555992 (hardback)
ISBN 9781846554520 (paperback)

The Random House Group Limited supports The Forest Stewardship
Council (FSC®), the leading international forest certification organisation.
Our books carrying the FSC label are printed on FSC® certified paper.
FSC is the only forest certification scheme endorsed by the leading environmental
organisations, including Greenpeace. Our paper procurement policy can be found at
www.randomhouse.co.uk/environment

MIX
Paper from
responsible sources
FSC® C016897

Set in Adobe Garamond by Palimpsest Book Production Limited,
Falkirk, Stirlingshire
Printed and bound in Great Britain by
Clays Ltd, St Ives plc

For Jo, and everything to come

PART ONE: GALYA

I

Blood hot on her hands. Red. The brightest red Galya had ever seen. Her mind tilted, her vision disappearing down a black tunnel.

No, don't faint.

She gasped, pulled air in, and with it a copper smell that went to her stomach and grabbed it like a fist. Bile rose to her throat. She swallowed.

The man's legs shook as she tried to withdraw the shard of glass, a strip of bed sheet wrapped around one end to form a grip for the improvised knife. She jerked. His eyes gaped. She twisted, feeling the glass grind against a hardness deep inside his neck until something snapped. The blade slipped free of the new mouth it had opened beneath his chin. Red bubbled from it and spread across his Lithuania football shirt, swamping the bright yellow.

Galya stepped back as the blood advanced across the linoleum towards her bare feet. It licked at her toes, warm kisses from the dying man who slid down the wall as his eyes dimmed.

A scream rushed up from her belly, but she clamped her free hand over her mouth, trapped it behind her teeth. The hand was slick on her lips, and then she tasted it.

Galya's gut flexed, and vomit streamed between her fingers. Her legs dissolved. The floor came at her like a train. She sprawled in the wetness and the heat, tried to scramble away from it, but it was too slippery against her bare skin.

The scream came again and this time she could not hold it back. Even though she knew it would kill her, Galya let it burst free, a terrified bird escaping from the cage of her chest.

The howl dragged every last swallow of air from her lungs. She inhaled, coughed, breathed in again, brought her mind back under control.

Galya listened through the rushing in her ears.

Silence, save for the choked bubbling from the man's throat. Then a knock on the bedroom door. Tears came to her eyes, frightened little-girl tears, but she blinked them away. She was not a little girl, hadn't been since Papa died almost a decade ago.

Think, think, think.

The glass blade still rested in her bloodied fingers, the tip missing, the rag grip soaked through. Maybe she could keep them back. They would see their dead friend and know she could do the same to them.

Another knock, louder. The door handle rattled.

'Tomas?'

Fear cut through her. No, she could not keep them back with this piece of glass. Again, the urge to weep. She pushed it away once more.

'Tomas?' The voice slurred out some more words. She knew a little Lithuanian but not enough to understand the drunken questions coming from the other side of the door.

'You all right in there?' Another voice, the English spoken with the hard twang of this strange, cold place. 'Don't be leaving any marks on that girl.'

How many were there? Galya had listened to the voices as they arrived. Two spoke Lithuanian. One of whom now lay beside her on the floor. The other spoke English with an accent strong enough for her to hear that he was Irish. One of the two brothers, she thought. After a week of listening to their conversations through the locked door, she had learned one was named Mark, the other Sam. Only one of them was here tonight.

'Tomas?' A fist hammered the wood. 'Listen, stop fucking about in there. I'm going to kick this door in if you don't come and open it.'

Galya got to her knees, then up on her feet, the air chilling the wetness on her stomach and thighs. The plain grey sweatshirt and pair of jogging bottoms they'd given her lay on the dressing table. She grabbed them, juggled the glass from hand to hand as she pulled

4

them on, feeling the fabric stick to the blood. Foolish, perhaps, but she felt safer clothed.

The door rattled with each thump. Beyond it, the other Lithuanian cursed.

'Fuck's sake,' the Irishman said.

Galya blinked as the door jerked in its frame, the noise booming in the bedroom. She backed towards the corner, gripping the glass knife in front of her. Another boom, and the light bulb swayed on its cord above her head. She wedged herself into the angle where the two walls met. The glass quivered in front of her eyes.

She prayed to her grandmother, the woman who had always protected her and her brother ever since they had been orphaned. The old woman had been Mama to them as long as Galya could remember. Now Mama lay in the ground hundreds of miles away where she could no longer give protection. Galya prayed to Mama's departed soul, even though she did not believe in such things. She prayed that Mama would look down on her granddaughter and take pity, oh please Mama, come down and take me away please Mama oh pl—

The door burst inward, slammed against the wall and bounced back. The Lithuanian blocked it with his shoulder as he entered. The Irishman followed. They stopped when they saw the dead man.

The Lithuanian made the sign of the cross.

The Irishman said, 'Fuck me.'

Galya shrank into the corner, made herself as small as she could, as if they wouldn't see her cowering there.

The Lithuanian cursed and shook his head, his eyes watering. He rubbed his big hand across his lips.

'Jesus, Darius,' the Irishman asked, 'Is he dead?'

'Look like yes,' Darius said.

'What do we do?'

Darius shook his head. 'Don't know.'

Sam – Galya was sure this was Sam – said, 'Fuck me'.

'We all dead,' Darius said.

'What?'

5

'Arturas,' the Lithuanian said. 'He kill us both. You brother also.'

Sam said, 'But we didn't—'

'No matter. We all dead.' Darius pointed a thick finger at the corner. 'Cause of her.'

Sam turned to look at Galya. She raised the glass blade, cut the air in front of her.

'Why you do this thing?' Darius asked, his face slack with despair.

She hissed, the glass sweeping in an arc at his eye level.

'Don't waste your breath,' Sam said. 'She doesn't speak English.'

Galya understood every word. She choked back a giggle at the deception, felt her mind flutter like a flag in the wind, ready to tear itself free. For a moment she thought she might let it go, let insanity carry her away, but Mama had not raised her to give in so easily. She bared her teeth and showed them the blade again.

'What are we going to do?' Sam asked.

'Get rid him,' the Lithuanian said.

Sam's eyes brightened. 'What, dump him?'

'We say Arturas, you brother come here, take her out of this place, no come back. Arturas ask where go, we say we know nothing.'

'Will he believe us?' Sam asked.

The Lithuanian shrugged. 'We say real thing, we dead. Arturas don't believe, we dead also. What different?'

Sam nodded to the corner. 'What about her?'

'What you think?' the Lithuanian said.

Sam blinked and stared at him.

'Go.' The Lithuanian stepped aside. 'Take *stiklas* from her.'

'Take what off her?' Sam asked.

'*Stiklas, stiklas*.' The Lithuanian searched for the word. 'Glass. Take from her.'

Sam approached, hands up. 'Easy, love. Take it easy.'

Galya slashed at him, almost caught his forearm.

'Shite!' Sam retreated.

Darius pushed him back. 'Take from her.'

'Away and shite, *you* get it off her.'

The Lithuanian cursed and bulled his way past. Galya swiped the

6

glass blade through the air in front of him, but he caught her wrist in one easy movement. He twisted once, hard, and the blade dropped to the floor. His thick arm snaked around her throat, and she smelled leather and cheap aftershave with her last breath before everything fell away into darkness.

She dreamed of Mama's coarse hands, and warm bread, and a time when she only knew Belfast as that wretched place they sometimes talked about on the radio.

2

Screams woke Detective Inspector Jack Lennon. He shot upright on the couch. How long ago had he dozed off? Not that long. The film still played on the television.

Another scream and he was on his feet. It had been a week or more since Ellen had last erupted from her sleep, howling at the nightmares that dwelled there.

His daughter had witnessed more suffering than any human ever should. Lennon was constantly surprised that she could function at all, that she had the inner strength to go on. Maybe it was the stubborn streak she had inherited from the mother who had died beside her. He had left Marie McKenna's body to the flames when he'd carried Ellen unconscious out of that house near Drogheda. She never spoke of what happened there. Perhaps she didn't remember, or simply didn't want to recount the events. Either way, Lennon was relieved. He wasn't sure he could bear to hear it from her lips.

Alert now, Lennon went to her bedroom, opened the door, and flicked on the light. Ellen stared at him from under her twisted duvet, no hint of recognition on her face. She screamed again.

Lennon knelt beside the bed, placed a hand on her small cheek. He had learned not to take the child in his arms when she awoke pursued by night terrors, the shock of it too much for her.

'It's me,' he said. 'Daddy's here. You're all right.'

Ellen blinked at him, her face softening. He'd almost forgotten how old she looked when she emerged from her nightmares, a girl of seven carrying centuries of pain behind her eyes.

'You were only dreaming,' Lennon said. 'You're safe.'

Her fingers went to her throat, brushed the skin as if it were tender.

'What did you dream about?' he asked.

Ellen frowned and burrowed into her pillow, pulling the duvet up so he could only see the crown of her head.

'You can tell me,' Lennon said. 'Might make you feel better.'

She peeked out. 'I was all cold and wet, then I couldn't breathe. I was choking.'

'Like drowning?'

'Uh-uh. Like something around my neck. Then there was this old lady. She wanted to talk to me, but I ran away.'

'Was she scary?'

'Uh-uh.'

'Then why did you run away?'

'Don't know,' Ellen said.

'You think you can get back to sleep?'

'Don't know.'

'Can you try?'

'Okay.'

Lennon stroked her hair. 'Good girl,' he said.

He watched her in silence as her eyelids drooped and her breathing steadied. The ring of the telephone in the living room caused her to stir for a moment. He held his breath until she settled, exhaled when it seemed the phone had not woken her, and went to answer it.

'It's Bernie McKenna here,' the caller said, her voice hard.

They had spoken on the phone and in person more times than he could count over the last few months, but still she introduced herself with that stiff formality.

'How are you?' Lennon asked. His only interest in her well-being was to gauge how the conversation might flow. Their discussions rarely went well.

'I'm fine,' she said. She did not enquire after Lennon's health. 'What about Ellen?' she asked instead.

'What about her?' Lennon regretted the hostility that edged into his voice as soon as he'd spoken.

'No need for that tone,' Bernie said, the words delivered in a staccato rhythm as if squeezed through tight lips. 'She's my grand-niece. I've every right to ask after her, more right than you—'

'You didn't want to know her for six years,' Lennon said. He winced.

'Neither did you,' she said.

Lennon swallowed his anger. 'Well, she's fine. She's in bed.'

'Any more dreams?'

'Some.'

Bernie clucked. 'Her eyes were hanging on her last time I saw the cratur.'

'Some nights are better than others,' Lennon said.

'Did you call Dr Moran for her?'

'My GP has her on the waiting list for the child psych—'

'But she'll be waiting for months. Dr Moran can see her straight away.'

Lennon saw the rest of the conversation spreading out in front of him. He closed his eyes. 'I can't afford to go private,' he said.

'*I* can,' Bernie said. 'Michael saw us right. I can spare whatever she needs.'

Lennon had heard rumours of the substantial estate Michael McKenna's kin had inherited when he'd got his brains blown out last year. He didn't doubt Bernie could afford to pass on a few shekels, but the idea of it burned him.

'I don't want Michael McKenna's money,' Lennon said.

'And what's wrong with my brother's money?'

'I know where it came from.'

He listened to Bernie's hard breathing for a few seconds before she said, 'I don't have to take that from the likes of you.'

'Then don't,' Lennon said. 'I've things to do, so if—'

'Hold your horses,' Bernie said. 'I haven't even got asking what I called you for.'

He sighed loud enough for her to hear. 'All right. What?'

'Christmas.'

'We talked about this already. Ellen's spending the day with—'

'But her granny wants to see her. That poor woman's been through hell. Ellen's all she's got left of her own daughter. What's the sense in making the child spend the day all alone in that flat of yours?'

'She won't be alone. She'll be with me.'

'She should be with her family,' Bernie said. 'Her grandmother, her cousins, all of our ones will be here. Let her have a nice day. A happy day. Just because you're miserable, don't make her miserable too.'

'I'm taking her to see her grandmother – *my* mother – then she's spending the day with me. We're having dinner with Susan from upstairs, her and her wee girl Lucy. They're best friends. She'll be happy here.'

'You're taking her to your mother? Sure, what's the point of that? Your mother hasn't the wit to know her own children when they're in front of her, let alone—'

'That's enough,' Lennon said, his throat tightening. 'I have to go.'

'But what about Chr—'

He hung up and placed the handset back on the coffee table, fighting the urge to throw it against the wall. How many times would he have to argue this out with Bernie McKenna? Ever since Marie died, her family had been circling, waiting for him to slip up so they could claim his daughter for their own.

True, he hadn't been a father to the girl for the first six years of her life, but they had been no more a family to her. Marie's people had cut her off when she took up with him, a cop, long before Republicans changed the stance they'd held for decades and acknowledged the legitimacy of the police service. Until then, any young Catholic who joined the police immediately became a target for assassination, and anyone who associated with them risked being ostracised from their community. Marie had done just that, and he had repaid her sacrifice by abandoning her when she fell pregnant. These arguments only served to remind him that they had all failed Ellen, and they always left him wishing he had some moral high ground he could take. But there was none. His was the worst betrayal of all, and Bernie McKenna would always hold that over him. Anger bubbled in him after every call, and only force of will would quell it.

Before he could fully calm himself, the phone rang again. He snatched it from the coffee table, ranting before he'd hit the answer button. 'For Christ's sake, you're going to wake her up. I am not discussing this any more so, for the last time, you can—'

'Jack?'

'—shove Christmas up your—'

'Jack?'

Lennon paused. 'Who's that?'

'Chief Inspector Uprichard.'

Lennon sat down on the couch, covered his eyes with his free hand. 'No,' he said.

'I need you in, Jack,' Uprichard said.

'No,' Lennon said. 'Not again. I told you, didn't I? We agreed this. I'm not doing nights over Christmas. I can't.'

'DI Shilliday's taken ill,' Uprichard said. 'I've no one else to cover for him.'

'No,' Lennon said.

'It'll be an easy night. It's quiet out. You can sleep in your office. Just so I have someone on site, that's all.'

'No,' Lennon said, but there was no conviction behind it.

'I'm not really asking you, Jack,' Uprichard said, his voice hardening. 'Don't make me order you.'

'Fuck,' Lennon said.

'Now, there's no call for that.'

'Yes, there bloody is,' Lennon said as he stood. 'That's the fourth time this month.'

He almost said he knew where it was coming from, that DCI Dan Hewitt of C3 Intelligence Branch was pulling strings to make his life difficult, but he thought better of it.

'I'm sorry,' Uprichard said. 'That's just the way it is. I want you here in an hour.'

Susan opened the door wearing a dressing gown pulled tight around her. In the few minutes between Lennon phoning her and knocking on her door, she had tidied her hair and applied as much make-up as she could manage. Either that or she went to bed wearing lip gloss.

Ellen huffed and mewled in Lennon's arms, her bare feet kicking at his sides.

'You're a diamond,' he said to Susan. 'I can't thank you enough.'

Susan gave him a smile that was at once warm and weary. 'It's all right. I hadn't gotten to sleep yet.'

Lennon knew a lie when he heard one, but still he was glad of it. 'I'll be back before you get up in the morning.'

Susan reached for Ellen. 'C'mere, pet, I've got you.'

Ellen whimpered and rubbed her eyes.

Susan kissed her hair. 'You can sleep in with Lucy, all right?'

Ellen buried her head beneath Susan's chin. She had been ferried here while she slept many times before.

Lennon touched Susan's forearm. 'Thank you,' he said.

She smiled again. 'When you come back, why don't you come in for breakfast?'

'The neighbours might talk,' Lennon said.

'Let them,' she said.

3

The plastic-covered corpse rolled against Galya as the car jerked to a standstill, its bloody odours forcing her to gag against the cloth that had been shoved in her mouth. She wedged her shoulders against the rear wall of the boot and pushed the body back with her knees. They'd used some sort of thin electrical cord to bind her wrists but already it had worked loose on her blood-slicked skin. She could easily slip free from it, but instead chose to keep it there until her hands could do her some good.

Galya felt the car rock as the men alighted, heard the doors slam shut. The last few minutes of the journey had been slow – sharp turns and sudden stops – before a final lurch and judder as the car came to a halt on rough ground. She strained to listen to the sounds beyond the blackness that encased her. Traffic noise somewhere but, closer, the soft sigh of water.

As soon as she'd woken in the dark, her head throbbing with the car's engine, Galya knew they meant to kill her. There was no question. The sound of water only confirmed it. They would dump the dead man in it, then throw her in after. Maybe they'd kill her first, or maybe they'd drown her. Either way, she would be in the water soon.

Voices now, outside, the Irishman's high and panicky, the Lithuanian's low and angry. They exchanged accusations and curses as they came closer. A key scraped against metal, the lock turned, and cold air flooded in.

A cloud of mist formed between Darius and Sam as their breath mingled. The Lithuanian grabbed his countryman's body and hauled it from the boot, grunted as he let it drop to the ground with a wet thump.

Galya did not resist when Sam reached for her. The icy ground seemed to bite at her soles as he held her upright. She bucked with the intensity of the shivers that shot through her, and he gripped her arms tighter.

The car, an old BMW, stood feet from a stretch of water, parked on a narrow band of waste ground separated from the empty road by a low kerb. All around were warehouses and cranes, quiet and still in the cold night. Lazy waves lapped at the embankment. Across the channel, more warehouses, and the lights of the city beyond them. Galya tried to turn her head to see more of the surroundings, but Sam squeezed and jerked her arm.

'Quit it,' he said, as much to himself as to her.

Darius stooped and grabbed his dead friend's ankles. He pulled, but managed no more than two feet, the plastic snagging and tearing on the rubble. He cursed and dropped the body's legs.

'Help,' he said.

'What?' Sam said.

'Help,' the Lithuanian said. 'Put Tomas in water.'

'I'm keeping hold of her,' Sam said, tightening his grip on Galya's arm.

'Where she go?' Darius asked, holding his hands out, indicating the expanse of water and low buildings. He pointed at the corpse on the ground. 'You help.'

A clammy heat lingered on Galya's arm when Sam released it. He pushed her back against the car.

'Don't move,' he said.

He crossed the few feet to the body, hunkered down, gripped the shoulders.

Darius said, '*Vienas, du, trys, hup!*'

Both men hissed as they raised the body a few inches from the ground. They shuffled towards the water's edge, huffing and grunting as they went. A bloodstained hand flopped from the plastic and brushed its fingertips along the loose stones.

'Jesus,' Sam said.

A thin distorted disco beat erupted from nowhere, and he yelped in fright as he dropped the dead man's shoulders.

Galya took a step away from the car.

Darius lowered the feet and straightened. Something vibrated on the body. He reached down and tore a hole in the shiny plastic. His hand explored inside for a moment before emerging again, a mobile phone gripped in his thick fingers. His face went slack when he looked at the screen, its light making him look even paler than he already was. He glanced at Sam.

'Is Arturas,' he said.

Sam swallowed so hard Galya heard the click in his throat. 'Are you going to answer it?' he asked.

Darius gave him a hard stare. 'You a stupid man. I answer, say brother busy? Say he go in water, yes? I say to him this?'

Sam shifted his weight as if the insult had hit him square in the chest. 'Well, fuck, I don't know. He's your boss, not mine.'

Galya moved to the far side of the car.

'Arturas everybody boss,' the Lithuanian said.

Sam took a step forward. 'He's not mine.'

Darius held out the phone, still blasting its tinny music, his podgy face swelling with anger. 'Okay, you say he not you boss, you say him now.'

'Fuck yourself,' Sam said.

Galya flexed her wrists, felt the electrical cord skim the backs of her legs as it slipped away.

Darius stepped over the body, came face to face with Sam.

'You think you big man?' he asked, the phone still alight and ringing in his hand.

Two metres separated Galya from the car now. She pushed the cord aside with her toes, kept her hands behind her back. She pressed her tongue against the rag between her teeth, pushed it out and let it fall to the ground. She steadied her breathing.

Sam moved to the other side of the body. 'Listen, this isn't the time for getting the arse with each other, right? We need to get this sorted before anyone comes along and asks us what we're doing here at this time of night.'

Darius would not be placated. 'You need take care your mouth, or you go in water also.'

Sam raised his hands.

Darius slapped them aside.

Galya ran.

4

Arturas Strazdas hung up without leaving a message. He thought for a moment as the car sped along the motorway towards the city, the driver's attention fixed to the road ahead. Tomas always answered his phone. It didn't matter if he was in bed or at a funeral, he never left a call unanswered if his mobile was in reach. Many times Arturas had phoned his brother only to hear hard panting and moaning on the other end as he rutted with one of the whores.

Once, Tomas had hospitalised a cinema-goer for complaining at the disturbance caused by his taking a call during a screening of some romantic comedy. It had taken several days, and some expense, to convince the victim they were mistaken in their identification of the attacker.

Tomas had always been trouble, but Strazdas had promised his mother he would care for his little brother, no matter what. He had repeated the promise just a few hours ago, before he left her in the Brussels apartment he'd bought for her and caught the flight to Belfast.

She had complained bitterly about being left alone at Christmas but it could not be helped. There was business to attend to and, as much as Arturas loved his little brother, Tomas could not be trusted with such a responsibility.

Strazdas had texted Tomas before he boarded the plane, reminding him to be ready for his arrival, that he needed him at the hotel that night. Now Tomas did not answer. Strazdas returned the mobile to his breast pocket and considered.

There were many reasons why Tomas might not have answered his phone, of course. But none were good enough for Strazdas. Clearly something was wrong.

'Herkus,' he called.

'Yes, boss?' The driver glanced back over his shoulder.

'When did you last see Tomas?'

'A few hours ago,' Herkus said. 'He and Darius were drinking in town. I had to pick them up in a hurry. They'd gone into the wrong bar, some place for queers. You know how Tomas is about queers.'

Yes, Strazdas knew how Tomas felt about homosexuals. That particular foible had cost him some money over the years. Between bail and pay-offs, caring for Tomas was like keeping an exotic animal. Its prey was expensive.

'How bad?' Strazdas asked.

'Not very bad.' Herkus shrugged. 'Not much blood on his hands. Darius got him out of there before he did any real damage. I lifted them a few streets away.'

'And then?'

'Tomas said he wanted to break in that new whore. The Ukrainian girl. Being around queers always makes him want a whore.'

Strazdas watched the city lights draw near, buildings solidifying in the dark.

'Which Ukrainian girl?' he asked.

'The one Rasa took from the mushroom farm last week,' Herkus said. 'The agency put her there, working under Steponas. She'd been there a month or six weeks, maybe, when Rasa spotted her. She was covered head to toe in horse shit, but Rasa can pick out a looker from a hundred metres. The Loyalists paid two thousand for her.'

'Good money,' Strazdas said.

'Like I said, she's a looker. Darius told me. Young, skinny, nice mouth. Good tits. They were putting her to work for the first time today. Tomas said he was going to get her off to a good start.'

'Where are they keeping her?'

'Bangor direction,' Herkus said. 'North-east of the city, past the other airport.'

Strazdas retrieved his phone from his pocket. He looked up Darius's number and dialled. It went straight to the answering service, didn't even ring.

'After you leave me at the hotel, you go looking for Tomas and Darius,' he said.

'Okay,' Herkus said.

5

Galya had been a runner ever since she was small. She'd been the fastest in her school district, winning every medal and trophy the regional championships had to offer. Mama displayed them in the old china cabinet she had inherited from her own grandmother forty years before.

As Galya reached her teens and her bones lengthened, she found the 5000 metres to be her best event. At fourteen, she trained three times a day, edging ever closer to running the distance in fifteen minutes. She remembered the cold early mornings, closing the door of Mama's house behind her, jogging to the track in the village, listening to the sounds of the world awaking as she devoured lap after lap.

The coach had wanted to put her up for the athletic school, said she'd sail through the trials; they might even start grooming her for the Olympic team. But that would have meant going away and leaving Mama all by herself to work the few acres of land she owned. So Galya turned down the chance and ran purely for the heart-racing pleasure of it.

Now she ran for her life.

Her arms pumped. Frosty tarmac chewed at the naked balls of her feet. Her lungs grabbed at cold air.

She had a twenty-metre start before they realised she had gone. Sam had tripped over the dead man in his panic to get after her. She heard him hit the ground and cry out in pain, leaving only Darius to pursue her, his footsteps heavy as he propelled his bulk forward.

Did they have guns? Galya did not believe so; she would have heard them boom by now, felt the bullets slam into her back. How would it feel?

She dismissed the thought.

Up ahead an open gate, a dock beyond. Behind, running feet, lumbering, unable to close the distance. She did not look back. To do so would be to lose her balance and rhythm. Galya knew this was the essence of running. Balance and rhythm granted speed and minimised fatigue. If she lost those, she would lose ground to them. If she lost ground, she would die.

Breathe.

In, two, three, four, out, two, three, four . . .

She heard the ragged stabs of Darius's breathing. He was not a sprinter, but he had no endurance either. Not like Galya. If she could keep ahead of him long enough, keep out of his reach, his legs would give up, the muscles' craving for oxygen too great to carry him any further.

In, two, three, four, out, two, three, four . . .

Galya heard him roar as he found a last reserve of speed. But she had more. Despite the pain as the salted road surface tore the skin from her feet, she pushed harder. He was closer now, his desperate gasps gaining on her. He cried out again as his pace faltered.

In, two, three, four, out, two, three, four . . .

She spotted the ice in time to lengthen her stride and she cleared it easily. Darius did not. She heard him slide, then the soggy thump of flesh meeting hard ground, and finally the wheeze of air knocked from his lungs.

The Lithuanian grunted and cursed behind her as he hauled himself to his feet. He was big and strong, but he was slow. She could outrun him, she had no doubt of that, but the pain dragged at her ankles and the chilled air spiked her lungs.

In, two, three . . .

Galya couldn't hold it in her chest, it was too cold. Her rhythm skipped.

Out, two, three . . .

The breath hissed from between her teeth, her balance lost along with it. She commanded her mind to concentrate, her body to follow its lead, but the pain wouldn't stay in her feet. It crept up her ankles to her calves, shortening her stride, speed deserting her.

The Lithuanian's thudding footsteps drew closer. He huffed and gasped, but he held his pace.

The open gate stood only metres away. Inside the yard she could make out great black mounds against the city lights. Coal, maybe, or stones, and towering machines and low huts. Places to hide, if she could reach them.

But the pain and the cold. They stabbed at her legs, tightened around her chest.

The Lithuanian came closer still, so close he could touch her if he reached out.

Galya prayed as she ran.

Mama, help me, help me, make me faster, let me—

Blinding light, a screech, a thump and a cry.

The car, a big four-wheel drive, came from a side road. She felt the displaced air as it missed her and hit the Lithuanian. She heard him hit the ground hard.

A door opened and a voice called, 'Stop!'

Galya kept running, though her long strides had turned to lopsided lurches.

The voice called again. 'Stop! Police!'

She slowed, spared a glance over her shoulder.

The car bore coloured markings and had the words HARBOUR POLICE emblazoned on the side. Galya halted, her fear mixing with confusion.

'Don't move,' the policeman said. He turned his attention to the man sprawled in front of the car. He spoke into a radio. 'Bobby, we better get an ambulance down here.'

The radio crackled in reply.

'Because I just ran somebody over.'

A longer burst of static.

'I don't know. He's alive. He's moving, like. Corner of Dufferin and Barnet Road.'

Galya fought the adrenalin, forced herself to be still, to wait.

The policeman noticed the car by the water, the plastic-wrapped bundle on the embankment. He spoke into his radio again. 'Better get some PSNI boys down here too.'

More crackling.

'That's what I'm going to try to find out. I don't like the look of it, whatever it is.'

He turned back to Galya. 'Right, love. What's happening here?'

She opened her mouth to answer, but remembered what she'd been told about the police in this country. The gangmasters had warned them all on the farm, and the workers remembered the stories they'd heard from others. The police hated immigrants, would arrest and beat them. The lucky ones got kicked out of the country; the rest went to grey prisons for years, abandoned to a system that would let them rot in the dank bowels of its detention centres.

Galya looked down at herself and saw blood had soaked through her clothing and coated her hands. She had killed a man not an hour before. If the police got her, she would be treated as a murderer. Did they still hang murderers here? She took a step backwards.

The policeman extended a hand towards her. 'Listen, love, no one's going to hurt you. Just stay—'

An engine roared. He turned to see the old BMW accelerate towards him.

Darius got to his knees.

'What the fuck is going on?' the policeman asked. He reached for the pistol at his hip, but Darius grabbed his wrist. He looked into the policeman's eyes as he rose to tower over him.

Once more, Galya ran.

6

For the second time that night, a phone's shrill call caught Lennon at the edge of slumber. He jerked awake, cold in his darkened office, and reached for the handset.

'Yes?'

'Call from Sergeant Connolly,' the duty officer said. 'Sounds like a bad one.'

'Christ,' Lennon said, wiping the sleep from his eyes. 'All right, put him through.'

Lennon listened to clicks and beeps while the call bounced down the wires before he heard Connolly's strained breath. Sounded like he was fighting the cold. Connolly was a good officer, still young enough to remember why he joined up but old enough to have had his eyes opened to the realities of the job. He'd made sergeant quicker than most, and was angling for detective. Lennon reckoned he'd have it sooner rather than later, but for now he was stuck on patrols.

'Go on,' Lennon said. He knew Connolly would give it to him matter-of-fact, no dressing it up.

'Me and Eddie McCrae took a call to come to the Harbour Estate,' Connolly said. McCrae, his partner, was still a constable despite being ten years older. 'One man dead – confirmed by me – one man injured. We've an ambulance on the way. Eddie's giving him first aid, but it looks bad. And here's the thing: he's a harbour cop. You'd better get down here.'

Lennon slumped in his chair. 'All right, give me thirty minutes.'

He hung up and dialled an outside line. He listened to the tone for six rings before an alcohol-soaked voice answered.

Detective Chief Inspector Jim Thompson, the officer in charge of Lennon's Major Investigation Team, yawned at the other end as he listened. When Lennon finished relaying Connolly's message, Thompson said, 'You could've told me all this in the morning. I'm having a get-together here.'

'You're the head of my MIT,' Lennon said. 'I'm supposed to report to you first.'

'And you're the senior officer on duty. You took the call. You bloody deal with it.'

'I don't have enough men to get a full team together.'

'It's pitch black outside. There won't be a proper examination of the scene until the morning, anyway. Just get a Medical Officer down there, and anyone else you can get hold of. Make sure the scene's secure and everything's done that needs doing. The ACC can take over tomorrow. I'm sure you're capable of doing that, at least. Now, don't call me again unless the sky's falling in, understood?'

'Understood,' Lennon said.

He would never fathom how Jim Thompson had made Detective Chief Inspector. Lennon had been on Thompson's Major Investigation Team for four months now and he'd yet to see his superior officer take responsibility for anything he didn't absolutely have to. Thompson called it delegation. Lennon called it passing the buck.

Nevertheless, it was true that little could be done tonight except secure the scene and have the Medical Officer certify death, and then the Assistant Chief Constable would assign an investigation team in the morning. All Lennon had to do was make sure all the right boxes were ticked for now. Still, the idea that Thompson would happily carry on his Christmas festivities while a man lay dead by the water stuck in Lennon's throat.

It seemed he had no luck with Detective Chief Inspectors. He sat here tonight because of DCI Dan Hewitt. There was no way to prove that, and Lennon had to concede there was a fair chance the notion was only paranoia on his part. But it was a powerful notion when coupled with the knowledge that Hewitt had sold Lennon out more than a year ago, costing Marie McKenna her life, and had almost done the same for Ellen.

Hewitt had many secrets, and Lennon had uncovered enough of

them to make things difficult for his former friend if he ever chose to reveal them. For now, he kept the information filed away, some of it in his head, some on paper. For the last year he had scoured case files, looking for connections between Hewitt and cases that had failed to reach prosecution. There was precious little on record because his old friend was a member of the most secretive branch of the force, C3 Intelligence, whose clandestine dealings were rarely revealed outside their own secure offices.

But Lennon had some of them stored in a locked box back in his apartment. Not enough to bring Hewitt down, but certainly sufficient to raise some awkward questions for him if push ever came to shove.

Perhaps nothing more than coincidence caused so many late-night shifts to come along at short notice. It could be by chance that so few of Lennon's old informants were still willing to talk to him. Evidence was mislaid all the time, of course, but two of Lennon's cases had fallen through when he'd brought them to the Public Prosecution Service and couldn't back them up because items had disappeared from storage.

Or it could be that DCI Dan Hewitt had whispered in certain ears, had nudged certain elbows, had forced certain hands. Lennon guessed that Hewitt wanted to make life at Ladas Drive Station as difficult as possible for him in the hope that he'd transfer away.

But Lennon would not oblige. Instead, he would continue to come in on nights like this when he'd rather be at home with his daughter. It was the same stubborn streak that made him resist the McKenna family's desire to bring Ellen into their fold, and he knew there was no logic to it.

He lifted the phone and began to make the necessary calls.

When Lennon arrived, the paramedics were loading the injured harbour cop onto the ambulance. Only his mouth was visible through the dressings and neck-brace. Another uniformed harbour officer watched them close the doors. Lennon noted the markings on his epaulet.

'You're the injured man's superior?' he asked.

The sergeant looked at him for a moment, confusion on his face, before he answered. 'Sorry, yes. I'm Bobby Watts. I was on the desk when it happened. It was me called the PSNI patrol after Smithy radioed in. Jesus, he sounded worried, but I didn't think it would be anything like this.'

'Detective Inspector Jack Lennon.' He extended his hand to Watts. 'I'll be the Senior Investigating Officer until the ACC sets up a team in the morning. What happened?'

Watts told him about Constable Wayne Smith's nervous call, how he fully expected it to be some drunk who'd wandered in front of the patrol car, and that as he'd made his way to the scene of the accident he'd cursed the prospect of the paperwork and the substantial claim that would surely result. He arrived a few minutes before the Police Service of Northern Ireland car to find something altogether different.

'I never saw the like of it,' Watts said, shaking his head. His eyes watered and his breath misted. 'Harbour work is quiet, you know? The odd bit of thieving, some traffic stuff, that's about the height of it. Nothing like this, even when the Troubles was going full scud. They took his weapon, too.'

'Shit,' Lennon said. Whoever was crazy enough to put a cop in hospital was now also wandering the city with a Glock-17 in his pocket. He wrapped his overcoat tight around himself as the cold bit hard. Connolly approached from the direction of the water, his fluorescent yellow jacket buttoned up tight.

Lennon tugged the paramedic's sleeve as he went to get back into the ambulance's cabin. 'How is he?' he asked.

'Not great,' the paramedic said. 'But I've seen worse. Apart from the cuts to his scalp, I don't see any sign of damage to the skull. But we won't know much until he has a scan. His vitals are good, though. We're taking him to the Royal. Call A&E in an hour or so – they'll have a better idea then.'

'Thanks,' Lennon said. He turned to Connolly. 'Well?'

'The dead man's mid-thirties or thereabouts. Going by the tattoos and the clothes, I'd guess Eastern European. Looks like a stab wound to the throat did for him.'

'All right,' Lennon said. 'Let's take a look.'

They moved towards the body, but Watts called after them. 'What do you want me to do?'

Lennon considered telling him to go back to his office – he couldn't be any help here – but he didn't have the heart. Instead, he said, 'Why don't you stay with Constable Smith's car? Make sure no one interferes with it before it gets cordoned off.'

Watts looked up and down the darkened road. Even though there wasn't a sinner to be seen, let alone to threaten interference with the car, he said, 'Aye, right, good thinking.'

'Thanks,' Lennon said, grateful Watts hadn't taken offence at the condescension. There was nothing useful the harbour cop could do here, but to send him away would be a greater insult than allocating a nonsense task.

Lennon and Connolly made for the water again, their footsteps crisp on the frost.

'It's a cold one,' Connolly said to break the quiet.

'Yep,' Lennon said.

'How's your wee girl?'

'She's fine.'

'Good.'

'Looking forward to Santa coming?'

'Yes.'

That thin trickle of conversation took them to the water's edge, and the corpse wrapped in black plastic. The covering had torn away where the bundle had been dragged over the stones, and more had been pulled back to reveal the face and torso.

'Did you open it up?'

'Yeah,' Connolly said, 'just so I could confirm no sign of life.'

'Okay. But make sure it doesn't get disturbed any more than it has been. The Medical Officer should be here soon. Aside from that, no one else touches him, right?'

'Right,' Connolly said.

'Torch,' Lennon said, holding out his hand.

Connolly pulled one from his belt and gave it to him.

Lennon shone the light on the ground so he could choose his

footing without trampling any evidence. The beam found the length of electrical cord and a wad of material – what looked like a piece of torn bed sheet – that lay a few feet away.

'What about these?'

'They haven't been touched,' Connolly said. 'Could be litter, there's plenty of it lying about, but I don't think so.'

'Neither do I.'

Lennon hunkered down beside the body. The face was round and blunt-featured, the hair cropped short, the mouth open to the night. Already frost formed on the lips. A deep gash beneath the chin spread into what resembled a dark red bib.

'Doesn't look like a knife,' Lennon said.

'No?' Connolly asked.

'Not clean enough.' Lennon held the torch beam close, the light finding the recesses of the wound. 'See how it's torn, rather than cut? Something more jagged did this.'

Lennon quietly hoped the case would not be assigned to Thompson's MIT. The senior officer, or his deputy, would be required to attend the post-mortem. Knowing Thompson, he would assign Lennon the duty of standing there while they cut this poor bastard up.

'There's tyre tracks over there,' Connolly said.

Lennon moved the torch's beam over the loose stones and earth. The tracks were faint, the ground frozen hard, but they were there all right. A car had been parked here tonight.

He scanned the patch of ground between the tracks and the body for footprints. All he saw were the slightest of impressions, nothing useful.

'Care to amaze me with some logical deduction?' Lennon asked.

Connolly shuffled his feet. 'Well, I suppose someone maybe drove here to dump the body. The harbour cop disturbed them before they could get it in the water, he got a beating for his troubles, and they ran.'

'I think that's some pretty good supposing,' Lennon said.

'There's one thing, though,' Connolly said.

Lennon stood. 'What's that, then?'

'I think I know his face,' Connolly said.

7

Arturas Strazdas opened his laptop on the hotel suite's desk and powered it up. He sat down in the leather-bound chair, a luxurious sofa to one side of the room. A few seconds later he had connected to the hotel's Wi-Fi network. He called up the website for European People Management, a labour agency that was jointly owned by him, his brother and his mother. Half a dozen such agencies operated in the British Isles and throughout the rest of the EU, and all of them were owned by some combination of his closest family members.

But only Strazdas knew their inner workings.

He logged on to the website's secure admin area with a username and password he changed every seven days and followed the links until he found a list of migrants registered as having been assigned work within Northern Ireland. They were all listed as Polish, Czech, Lithuanian or Latvian nationals. He filtered the list down to females who had left employment in the last three weeks.

One listing.

It said she was Lithuanian and gave her name as Niele Gimbutienė. Strazdas knew this to be false. He clicked on the link to see her full profile. There were two images, one a scan of a Lithuanian passport, the other a head-and-shoulders shot of the girl. A casual examination, such as a tired immigration official might give, would suggest the photographs matched, that this girl was indeed a Lithuanian national with every entitlement as an EU citizen to live and work legally in the United Kingdom.

But if you looked closely at the eyes, the height of the cheekbones, the set of the mouth, you might suspect this girl was not the one pictured on the passport. And you'd be right.

The notes said this girl had left her job at a mushroom farm in

County Monaghan just over a week ago and was no longer associated with the agency. Strazdas knew this was not untrue, strictly speaking, but the reality was a little harsher. If the notes were entirely accurate, they would say she had been purchased from the agency by another party, along with the passport on which she had travelled. Perhaps the passport would be used to gain passage for some other pretty young woman with blonde hair, blue eyes, and Slavic features. But this girl was still somewhere in Belfast.

Strazdas knew in his gut that Tomas was in trouble. Did this skinny girl have something to do with it? He had no reason to suspect so, but he had learned over many years in business to be mindful of all possibilities.

His mobile phone rang. He lifted it from the desktop, checked the display, and answered.

'There's no answer at the apartment,' Herkus said. 'I can't see any lights from outside. I don't think they're here. I'd break in, but all these places have reinforced doors. I'd need a battering ram to get through.'

'All right,' Strazdas said. 'Check whatever bars Tomas and Darius drink in. Get more men if you have to. I want them found tonight.'

He did not wait for Herkus's response before hanging up. Strazdas returned his attention to the picture of the girl.

'What did you do with my brother?' he asked.

His cheeks warmed as the sound of his own voice reverberated in the empty room. Talking to himself. His mother had lectured him earlier that day, saying he was working too hard, putting himself under too much stress and strain, not sleeping. A man's mind could only take so much, even a man as strong as Arturas Strazdas.

Strazdas did not argue with his mother. No one argued with Laima Strazdienė.

His father certainly hadn't. As a teenager, Arturas had sat at the table in the two-room apartment the family shared in Kaunas, Tomas facing him on the opposite side, their father between them. The fourth place often remained empty when they ate. They would talk to drown out the grunts from the other room as their mother took care of another visitor.

At night, Arturas and Tomas would share the fold-out bed in the same room while their parents talked on the other side of the wall. Or rather their mother talked, and their father listened.

To feed us, she would say, to keep us warm.

Once, Strazdas had asked her about the visitors who came and went at all hours. She threw hot coffee in his lap. His father took him to the university hospital, told him to keep his questions to himself.

His father left their home not long after the Soviets released their hold on Lithuania. He said nothing, left no note, was simply no longer at the table. Strazdas's mother would not discuss it, as if the man had never existed.

Soon, men were not the only visitors. Often there were young women, and they would take the men into the other room while Arturas and Tomas ate with their mother at the table.

Three months later they moved to an apartment that had two bedrooms. The brothers hoped this would mean a room of their own, but instead it allowed two girls to receive visitors at any one time. But there was money for Tomas to go to a good school and for the older brother to attend university.

As a student, Arturas took an apartment of his own. Under his mother's guidance, he also allowed a room to be used for the entertainment of lonely men. He discovered that he liked having money in his pocket and good clothes to wear. The other students were jealous when he acquired a car, albeit a used one.

Then there was an incident with Tomas and a teacher at his school, and they had to move away to Vilnius.

Laima had always indulged his younger brother, fool that he was. For every soft kiss on Tomas's cheek, it seemed Arturas received a hard slap. Still, looking back, he did not hate her for it. Not really. After all, she had taught him how to make a good living from the weaknesses of others.

Arturas Strazdas stood and crossed the room to the elegant glass-topped sideboard. Herkus had left a small package there, a cellophane bag containing an amount of white powder. Good stuff, Herkus had said, straight from the source. Go easy on it, he had said. Maybe get some rest before taking any.

Strazdas opened the bag's seal and poured a little of the powder onto the glass. Using the hotel's key card, he divided and shaped the powder into three lines. He took a fifty-euro note from his pocket, rolled it into a tube, inserted one end into his left nostril, and inhaled.

The world snapped into focus.

He shivered as he exhaled, moved the rolled-up note to his other nostril, and inhaled the second line.

His head lightened.

Strazdas switched the note back to his left nostril and took the last line. He threw the note aside and bent down, licked the last of the powder from the glass. As his tongue slipped across the glossy surface, tingling from the cocaine, he opened his eyes and saw their reflection. He stood upright and stared at himself for a moment.

'Fuck you,' he said.

His wits sharpened, his heart beating harder, the air sweeter than it had been before. He grinned at the powder-streaked face in the glass. His phone chimed and, somewhere inside himself, he thought he might have sensed the coming call seconds before it sounded. Some might dismiss that as nonsense, but Arturas Strazdas was not an ordinary man. He was a great man. He could do anything.

Or perhaps that was the cocaine talking.

He sniffed hard and wiped his nose before crossing back to the desk and lifting his mobile. His soul withered a little when he saw the name on the display.

'Yes, Mother,' he answered.

'You didn't call,' she said, her voice jagged like broken slate. 'You said you'd call when you landed, and you didn't. Why not?'

'I've been busy,' Strazdas said.

'Not so busy you couldn't call your mother, let her know you got there safe.'

'No.'

'And how is Tomas?' she asked.

Strazdas closed his eyes. 'Why are you up so late? It's the middle of the night. You should be sleeping.'

'And so should you,' she said. 'You didn't answer my question. How is Tomas? I haven't seen him since he went to that awful place.'

Strazdas had never been able to lie to his mother. 'I haven't spoken with him,' he said.

'Why not?' she asked, making no attempt to disguise the worry in her voice. 'Have you phoned him?'

He took a breath. 'Yes. He didn't answer.'

'But Tomas always answers his phone.'

'I know.'

'Even when he's with one of his women, he answers his phone. There've been times I wish he hadn't, but he always does.'

'I know.'

'Then find him,' she said. 'Don't dare talk to me again until you've found him.'

The phone died in his hand.

'I won't,' he said.

8

Galya didn't know how long she'd hidden in the shadows before making her way through the fenced-off yards to the rubble and steel of this building site. She had spared one glance over her shoulder to see the big Lithuanian slam his huge fist into the policeman's head. She had heard the sickly slapping of fist on flesh as she ran, and for a short while, the policeman's cries.

Lorries and cargo containers stood sentry outside a warehouse, along with piles of rusting machinery and giant sacks of concrete. She found the dark pools between them, immersed herself there where the orange street lights couldn't touch her.

Soon she heard the BMW's engine rumble as it advanced along the road, nearing her hiding place. It came into view, only metres away, its engine rumbling. It stopped, a door opened, and the big Lithuanian climbed out. His breath plumed around him.

Galya clasped a hand over her mouth in case he saw the warm air seeping from her lungs.

He stood staring into the blackness. For a moment, she was certain he looked directly into her eyes. His body leaned forward as if he was about to take a step closer to her hiding place but Sam called from inside the car, 'We have to go.'

'She here,' the Lithuanian said.

'There's no time. The cops will be on their way. They'll be here any second. For fuck's sake, come on.'

The Lithuanian turned to face him. 'You no say me what do.'

'What?' Sam peered out at him, his face slack with disbelief. 'I'm not having this out with you now, for Christ's sake. Get in the car or I'm leaving you here.'

The Lithuanian's shoulders slumped. He returned his gaze to the shadows. 'I know you here,' he said. 'I know you speak English. I not stupid like this man. You stay in dark. I find you, you dead. Tomas brother find you, you dead. Police find you, you dead.'

Galya shrank further into the dark. The Lithuanian took one more step forward.

'Yes,' he said. 'Arturas own police. Police give you to him. Then you dead. Arturas hurt you bad, hurt you long time. Then you dead.'

He drew a finger across his throat and grinned.

'Come on,' Sam said. 'I'm not asking again.'

The Lithuanian climbed back into the BMW. Its tyres skittered on the ice before he closed the door, and the car disappeared from Galya's view.

How long ago had that been? How long had she hidden in the dark there? The shivering had become uncontrollable, her limbs jerking and bucking. She knew she had to move or the cold would get her. She had seen it before, how the hypothermia took old Vasyl on the neighbouring farm. No money for fuel, he had burrowed into a pile of rags at the bottom of a wardrobe to die. Like an animal, Mama had said, digging its own grave.

It was the arrival of another car with HARBOUR POLICE on its flank that got her on her feet. Galya clung to the shadows as she fought to put one foot in front of the other, her arms and legs feeling like they belonged to a drunkard. The icy air robbed her of her balance as she tried to quicken her pace.

A foolish part of her almost welcomed the growing numbness in her feet, blocking the stinging pain, but then she remembered how Papa had lost parts of his own body to frostbite. She wiggled her naked toes to keep the blood flowing to them.

Through the lorry cabs and stacked sacks of concrete, in the orange-lit distance, she saw the policeman kneel beside his fallen colleague. While his attention was on the stricken man, Galya emerged from the darkness to cut across the road and lose herself in the night.

She had half-run, half-walked perhaps a quarter of a mile or more, keeping the rumble of the motorway on her right, water on her left, when she heard the sirens. That was when she had come upon the stretch of steel skeletons, a row of buildings under construction.

Galya squeezed through a gap in the barrier that had been erected around the site. Four storeys of girders rose above her head. She kept to the edge of the site, her focus on the ground in case a hole might swallow her. For every step she took, she first explored the earth and stones with her toes. Her vision failed as she moved further into the site and away from the street lights.

An old church stood adjacent, on the other side of the plywood wall, its arched windows showing no light from within. Galya skirted its perimeter until she reached the far side of the building site and found a hinged door secured by a padlock and chain. She pushed against it, opening a gap of only a few inches, and crouched down. Her slender shoulder fitted through the opening beneath the chain, but her head jammed tight in the gap. Coarse wood scratched her cheek. She put all her weight against the barrier, and splinters dug at her ear as she squeezed her head through. A thin cry escaped her as she lost skin and hair to the wooden edges before she finally forced her other shoulder through. She fell to the ground and snaked her torso and hips between the panels. But for the stinging frost, she might have rested there for a moment.

Instead, Galya fought her way upright. Her limbs were back under her control at last, the wild shivering spasms abated at least for now.

A fence, perhaps ten feet tall, stood opposite, a car park and new-looking apartment blocks beyond it. Lights shone in a few of them. Could she ring their doorbells, ask for the use of a phone? Possibly. But how would they react to a strange foreign girl disturbing them in the early hours? A payphone would be better.

Day or night, he'd said.

The kind man.

Galya saw a car parked at the end of the street, its windows steamed up, its front wheels on the pavement, a street light shining down on it. Beyond that, an open gate.

Move, Galya told herself. If she kept still, the cold would start to gnaw at her again. She made for the gate. Her soles stung with every step. God only knew what kind of state they were in. Worry about that later, she thought. Get shelter, get help.

A bar stood at that end of the fenced-off street, the old building standing lonely and defiant against the new structures that had sprouted up around it. A sign advertising Guinness hung over the door. No noise from within.

As she drew close to the car, she saw its nose had butted up against a junction box at the base of the light. Its rear passenger-side door looked like it had not quite found home. Was it open? Maybe she could slip inside, get out of the cold for a little while.

It was an old car, boxy and dented. The kind she used to see back home in her village, held together with rust and hope. Galya reached for the handle. Condensation on the windows obscured the interior. She swallowed, pulled, and stepped back.

A man lay snoring on the back seat, curled in a foetal position, a tall bottle clasped to his chest. Disturbed by the chill draught, he snorted and pulled a coat up to his nose. The stale smell of alcohol borne on warm air drifted from the car.

Galya guessed this man had emerged from the bar with the intention of driving home, and had got no further than this. Defeated by his own stupor, he had climbed into the back to sleep it off. Short in stature as he was, he hadn't needed to draw his legs up too much.

And he had small feet.

Galya regarded his trainers. Cheap, even a girl from Ukraine could tell. But better than raw bare feet on this icy ground. She took a breath, held it, and gripped one of the laces between her forefinger and thumb. It came loose with a gentle pull. She grabbed the heel and worked the trainer free.

The man gasped and huffed. 'Yeah, yeah, I'm up,' he said, his words sodden with sleep and drink.

Galya froze.

He did not open his eyes. Soon his snoring resumed.

Galya exhaled. She undid the other lace and dislodged the remaining shoe.

The man's eyes opened, focused on nothing. 'Aye, aye, I'm coming, hold your horses.'

Again, he sank back into his slumber.

Galya slipped the shoes onto her feet, ignoring the odour from his socks. They were at least two sizes too big, but they would do. She flexed her toes in the sweaty warmth.

A glint caught her attention. There, in the footwell, a mobile phone and some loose coins. She leaned in and across the drunk. The bitter smell of him seeped in through her nose and mouth. The coins rattled against the phone as she scooped them up. The man's eyes opened again, now staring directly into hers.

'Sure it's early yet,' he said.

'Yes,' Galya said in English. 'It's early. Go back to sleep.'

9

Herkus had called at half a dozen bars that Tomas frequented. No one had seen Tomas or Darius, they said, and he believed them. People seldom lied to Herkus, even if they didn't know who he worked for. He had one of those faces that inspired truth-telling. Only the very bravest, or most stupid, would consider lying to him. There were few brave men in the bars he had trawled over the last two hours, but plenty of them were stupid. Even so, he was satisfied they had been sincere when they'd told him Tomas had not darkened their doors that night.

With a heavy heart, Herkus drove to the last bar he could think of. This time of night the doors would be closed but, if Tomas and Darius were in the mood for drinking, then the opening hours would be flexible.

He parked the Mercedes on Holywood High Street, directly opposite the Black Stove Bar & Grill. At first glance, the Black Stove seemed like an upmarket place in a well-to-do part of Greater Belfast. And to many a customer it was exactly that. But its owner was far from respectable. Not that he was a criminal, at least not in the sense that Herkus understood. He was not a bad man, as such. Clifford Collins merely had certain tastes that only women of a particular profession could satisfy. So, now and again, Clifford played host to Tomas. If Clifford hinted that he might have liked payment for the food or drink served to Tomas and his friends, then he would be quietly reminded that Tomas would settle his bill simply by not calling Clifford's wife and telling her the specifics of her husband's more exotic pastimes.

Herkus crossed the street. The heavy outer door stood open. He tried the glass-panelled inner door, but it was locked. A dim glow burned within. He peered through the frosted pane, looking for hazy shapes that might pass for human. He could make out nothing but variations in light and darkness. Keeping his eyes to the glass, he rapped the door with his fat knuckles.

One of the dark shapes moved.

'I see you,' Herkus said in English. 'Open the door.'

He knocked again, harder.

'Just a minute,' a voice called. Herkus recognised it as the high whine of Clifford Collins.

'Open now,' Herkus said.

A shadow approached the other side of the glass. Locks snapped, and a chain jangled. The door opened four inches and Clifford peeped out through the gap.

'Tomas is here?' Herkus asked.

'No,' Clifford said. 'I haven't seen him since the weekend.'

The little man's voice quivered as he spoke, but his eyes said he was truthful. And relieved.

Why would he be relieved? Perhaps Herkus had asked the wrong question.

'Darius is here,' Herkus said. This time, it was a statement of fact, not a query.

Clifford shook his head from side to side, his mouth slack as he scrambled for the correct answer. Eventually he said, 'No.' And the lie was plain to see.

Herkus didn't hesitate. He took one step back and kicked the wood, his full weight behind it. Clifford squealed and backed away. The chain held. Herkus kicked again, then once more, and the door swung inward.

'Stay there,' Herkus said to Clifford as he entered.

Clifford nodded and sat down at a table.

There at the back, huddled in a booth, Darius and one of the two moronic Irish brothers who ran whores from that flat towards Bangor. He believed this one went by the name of Sam.

But no Tomas.

Sam kept his hands on the table, his face pale, sweat glistening on his forehead. He looked very much like a man in fear.

42

Herkus spoke to Darius in Lithuanian. 'Where is he?'

Darius stared at the granite tabletop. 'Who?'

Herkus approached the table. 'You know who.'

Darius gave a strained laugh. 'You mean Tomas?'

Sam flinched at the name.

'Yes,' Herkus said. 'I mean Tomas.'

'I don't know,' Darius said.

'Look at me,' Herkus said, leaning over him. He smelled whiskey and terror.

Darius raised his eyes to meet Herkus's.

'Where is he?'

Darius shrugged. 'Like I said, I don't know. I'm not his babysitter.'

'Yes, you are,' Herkus said. He kept his voice calm and even lest Sam realise the gravity of the situation. 'I left him with you. You're responsible. I'll ask you once more. Don't lie to me. Where is Tomas?'

'I took him to the flat in Bangor,' Darius said. 'He wanted to try out the new girl. He decided to take her out somewhere. I don't know where. That was around eleven. I haven't seen him or her since.'

Herkus placed a hand on Darius's shoulder. The muscles tensed beneath the leather. 'You're lying to me. I'll have to call Arturas. He'll be angry. You know how much he cares for his brother.'

Darius held his hands up. They betrayed the panic boiling beneath the forced calm. 'That's what happened. He took the girl. That's all there is to it. What do you want me to say?'

'The truth,' Herkus said. 'And you will. Eventually.'

He turned his attention to Sam, noticed the grazing and dirt on his hands, as if he'd taken a fall.

'You,' he said in English. He spoke it better than Darius. 'Where is Tomas?'

The moron looked up at him with drink-heavy eyes. He sneered. 'Fucked if I know.'

Herkus grabbed as much cropped hair as he could and slammed the moron's face into the tabletop. He felt more than heard the satisfying cracking of teeth.

Sam spat blood and tiny chips of enamel onto the granite, lurched to his feet and reached for something at the small of his back. Was the idiot going for a knife?

'Don't,' Darius said.

The anger on Sam's face turned to terror as he seemed to realise whatever he sought in his waistband was no longer there. He turned to look at the spot where his skinny arse had been just moments before.

'Don't,' Darius said again, louder.

Sam reached for something on the seat. He brought it up to point at Herkus's forehead. Or thereabouts. The pistol danced in his grip like a landed fish while blood dripped from his chin.

Herkus sighed. 'You need to take the safety off.'

Sam stared for a moment before turning the pistol in his grip, looking for the catch.

In one smooth, quick sweep of his hand, Herkus snatched it from his grasp. Sam gaped at his own empty fingers.

'It's a Glock,' Herkus said. 'It has no safety catch. Sit down.'

Sam did as he was told while Herkus stashed the gun in his jacket pocket.

'I ask you again: where is Tomas?'

Sam spat again. 'My hucking heeth!' he said, tears welling in his eyes. He brought his fingertips to his swelling lip.

Darius wiped red spots from his cheek and spoke in Lithuanian. 'I told you already. We don't know. He went off with the girl and didn't come back.'

'All right.' Herkus smiled and spoke to Sam in English. 'Let's go for a drive.'

10

Lennon shivered as the attendants at the scene grew in number. First, the Forensic Medical Officer arrived. Dr Eoin Donaghy wore a raincoat over his pyjamas. His sole duty here was to officially pronounce extinction of life. It took only a few seconds of examining the corpse for him to announce, with confidence, 'Yep, he's dead all right.'

He trudged back over to Lennon's side, peeling off the surgical gloves he'd worn for the examination, brief as it had been. 'It's a cold night to be out killing anyone,' he said.

'True,' Lennon said.

'Shame about the young lad, the harbour policeman. How bad was it?'

'Bad enough,' Lennon said. 'But he'll pull through.'

'Good, good,' the doctor said. 'Well, if there's nothing else?'

'No,' Lennon said, 'that'll be all. Thank you.'

They shook hands and the doctor walked back to his car.

Connolly approached. 'I've got a name,' he said.

He'd spent the last fifteen minutes in his patrol car, talking to the duty officer at his station, having him check the records for public-order arrests Connolly had made over the last few months.

'I knew I'd seen him before,' he said. 'Tomas Strazdas. Lithuanian. I lifted him for disorderly conduct back in October. He'd been giving the nightclub doormen grief. He got an evening in the cells and a caution.'

'Is that all?' Lennon asked.

'He'd given one of the doormen a good dig in the mouth,' Connolly said. 'The doorman was all for pressing charges – until the next morning.'

'You think someone got to him?'

'Maybe,' Connolly said. 'I remember some big fella, another Lithuanian, lifted him from the station the next day. I thought it strange at the time. The big fella was kind of . . . what's the word? When you're talking to your boss?'

'Deferential?' Lennon suggested.

'Yeah, that's the one. Deferential. Like Tomas here was the big fella's boss.'

'I think we'll have to do a bit of digging into poor Tomas's background. You up for some detective work?'

Connolly's face stiffened with the effort of suppressing a smile. 'Yes, I think so.'

'Good,' Lennon said. 'I'll clear it with DCI Thompson. When you're done here, go home and get some rest. See me in my office at eleven.'

Connolly's happy glow intensified with a layer of hope. 'I'm due on night shift tomorrow evening.'

'On Christmas Eve? I'll straighten that out, don't worry. You'll get to spend the night with your family.'

Connolly could hold his grin back no longer. 'Thank you,' he said.

'It's all right,' Lennon said. 'Just be sure to make the most of the opportunity. You do some solid work for me, I'll see it doesn't go unnoticed by the higher-ups.'

A marked four-by-four pulled up on the other side of the crime-scene tape. Two men emerged, a forensics officer and a photographer. There was no point pulling in a full team before daylight. Until then, they'd erect a tent over the body and take some cursory photographs.

Lennon doubted he'd be away from here before morning. He'd call back home to see Ellen before heading into the office to draw up his notes for DCI Thompson. He'd already been pencilled in for duty on Christmas Eve – thanks, he was certain, to Dan Hewitt's influence – but he would have been home by early evening to spend the rest of the night with his daughter. With any luck, he still would, but he'd be too tired for much more than falling asleep on the couch again.

The previous Christmas had slipped by almost unnoticed. Apart from the nightmares, Ellen had been quiet for the first couple of months after her mother's death, like the shadow of a child. Lennon had sat with her for hours at a time, trying to coax her into talking, only to be met with her polite silence.

Now and then she would hold his hand. Seldom at first, but more frequently as time went on. Often he sensed it was more for his benefit than hers.

He'd found it difficult to face himself in those weeks after Marie died. It took an almost physical effort not to ask himself that question over and over again: what if he hadn't left Marie and Ellen alone in that flat in Carrickfergus?

Lennon had a couple of sessions with the counsellor the force provided. He talked over the possible answers with the psychologist, and none of them helped. If he'd been there when the killer came for the child and her mother, could Lennon have defended them? Perhaps. Or maybe he would have died too, and they would have been taken anyway. Then there was the question of whether Lennon had been betrayed. DCI Gordon had called him away from the flat, only to be executed less than two hours later. Had Gordon been part of it? Had he set Lennon up and then been betrayed in turn? If so, and Lennon had not left Marie and Ellen alone, would the killer have gone there for them, or bided his time until they were more vulnerable?

Trying to answer those questions was like catching falling rain with your hands; for every drop that landed in your palm, a thousand more fell freely to the ground. The futility of it became clear. Lennon couldn't change what had happened. Instead, he would give Ellen the best life he knew how.

Things were bearable, at first. Her silence was a relief, in a way, even though he knew he was a coward for feeling so. But then her anger came. Bright flashes, like lightning from a blue sky. Anything could set the child off. She'd be playing with a doll and, when it wouldn't hold the pose she'd arranged it in, she would scream and thrash and bite. Sometimes she would break things in her fury;

whether they were her possessions or her father's, it didn't seem to matter. Each flare would burn itself out as quickly as it ignited, and she would carry on as if nothing had happened.

It was around that time that Bernie McKenna, Marie's aunt, began to call. She was a dry-hearted spinster who couldn't crack a smile if God himself had come down from above and told her a knock-knock joke. Lennon agreed to her requests to see Ellen, thinking contact with her wider family could only help his daughter deal with her new situation. He never thought for a moment it would lead to Bernie suggesting, in a tone of laboured innocence, that the child might be better off with her maternal relatives. Sure, a single man like him, how could he raise a little girl? Not that they'd think ill of him for giving her up, of course, but a man is a man, and if he worked the odd hours of a police officer how could Ellen have any stability?

Lennon would never admit it as long as he lived, but a small and frightened part of him did wonder if Bernie McKenna was right. After all, he had abandoned Ellen while she was still in the womb and had no contact with her for the first six years of her life. Then he would remember she was the only family he had. At least, the only family that acknowledged his existence since his mother and sisters had disowned him when he joined the force.

No, he would not give up his daughter. Was that selfish of him? Maybe. Probably. But that was the promise he had made to himself when he carried her from that burning building, the building where her mother died, and it was a promise he was going to keep.

Lennon shivered as he watched the photographer help the forensics officer raise the tent, white PVC over an aluminium frame. It took less than a minute between them, and one more to secure it with pegs.

He walked to the open flap and stepped inside. The translucent roof allowed the street lighting to penetrate the shell. Lennon stood over the corpse, feeling like a mourner at some strange funeral.

He wondered who would mourn for Tomas Strazdas.

II

'My name is Galya Petrova,' she said. 'Please help me.'

'Where are you?' the man asked.

'I don't know,' she said. 'Under a bridge. Near water.'

'Look around you,' he said.

'There is a big building,' she said. 'Glass and metal painted red. I hear cars on the bridge. There are cranes and fences all around.'

'I understand,' he said. 'That's the Royal Mail building you're talking about. Don't move from there. Stay under the bridge. Stay in the dark. I'll find you.'

Tears climbed up from Galya's throat. 'Thank you,' she said, and hung up. She retreated further into the shadows, clutching the phone to her breast as if it were a newborn infant.

It had only been this afternoon – no, yesterday afternoon – that Rasa had come to the bedroom where they had kept her locked up for almost a week. She'd told Galya she would start work that day.

Galya knew what kind of work.

Rasa had laid out underwear on the bed, tiny sheer things, and placed a pair of shoes on the floor. The shoes had platform soles and heels so tall that Galya could not possibly have walked in them.

'Take your clothes off,' Rasa said in stilted Russian. 'Put these on.'

'No,' Galya said.

Rasa smiled in the tired but patient way a parent does with a slow child. Galya guessed her to be twenty years her senior, maybe more, her face lined by age and tobacco. Rasa dressed like a businesswoman who yearned for younger men. 'Don't be silly,' Rasa said. 'You want to look nice for your client, don't you?'

Galya backed towards the wall. 'Client?'

'The gentleman who's coming to see you. He'll be here soon.'

'Who is he?' Galya asked.

'No one,' Rasa said. 'Just a nice man.'

'What does he want?'

Rasa laughed and sat down on the foot of the bed. 'That's for you to find out. And whatever he wants, you'll do it for him.'

'I won't do—'

'Whatever he wants,' Rasa said, her voice hard like bones beneath skin. 'Come. Sit beside me.'

Galya pressed her shoulders against the wall, kept her feet planted firm on the floor. 'I don't want to.'

'Sit,' Rasa said. 'Now.'

Galya moved to the bed and lowered herself onto the mattress, keeping a good metre between her and the other woman. She kept her eyes downward.

'Are you a virgin?' Rasa asked.

Galya blushed.

'Are you?'

Galya chewed her lip.

'Answer me,' Rasa said.

'No,' Galya said.

'One man?' Rasa asked.

Galya looked at the wall.

'Two men? More?'

'Two,' Galya said, wondering why she told the truth even as she spoke it. 'There was a boy back home. We were very young. It was in a field near Mama's house. It was so quick, he hardly started before he was done, then he ran away. He never spoke to me again. I didn't sleep for two weeks. Not until the blood came.'

Rasa's voice and countenance softened. 'And the second man?'

'Aleksander,' Galya said. She turned to look directly at Rasa. If Rasa recognised the name, she didn't let on. 'In Kiev. The night before we flew to Vilnius. He told me I'd live with a nice Russian family in Dublin, that I'd look after their children, and . . .'

'And what?'

Galya almost said she'd teach them English – that was what

Aleksander had told her as they drove the many kilometres from her village near the Russian border to Ukraine's capital. Aleksander had told her of the life she'd have, of the places she would see, of the money she would make and send back home to her little brother Maksim so he could settle the debts Mama had left behind.

Aleksander told her about the good life she would have as he took her in his arms in that hotel in Kiev. Galya had never seen such luxury, such thick carpets, sheets made of silk, more food than she could eat. All this would be hers, he said, and he pressed his lips and his groin against her. And she succumbed, despite what Mama would have thought looking down from Heaven, because, dear God, she was grateful. And Aleksander was handsome and tall, with dark eyes and long lashes, and Galya needed to touch something beautiful, just once in her life.

Her orgasm had come like breaking glass and left her hollow like one of the mannequins she'd seen in the shop windows at the Metrograd centre. For a minute, perhaps only a few seconds, she felt she might have loved Aleksander. But the feeling dissolved in her breast, washed away when he handed her a Lithuanian passport with a picture of a girl who looked just enough like Galya Petrova to satisfy a casual glance.

She boarded the plane alone, the passport clutched in her hand, a joyful fear in her heart. Her nerves sparked with anticipation. She had never flown before and gasped at the sensation of being pushed back into her seat by the speed of the craft. It left the ground, and she made a prayer that God would deliver her safely to Vilnius.

Looking around, she noticed the faces of other passengers. Whether they laughed with their companions or sat in silence, she saw that same prayer behind all their eyes.

Everyone believes in God when they fly, she thought.

Otherwise, who would have the courage?

'And what?' Rasa asked again.

'Play with them,' Galya said.

'And now you're here in Belfast. So what are you going to do?'

Galya twined her fingers together.

'So this Aleksander lied to you, and you wound up at that farm, slaving every hour of the day,' Rasa said. 'You were filthy when I found you, you stank like a horse. Now look at the nice things I bought for you to wear. And you can make some money, once you've paid me back.'

'Paid you back?'

'The agency that brought you here. I had to pay them good money to get you out of that farm. How are you going to pay me back?'

'I didn't ask—'

'I don't care what you asked for,' Rasa said, that hardness in her voice once more. 'I took you out of there. It cost me plenty, and you owe me. All you have to do is make the clients happy. Is that so bad? Just do what they ask, smile for them, be pretty.'

Rasa edged closer to Galya, reached out a hand to brush the hair from her face. 'And you're *such* a pretty girl, you know.'

Galya chewed a nail.

'Like a doll,' Rasa said. 'That's all you have to do. Smile, be pretty, and do what they ask.'

Galya turned her head to Rasa. 'What if I say no?'

Rasa gave a sad smile. 'Then the client will be unhappy,' she said, speaking slowly, the Russian coloured by her Lithuanian accent. 'And the men who gave you this room and this roof over your head, they will be unhappy. You don't want to seem ungrateful, do you? You don't want them to think you're difficult, hmm? They'll be upset. They need the money to pay your rent. You don't want to make them angry, do you?'

'No,' Galya said, her voice barely audible even to herself.

'Good girl,' Rasa said. She leaned in and placed a dry kiss on Galya's cheek. 'Do as you're told and everything will be all right. I promise.'

And so Galya had taken off the grey tracksuit and plain underwear they'd given her a few days before and put on the lacy things and the shoes she could barely stand in. She had sat there for an hour, goose pimples sprouting on her bare skin, waiting for the client to come. The weeks since she'd flown from Kiev to Vilnius, then Vilnius to Brussels, then Brussels to Dublin – they had blurred into one long arduous smear, work and sleep, sleep and work, always wet and cold, always dirty, always tired, always aching for home.

Now she sat in a room with a soft bed, cold but dry, and all she had to do was make a client happy. Could she do such a thing? Maybe, if she forced Mama from her mind.

She might have done it, might have given herself away, if not for the kind man and the cross on a chain he'd pressed into her hand, and the piece of paper with a telephone number written upon it. The hope he gave her had turned to courage in her heart and blood on her hands.

'Call me,' he'd said in an accent that was not from Belfast.

'I can save you,' he said.

And Galya believed him.

12

He placed the phone back on the table, next to the glass. Condensation beaded on its surface. He brought a thick finger to the moisture, felt the cold on his callused skin.

She had called sooner than he'd expected. He had been awake, unable to sleep, nursing a buttermilk shandy. Half a glass of buttermilk, half a glass of lemonade. He took a sip, tasted the sour-sweet mix, and swallowed.

It usually took days, sometimes a week or more, before they would call. Sad as it was, it took a good deal of abuse before a girl would seek a way out. But this girl had taken less than twenty-four hours. She must have suffered at the hands of those monsters, but he refused to think about that.

He had taken a taxi to the apartment that afternoon, not wishing his own vehicle to be seen, and rang the doorbell. A buzzer sounded, and the door unlocked. He let himself in. The older woman waited for him on the landing, dressed far too well for such an occasion.

'Hello, sweetheart,' she said in her thick accent. 'Your first time?'

'Yes,' he lied.

'Don't worry,' she said, showing him into the apartment. 'You have nice time.'

Three men stood inside, huddled in the kitchenette. Two of them were local, going by their tattoos and clothing. The third looked foreign, a big man, all belly and fat fingers.

He paused in the doorway, unsure if he should proceed.

One of the local men looked up, barely registered his presence, and fell back into conversation with his friends.

'Come on,' the woman said. 'Don't be shy.'

He entered, wondering why he was so nervous. It wasn't as if this was the first time he had entered such a place. He had done it many times before.

'Is fifty pounds for massage,' the woman said, holding out her hand.

'What?' he asked, feigning ignorance.

'You give fifty for massage,' the woman said. 'You want something else, is between you and her.'

'Ah,' he said. He reached for his wallet, counted out two twenties and a ten, placed them in her hand.

'Is good,' she said, smiling, showing her yellowed teeth.

Nicotine, he thought.

She tucked the notes inside her blouse, pulling aside the fabric of her brassiere. An unnecessary touch, he thought.

'Come,' she said. 'Her name is Olga.'

At least a third of the two dozen times he had visited these places, the girl's name had been Olga. Most of them had hollow eyes and moved like marionettes. They said hello, and please, and thank you. When he said he wanted nothing from them, they tugged at his clothes anyway. They were the lost. He could do nothing for them.

But a few were still alive inside. They listened when he spoke. They gazed on him with hope and awe when he told them of salvation. They called him. Eventually.

The woman led him across the living room and opened a door. He looked back over his shoulder at the three men. One of them lifted a coat, exchanged a farewell with his friends, and let himself out. None of them paid any attention to the man who watched.

'Come,' the woman said. 'She is nice. You see, you like her.'

She stepped through to the bedroom.

He followed.

She extended a hand towards the girl on the bed.

The girl looked up, no more than a glance, but enough to see that she still had her soul. They had not yet stolen it. She could still be saved.

Silently, he thanked the Lord on High.

13

The others had been waiting when Herkus and his friends pulled up in the old BMW. The moron Sam drove, the Glock's muzzle pressed against the back of his seat. Darius lay in the boot. He had given a pained sigh when Herkus told him to get in.

Now Darius and Sam sat side by side, each bound by cable ties to a chair. Herkus stood over them, blowing into his cupped hands to warm his fingers. The others, Matas and Valdas, stood silent against the roller door. They were good men, Herkus had known them since his army days, and they would back him up, no matter what happened here.

He'd called Arturas from the car, told him he had the two men on the way to the lock-up. Arturas had said to do whatever was necessary, to hell with whomever it upset.

The lives of these two men were now worth shit, which gave Herkus solace.

The lock-up was as cold inside as it was outside, one of two dozen identical buildings on an abandoned industrial estate that lay to the north of the city. It had belonged to someone called McGinty. Herkus had been told in hushed tones that a crooked cop had been killed here by a madman called Fegan, and the planned housing development that was to replace the complex of storage buildings and commercial premises had been put on hold indefinitely as a result.

Herkus regarded each of the men in turn. Sam was as stupid as his idiot brother, both of them cheap hoods with a big-name organisation behind them. No wonder Arturas held his business partners in the Loyalist movement in such contempt; if this was the standard of their personnel, then God help them all.

Darius was a different animal. He was not the brightest of Arturas's men, that wasn't under question, but he had heart. And real physical strength. A mountain of a man, bigger than Herkus, even.

So who should he start with? For a moment, he thought it should be Darius. Show Sam how serious this situation was. But, on the other hand, Darius was too useful. At least for the moment.

Sam, then.

Herkus tore two strips off a tissue. He rolled each into a ball and jammed them into his ears. He took the Glock 17 from his pocket and pressed the muzzle against Sam's forehead.

'Where is Tomas?' he asked.

'Jesus,' Sam whined. 'I don't know, I swear to—'

Herkus squeezed the trigger, and shouted, 'Bang!'

Sam screamed, and a dark stain spread on his lap.

Herkus laughed. 'Other thing about Glock 17,' he said. 'No round in chamber, no bang.'

He pulled back the slide assembly.

'*Now* it goes bang,' he said.

Herkus placed the muzzle against Sam's forehead.

Liquid trickled to the floor.

'Where is Tomas?' Herkus asked.

'He's dead!' Sam cried. 'She killed him.'

Herkus's heart sank. He closed his eyes.

'Who killed him?' he asked, opening them again.

'The girl,' Sam said. 'She had a piece of glass, off a mirror. She stabbed him in the throat. We panicked. We stuffed her and the body in the boot of the car. We drove out to the harbour to get rid of them. She got away. We left Tomas there on the side of the road.'

He looked up at Herkus, his eyes wide and wet. 'Oh, Christ, I'm sorry. We didn't know what to do, we were scared, I'm sorry, oh God, I'm—'

Herkus squeezed the trigger again.

The back of Sam's skull exploded.

Darius wept.

Herkus placed the Glock's muzzle against his old friend's forehead.

'Tell me everything,' he said.

14

Arturas Strazdas pressed the red button on his phone before Herkus finished speaking. He stared at the display but saw nothing.

Tomas dead.

Killed by a whore.

Abandoned at some roadside like a dog.

Strazdas roared and threw the phone at the wall. He burned inside, his heart incandescent. He grabbed fistfuls of his own hair and pulled until his scalp screamed. He formed a fist with his right hand and struck his forehead and temples again and again until he staggered, dizzy like a drunk, into the wall.

But still the fire would not dim.

He tugged at his left shirtsleeve to expose his forearm and closed his teeth on the pale flesh.

Oh, the pain, white hot and fierce, at last blotting out the anger. His mind found balance. He eased his jaw open, tasted metal.

The shame hit hard, like a punch to his gut. He had never, *would* never tell a living soul about his anger. How sometimes it made him hurt himself. How, now and then, he bruised himself. How, albeit rarely, he occasionally drew his own blood.

Strazdas breathed hard, in through his nose, out through his mouth, until his heartbeat settled in his chest. He went to the suite's bathroom and turned on the cold-water tap at the washbasin. Leaning against the black marble, he held his forearm beneath the stream and watched the red streaks run down to the plughole.

He cursed himself.

Ten years or more he'd been doing this. Always out of the blue, always over as soon as it began. First the anger, then the pain to drown it out, then the shame.

Once, in his Brussels apartment, the house-cleaner had seen him slap his own face and bite the back of his hand. She had asked if everything was all right. He had said yes, everything was fine, not to worry.

Her body had never been found.

Strazdas tore off half a dozen sheets of toilet paper, wadded them into a ball, and pressed them against the bloody ellipse. He straightened and looked at himself in the mirror. A handsome man, he had been told. Thick dark hair and blue eyes. Good skin, fine features.

He spat at the mirror.

Saliva sprayed and dripped down the glass.

Arturas Strazdas knew he was unwell but had no idea how to get better. Often it seemed his life played out before him and he was a spectator of his own days. He had never had a woman he hadn't paid for, he had never had a friend who didn't fear him, and he knew he would die alone.

He had always known he would bury his brother.

Oh God, Tomas.

Strazdas grabbed a hand towel and wiped spittle from the mirror, avoiding his own gaze in the reflection. He dropped the towel in the basin, walked to the bedroom, and sat on the edge of the bed.

Tomas, dead.

What did grief feel like? Strazdas had never knowingly experienced it. When he'd got word from an uncle that his father had died, he had played the part of the mournful son but, deep down, he had rejoiced. He had never wept over the passing of another.

Strazdas closed his eyes, reached inside himself, searched for any sense of loss. Something nestled there, in his heart, that might have been a keening for his brother. But it was matched by the relief that he would never have to deal with Tomas's catastrophes again. And that in turn was dwarfed by the anger at his own kin being snuffed out by a whore.

There, seize on that, take hold of the anger.

Surely a real human being would feel anger at the murder of his brother? Yes, they would. Murdered by a whore. Strazdas took hold of his rage and brought it close to his heart.

Don't call until you've found him, his mother had said.

'I found him,' Strazdas said to the empty room.

He had to call her. Tell her what had happened. He thought about waiting until he had more information, but it would do no good. She would resent every second he held the knowledge from her and punish him for it. Every minute he spared himself the act of telling was a minute of fury earned from her.

He stood, walked to the suite's lounge, retrieved his mobile phone from the floor. A crack or two in the casing from the impact against the wall. He opened the contacts list. Her number was stored under 'Laima'. He would never call her that to her face, of course, but it felt foolish to have 'Mother' in one's collection of phone numbers.

Before he hit the dial button he mopped up white powder from the glass desktop with his fingertip. He worked it across his gums, relishing the cool numbing sensation that followed.

Now, dial.

Strazdas listened to the tones as the mobile connected to the apartment in Brussels. His mind's eye pictured the large open living area, and the telephone on the elegant side table next to the plush couch he had bought for her. He saw her switch on lights in the darkened apartment, walk to the phone, reach for the handset, her eyes blurred by sleep.

'Hello?' she said.

'It's me.'

Silence for a moment. Then, 'Tell me.'

'Tomas is dead,' he said.

A distorted clatter as the phone fell to the apartment floor. A strangled cry, like an animal caught in a trap. He listened for a minute or more, choked sobs and keening wails, until it stopped like a needle lifted from the groove of an old vinyl record. She picked up the phone again.

'How?'

Strazdas told her all of it. About the whore, how Tomas had wanted to break her in, how she'd cut his throat with a shard of glass, how Darius and that idiot he ran with tried to dump the body in the water, and how the whore got away from them.

When he was done, he listened to his mother's steady breathing. Eventually she said, 'Kill her.'

'I will,' Strazdas said.

'Make sure the bitch suffers for what she did to my boy,' she said.

He was a child again, shamed because he'd wet his bed, red imprints of her hard hand against the skin of his legs. 'I will,' he said.

'And anyone else who was responsible, anyone who gets in your way. Do you understand me?'

Or a young teenager, caught with his fingers in his trousers, her mouth slashed wide in disgust. 'Yes,' he said.

'Kill them all.'

His bladder ached. 'Yes.'

A hard click, and she was gone.

He ran to the bathroom.

15

A white Toyota van approached, its headlights flooding the shadows beneath the bridge. Galya flattened her shivering body against the pillar, concrete icy cold on her cheek.

The van slowed and the driver's window lowered, showing the occupant's moon face.

Galya stepped away from the pillar, letting the light find her.

The driver smiled. He reached for the passenger door, opened it, turned back to her.

'Come on,' he said.

He had come to her in the afternoon. She had given him a glance as he entered the room, ushered in by Rasa, and then had turned her gaze downward.

Rasa spoke to the man in English, saying, 'Enjoy her. She is new. Never been touched.'

She closed the door, leaving him alone with Galya.

He lingered at the other end of the bedroom, his eyes like points of black oil on his round face, his coarse dark hair swept back from his forehead, a thick beard surrounding the red slit of his mouth. A pink scar carved a line from the centre of his forehead to the outer edge of his right eyebrow. Thirty-eight, thirty-nine, maybe forty. Galya examined him in the corner of her vision

'Hello,' he said.

Galya tried to reply, but only managed a thick murmur in her throat.

'Can I sit down?' he asked.

Galya moved closer to the bed's headboard. She felt his weight on the mattress. It rocked her like a boat on a sickly wave. She did not look at him, but she sensed his attention on her bare skin. Without thinking, she placed one forearm across her breasts, the other down between her thighs so her hand cupped her knee.

'My name's Billy,' he said.

Galya did not respond.

'Am I really the first client?' he asked.

Galya swallowed, her lips tight together.

'So no one's touched you yet?'

Galya studied the patterns on the faded wallpaper.

'Good,' he said. 'Then it's not too late.'

He kneeled on the floor, facing her, like a suitor asking for her hand in marriage.

'I can help you,' he said. His accent was soft and soupy, not hard and angular like the men who owned this flat. English, maybe, she couldn't be sure.

Galya lifted her eyes to meet his. His gaze locked solid on hers, his expression firm and truthful.

'If you can get away from here,' he said, 'I can help you.'

Galya went to speak but closed her mouth when she realised she had no words for him.

'Please believe me,' he said. 'I can help you. If you can get out of here, don't tell anyone where you're going, I can help you get back home. What's your name?'

Galya shook her head.

'My name's Billy Crawford,' he said. 'I'm a pastor. A Baptist pastor, but I haven't been placed with a church. Instead, I help girls like you, help you get away from this. Do you understand?'

He reached for Galya. She pulled away.

'It's all right, I won't hurt you,' he said, as if he were calming a trembling puppy. 'Look.'

He held a fine silver chain before her eyes, a cross dangling from it.

'For you,' he said. 'So Jesus will protect you.'

He went to place it over her head. She flinched.

'I'm sorry,' he said, lowering his hands. The cross settled in his lap. 'I didn't mean to frighten you. I know you're scared. I know you don't want to be here. You don't, do you?'

Galya wanted to shake her head, tell him no, she didn't want to be here. Instead she turned her eyes away.

'It's all right,' he said. 'I'm here to help you. I can help you get back home, away from these people.'

Away.

Such a big word. So big there were many ways to say it in Russian. Away, like she wanted to get away from Mama's farm. Like she wanted to leave her village. To be free of the things that bound her there. To go to another place and have a life of her own.

Those notions seemed foolish now, but the word still weighed as heavy. She wanted to be away from here more than she had ever wanted anything before.

So when he reached again, she dipped her head, allowed him to place the chain around her neck. The cross lay cold on her skin. She touched it with her fingertip, felt the hard angles.

'Jesus will protect you,' he said. 'He will protect you, and He will help you get away from these people. Do you understand me?'

Galya nodded once.

'Good.' A smile split his moon face. He took her hand and put a piece of paper in her palm, a string of numbers written on it in pencil, each digit impossibly neat. 'When you get away from here, call me. Understand? Call me. I can save you.'

He stood and walked to the door, opened it, and left her alone in the room. Galya stared at the paper and the numbers printed on it. She lifted the cross from her breast, turned it in the light, brought it to her lips, kissed it.

Hard, quick footsteps approached from beyond the bedroom door. Galya bunched the piece of paper up and stuffed it beneath the pillow on the bed beside her. She lifted the chain over her head, ready to stash it with the phone number, but the door opened. Galya clenched her fist around the cross as Rasa entered and asked, 'What happened?'

'Nothing,' Galya said.

'That's right,' Rasa said as she approached the bed. 'Nothing.'

'He just—'

Rasa's open hand struck Galya's cheek, the impact followed by heat, heat followed by pain. 'Nothing. You didn't do a thing for him.'

'He only wanted to talk,' Galya said as her throat tightened with tears. She held up the cross. 'Look. He gave me this.'

Rasa's hand lashed out again, leaving its stinging mark on Galya's other cheek. 'Men don't want to talk,' she said. 'Men want to fuck. You ungrateful little bitch, after everything I've done for you.'

Galya could hold the tears back no longer. 'But he didn't want—' She cried out as Rasa grabbed a fistful of hair and hoisted her to her feet.

'They only want to fuck. That's all you're here for.'

Rasa threw her against the chest of drawers, sending make-up and lotions spilling. The mirror teetered on its stand before tipping and crashing to the floor, shards scattering.

'Now look what you've done,' Rasa said, marching to the door. 'Clean it up.'

Galya got to her knees as the door slammed shut. Pieces of broken mirror lay around her. She wept as she gathered them up and dropped them in the small bin that sat by the chest.

Maybe the kind man could save her. Maybe he couldn't. It didn't matter either way, not if she couldn't get away from here, away from Rasa and the men she had sold Galya to. Soon another man would come, a man who wasn't kind, and she would have to do things for him. Her stomach soured at the idea.

Galya reached for the largest piece of glass, long like a blade, and saw the cross and chain lying curled upon it.

'I'll take you to my house,' Billy Crawford said as he put the van in gear and moved off. 'You'll be safe there for now. Put your seat belt on.'

Galya did as she was told. He noticed the deep red stains on her clothing and her hands.

'What happened to you?' he asked.

She stared straight ahead. 'I killed a man.'

The seat belt gripped her tight across her chest as he stood hard on the brake pedal. He unclasped his own belt and climbed out of the van. The headlights made his wide face glow white as he crossed in front of her and approached the passenger side. He yanked the door open.

'Get out,' he said.

Galya stared down at him.

'Out,' he said.

She undid the seat belt and lowered herself to the ground.

'I can't help you,' he said. 'You have to go.'

'You said—'

'I can't. It's too dangerous.'

Galya's breast tightened with alarm. 'You said you would help me.'

He paced, his gaze shooting in every direction. 'If the police are looking for you, they'll . . .'

His words trailed away, and he bit his knuckle.

Galya felt something crumble inside herself. This strange, kind man had given her hope. Would he now take it away, abandon her out here in this cold city? Her chest hitched as she fought tears.

He stopped pacing, ran his hands over his face. 'Tell me what happened.'

'We have to go away from here,' Galya said.

He gripped her arms with his coarse-skinned fingers. 'Tell me what happened.'

'A man came, a Lithuanian. He says he will break me, show me how to do it right. He holds me down on the bed. He hurts me. I push him off.'

She mimed the actions with her hands, shaping the words into English as she spoke.

'I have a broken glass from the mirror. When I broke it, I wrapped it in cloth from the bed so to make a knife. I told him let me go. He was angry. He was shouting. He tries to take the glass from me. I didn't want to kill him. I just want to go home.'

He released her arms and backed away. 'It's too much risk,' he said, more to himself than to Galya. 'I can't, not this time.'

Galya tugged at his shirt. 'Please, sir, you say you would help me if I go away from them.'

He brushed her hand away. 'Not like this. The police will come for you. I can't—'

A siren in the distance stopped him talking. His shoulders rose and fell, his breath misting in plumes between them.

'Calm down,' he said.

Galya knew he was not addressing her.

He turned in a circle, looking all around him until his stare settled on the number plates of his van. He looked back to Galya.

She reached beneath the neckline of her bloodied sweatshirt and withdrew the pendant that clung to the chain around her neck.

'You gave me this,' she said, showing him the cross. 'You say Jesus will protect me. He did. He showed me how to go away from that place.'

He closed his eyes, engaged in a silent communion with himself. His eyes opened, his breathing slowed, his decision made.

'All right,' he said. 'Come with me.'

16

Susan stepped back to allow Lennon to enter her apartment. He held the envelopes he'd taken from the postman he'd intercepted downstairs.

'You look like shit,' she said.

'Thanks. Ellen up yet?'

'Half an hour ago,' Susan said, leading the way to her kitchenette. 'She's in Lucy's room. I was just about to make breakfast for them. Coffee?'

'Please,' he said, taking a seat at the table.

He set the mail addressed to Susan to one side and opened his own. One bill, an overdue notice, and a card with an *An Post* stamp and a Finglas postmark.

Susan spooned instant-coffee granules into two mugs and poured boiling water over them. Without asking, she added two sugars to Lennon's, stirred, and set the mug in front of him.

'Take it easy for ten minutes,' she said. 'Ellen's happy playing, anyway.'

Lennon smiled in thanks and took a sip.

The Christmas card was a cheap supermarket job, all gaudy colours and saccharine sentiment. He looked inside and felt his nerve endings jangle.

The only mark it bore was the letter T, two lines intersecting as if drawn by a child.

He stared at it, his mind racing through possibilities. A sick joke, maybe. Or perhaps he misunderstood, the shape etched on the card being nothing other than the pair of scrawled lines they appeared to be.

Susan hovered by his side, asked, 'What's wrong? You're shaking.'

'Nothing,' he said. He closed the card, the image of the Traveller's knowing grin burning in his mind.

Lennon had arrested him after a botched attempt at kidnapping Ellen at the Royal Victoria Hospital. He remembered the taunts, the cackling, the madness of him. The Traveller had escaped custody with, Lennon suspected, DCI Dan Hewitt's help, and had tried again. He'd succeeded this time, taking Ellen and Marie from a place Lennon had thought was safe, and had brought them to a house owned by a revenge-driven old man called Bull O'Kane.

Marie never left that house, and until now Lennon was sure the Traveller hadn't made it out either.

Of course he hadn't, Lennon told himself. They'd scoured the place, found more than half a dozen bodies in the smoking ruin. There was no way the Traveller could have gotten out of there alive.

A hoax, there was no other explanation, perhaps another of Dan Hewitt's connivances.

Lennon's mobile rang, and he said a silent thank-you for the interruption before answering.

It was Sergeant Darren Moffat, the duty officer. 'Just wanted to give you word on something,' he said. 'Two bodies found in a lock-up in D District, near Newtownabbey, about forty-five minutes ago. An officer at the scene recognised one of them straight away. A real likely lad called Sam Mawhinney.'

Lennon tucked the phone between his ear and his shoulder and tore the card into small pieces. Susan watched as he stood and dropped the scraps into the kitchenette's bin.

'And what's this got to do with me?' he asked, willing himself to forget about the card and concentrate on Moffat's information. He retook his seat and pressed his fingertips against his forehead in an attempt to rub away the ache of fatigue.

'The name rang a bell,' Moffat said. 'Took me a few minutes to figure it out. I'd been pulling information for Sergeant Connolly this morning – the arrest records for that Lithuanian fella that got killed last night.'

Lennon tensed. 'And?'

'Sam Mawhinney and his brother Mark were arrested along with Mr Tomas Strazdas on one occasion. An assault in that wee park by the cinema on Dublin Road.'

'Christ,' Lennon said.

'Quite a coincidence, eh?'

'Yep,' Lennon said. 'Anyone ID the other body?'

'Not yet.'

'Who's the Senior Investigating Officer on this?'

'That'll be DCI Keith Ferguson. You want him to give you a call?'

'Yep.' Lennon hung up.

Susan sat down opposite. 'Trouble?'

Lennon nodded over his coffee mug.

'Will it wait until you get some sleep?'

'Probably not,' Lennon said.

A movement at the window caught his attention. Snowflakes, drifting slow and lazy in the darkness beyond the glass. Susan turned her head to follow his gaze.

'Think it'll lie?' she asked.

'Should do,' he said. 'It's dry out.'

He pictured the fat flakes settling on the cold upturned face of Tomas Strazdas, even though the body now lay under the translucent roof of a forensics tent.

Susan reached across the table and rested her hand on his. 'Why don't you go and lie on my bed for a while? Just rest your eyes for a bit.'

'Okay,' he said. He squeezed her fingers between his and then left her there.

He knew where to go, having slept in her bed on several occasions.

'Just ignore the knickers on the floor,' Susan called after him.

Lennon kicked his shoes off and collapsed onto her unmade bed. It smelled of perfume and fabric softener. He closed his eyes and let his weight sink into the mattress. Sleep took him before long, bringing dreams of a man emerging from flames, hate in his eyes. A short time later he was disturbed by another body settling beside

70

his own. He felt Susan's shoulder press against his, and did not protest.

When Lennon woke, Susan was gone. He felt the mattress beside him: still warm.

Physically, he and Susan had never ventured further than kissing and touching, though she had often tried to guide his hands to the places he most desired them to be. But he had resisted, sure in his heart that he would eventually hurt her and destroy their friendship if he crossed that line. Even so, they had both taken comfort from having a warm body to sleep beside when they needed it.

A cold blue light slipped through the window, the snow heavier now in the stillness outside. Lennon sat up on the bed, wondering how long he'd slept. His phone sat on the bedside table. It rang as he reached for it to check the time. He answered it.

'DCI Ferguson for you,' Moffat the duty officer said.

'Thanks.'

'Jack Lennon?' a voice asked.

'That's me,' Lennon said, trying to sound awake.

'Keith Ferguson here. We met a while back at Roger Gordon's funeral.'

'I remember,' Lennon said, though he wished he didn't. Gordon's widow had glared at him across the grave. He knew she blamed him for her husband's death.

'This Mawhinney lad in Newtownabbey,' Ferguson said. 'He was a bad 'un. It looks like he crossed the wrong people this time. We don't know who the other body is yet, but he looks foreign. Sergeant Moffat tells me there might be a link to the chap you've got over at the docks.'

'Maybe,' Lennon said. 'Him and the Mawhinney brothers were arrested together on an assault case.'

'Hmm. Sounds like this boy, all right.'

'You know him?'

'Only too well,' Ferguson said. 'Him and his brother. They've been up to their necks in trouble since they were off their mother's teats.'

71

Lennon grimaced.

'Drugs, smuggled cigarettes, bootleg DVDs, you name it, they were into it. Last I heard, they were dabbling in prostitution. They have a few flats – two in Carrick, one in Bangor – that we'll be having a look at later today.'

'Bangor,' Lennon said. 'That's the same side of the Lough we found Strazdas's body.'

'True,' Ferguson said. 'If you want to take that one, feel free. Just clear it with C District.'

'Will do,' Lennon said.

'Here, you're part of DCI Thompson's team, aren't you?'

'That's right.'

'So how come I'm talking to you?' Ferguson asked. 'Thompson should be the Senior Investigating Officer.'

'He likes to delegate,' Lennon said.

'Hmm. Well, let's keep in touch on this. And hope it's not the start of something.'

17

Herkus helped himself to a vodka from the minibar. He felt he deserved it after such a long night. Only queers weakened their drinks with cola and such, so he sucked it neat from the tiny bottle. It warmed his throat and chest as it went down.

Arturas paced in circles around him. Herkus had considered calling him to see if he wanted to question Darius personally, but he'd known there would be no point. The boss wouldn't leave his suite. If he could help it, he never stepped outside at all. He had been pale-faced and jittery when Herkus arrived.

White powder dusted the glass tabletop.

Herkus measured each word and movement carefully.

'Drink, boss?' he asked.

'No,' Arturas said.

'Why don't you sit down?' Herkus asked. 'Maybe order some breakfast?'

'No,' Arturas said. 'No food. You got any more . . . ?' He pointed to his reddened nostrils.

Herkus shook his head. 'Later, boss. Sit down a while, all right?'

Arturas sighed and sat down on the couch. 'All right, I'm sitting.'

Herkus crossed the floor and took a seat facing the boss. 'Darius told me everything,' he said.

'I want all of it,' Arturas said.

'You sure?' Herkus asked.

'I'm sure,' Arturas said.

Herkus sighed and nodded. He began.

Darius spilled it all, his voice trembling, words scrambling through the terror. He wept as he spoke, already mourning himself. Darius was big and slow, but he wasn't stupid. He knew he was going to die. It was merely a question of how badly.

Darius said he and Tomas had been drinking since early afternoon. Nothing unusual about that. Tomas was in good spirits, talking, talking, always talking. Eyeing up the women, grabbing at them. Three times Darius had to grab his skinny frame, swallow him up in a bear hug, laugh and kiss his cheek, just to get him away from trouble.

Darius thought of Tomas as a brother, which meant he hated and loved him in equal measure. Sometimes he wanted to tear the little prick's head off, other times the scrawny shit made him laugh so hard his big belly hurt.

Today it had been mostly laughter, but it went wrong as soon as they entered the bar near Belfast's City Hall. They had drunk there many times before. Some of the girls who waited the tables were Lithuanians, and Darius and Tomas had both enjoyed flirting with them. But this evening was different. More men than usual, with just a few cackling women hanging on the arms of effeminate male friends who hooted and cooed at each other.

Darius understood straight away and tried to steer Tomas out onto the street again. But there was no turning him, and he shouldered his way to the bar. It wasn't until he reached it, money already in his extended hand, that Tomas realised something wasn't quite right. He stopped, turned a full circle, his eyes wide.

'This place is full of queers,' he said.

'Is it?' Darius asked, feigning surprise. 'Let's go, then, before one of these poofs takes a shine to you.'

'No,' Tomas said, swatting Darius's hand away. 'We've come here before and it's been all right. Now it's full of queers.'

Darius put a big arm around Tomas's slim shoulder. 'So they have a queer night once a week, lots of places do that. We'll just go some-where else, eh? How about The Fly? Get a look at some of those little student girls, eh? We'll call Herkus, he'll drive us up there.'

'No, no,' Tomas said, twisting away from Darius's reach. 'I won't leave a place because some queers think it belongs to them. The

74

fucking queers should get out. Not me. I'm not the fucking pervert. I'm not the freak.'

Before Darius could stop him, Tomas seized the arm of one of the men leaning against the bar, spun him around, and swung a clumsy right hook at him. The blow glanced off the man's lower lip, hard enough to draw blood, but not with enough force behind it to do any real damage.

All around them, homosexuals screamed.

'Fucking freaks!' Tomas roared, though none of the wide-eyed onlookers understood his Lithuanian.

Darius swept Tomas up in his thick arms and dragged him towards the door. 'Easy, easy,' he whispered in his friend's ear.

As soon as they were outside and a street away, Darius called Herkus.

'Fucking queers,' Tomas said as they walked through the crisp cold evening. Christmas shoppers stepped onto the road to avoid them. 'Think they can take over a place just like that. Perverts, all of them. Fucking perverts.'

'Perverts,' Darius agreed. 'How about The Fly, eh? Plenty of girls there.'

'No,' Tomas said. He stopped. 'What about that whore Rasa brought up from the South? We could go and see her.'

And so they had gone to the flat to the east of the city. Darius and Sam had sat drinking in the lounge while Tomas went to the bedroom and locked the door.

Darius felt bubbling unease in his gut. Perhaps Tomas would take his anger out on the girl. Well, no matter. If worse came to worst, if the girl was marked so badly she was left unsaleable, Darius would ask Herkus for the money to reimburse the brothers and everything would be forgotten.

When they heard Tomas's raised voice, they thought little of it. Tomas often got worked up over matters of sex. It was when his voice stopped dead that Darius and Sam exchanged uneasy glances.

Herkus massaged his temples with his fingertips, willing the headache to dissipate. It would not go. He considered taking another vodka, or perhaps a gin, from the minibar, but thought better of it.

'She got away from them,' he said.

'How?' Arturas asked.

'They were squabbling amongst themselves. Darius said he looked up and she was running.'

Arturas stood. 'They would have dumped Tomas in the water.'

'Seems that way,' Herkus said.

Rage burned beneath the boss's skin, barely concealed. 'They would have dumped him like an animal.'

'Yes, boss,' Herkus said.

Arturas nodded. 'It's good that you killed them. Better than they deserve.'

'Yes, boss.'

'Now you'll kill the whore.'

Herkus moistened his lips and shifted in his seat. 'Like I said, boss, she got away.'

Arturas leaned over him. 'And you will find her.'

'In this city? She could be anywhere by now.'

'You will find her.'

'Sure, I'll look for her, but—'

Arturas punched the armchair's cushioned headrest hard enough to make Herkus's head bounce. 'You will find her!'

Herkus got to his feet. 'Yes, boss.'

Arturas stood back. 'Good. Thank you.'

Herkus went to the door, opened it and stepped through to the corridor. As he went to close it, Arturas called, 'Herkus?'

He stopped, looked back into the suite. 'Yes, boss?'

Arturas pointed to his reddened nostrils again. 'Bring me something, all right?'

Herkus sighed. 'Yes, boss.'

18

Galya watched as Billy Crawford set a tall glass on the Formica-topped table before her. He half-filled it with something that was not quite milk, then topped it up with lemonade.

'Buttermilk shandy,' he said. He lifted the glass and held it out to her.

She caught its sickly sour-sweet odour and turned her head away.

He laughed. 'It's an acquired taste,' he said. He took a long swallow and placed the glass back on the table. White liquid clung to his whiskers. 'Coffee?' he asked.

Galya nodded and pulled the blanket he'd given her tight around herself.

He went to the worktop by the sink and clicked on the electric kettle. The jar of instant coffee he took from the cupboard looked old and seldom opened.

'I don't know how fresh it is,' he said, as if reading her thoughts. He dropped a spoonful into a mug. 'How do you take it?'

'Black,' she said.

The kitchen looked like Mama's back home: cupboards with old sliding doors, cracked tiles on the floor, an ageing cooker in the corner. The refrigerator hummed next to a top-loading washing machine. The wallpaper bore faded green flowers. It peeled at the corners.

Galya watched him work. He was a short man, no taller than her, but he was bull-shouldered with a thick neck. Muscles bunched and flexed beneath his shirt. He had short, graceless fingers, with dirt under his nails. His shoes were good quality but heavily worn.

She looked closer.

They weren't shoes, but rather work boots. Through the old net curtain that covered the window she could see into his high-walled yard where his van was parked. She recognised the shape of a cement mixer underneath a tarpaulin and a thin layer of snow. Around the rectangle of concrete lay piles of bricks, sacks of sand and gravel, shovels, a pickaxe, and other tools she didn't recognise.

She guessed the journey here had taken less than fifteen minutes. He had told her to lie low in the seat lest anyone see her. She had obeyed until she felt the van begin to slow. Sitting up, she saw the house as they approached. The neighbouring building looked derelict and the pair of houses stood away from any others on the quiet street, on the apex of a bend. A patch of waste ground, overgrown with weeds, lay opposite.

He steered the van to the rear of the house. She waited in the passenger seat while he opened the gates of the small yard. Backing onto the house was another stretch of waste ground, across which she could make out the low forms of some industrial buildings. A strange place, lonely with separation from the world around it, yet Galya could still hear the thrum of the city not so far away.

Once inside, he had walked her up a flight of stairs, fetched a towel from a closet on the landing and brought her to a bathroom.

She emerged after ten minutes, scrubbed clean but still dressed in the blood-soaked clothes she'd arrived in. A small cry escaped her when she found him standing exactly where she'd left him, waiting. He smiled. She pictured a vulture lingering over a dying animal. He draped the blanket around her shoulders, and she scolded herself for such ingratitude.

Now she wasn't so sure.

'You said you are a priest,' Galya said, her fingertips seeking out the cross he'd given her.

'A pastor,' he said. He poured boiling water over the coffee granules. 'Baptist. Pastor Billy Crawford.'

'Where is your church?' she asked.

He set the mug of coffee in front of her and sat down at the table. 'I don't have one,' he said, his voice soft like a child's kiss. He took another sip of his buttermilk shandy. 'I got my accreditation five years ago, but I never took a placement in a church. I wanted to work in the community instead. Helping people like you.'

Galya brought the coffee to her lips. It tasted bitter and stale. She tried not to grimace. The snowfall beyond the window started again, heavier than before, coating the tools and machines strewn across the yard.

He followed her stare. 'I have to make a living,' he said. 'I do occasional work on building sites. I've always worked with my hands.' He splayed his stubby fingers on the tabletop, then pointed to the long scar on his brow. 'That's how I got this. A block fell off a pallet, caught me over the eye. A dozen stitches. I always wear a hard hat after that. Not much work around just now, though. Things are quiet. But that's okay. Means I have more time to help girls like you. Do you want my help?'

For want of a lie, Galya said, 'I don't know.'

'You should,' he said, his smile creasing his wide face. 'Because that's what Jesus has asked of me. To help girls like you. It took me a while to figure it out, what I was supposed to do, but He showed me in the end. I've helped lots of girls like you.'

'How many?' Galya asked.

'You'll be the sixth,' he said, the pride plain on his face. 'All of them like you, from faraway places, brought here by evil men to be sold like meat. With His help, I saved them.'

'How will you help me?' Galya asked.

'You speak very good English,' he said. 'Where did you learn?'

'At school,' she said. 'And from movies. I wanted to be a translator. Or a teacher.'

'You still can,' Billy Crawford said. 'When you get home, you can be anything you want.'

'No,' Galya said. She put the mug down. 'To go to university, it is too much money. I have to care for my brother Maksim, he is all alone back home. He has no money for food. That is why I came here, to make money to send to him.'

'But they lied to you, didn't they?' he said.

'Yes.'

'How old are you?' he asked.

'Nineteen,' she said.

He smiled. 'So young,' he said. 'Too young to be treated like that, stolen by these thugs. Tell me about home.'

Weariness tugged at the edges of Galya's mind, but she brushed it away with a hand across her eyes. Soon she would sleep. After that, she would decide if she wanted this man's help or not.

'I come from close to Andriivka, a village near Sumy, in Ukraine,' Galya said. Now the smothering weight of fear had lifted from her breast she found it easier to form the words in English. 'We are Russians, my brother and me. We speak Russian, like many people where we have our home. We lived with Mama and Papa on their farm. We call them Mama and Papa, but they are not . . . I don't know to say in English, they are my mother's Mama and Papa.'

'Your grandparents,' the man said.

'Yes, our grandparents. Mother and father died when we were very small, so Mama and Papa took care of us. Papa died when I was ten, so Mama has to work in the fields. Sometimes I helped, but there is no money. So she sells the fields to other farmers to buy clothes for us. When she died, there is only one field for to grow a little food for us. She owes a lot of money. The man who lends money came, he said he would take the farm from us and throw us out to live in the fields. He said we are only Russians and we stole his money. We were never treated like that before. Russians and Ukrainians are friends, we don't make a fight with our neighbours, not like this place.'

Galya thought of the murals and graffiti she'd seen when they drove her to this city from across the border, hatred spattered on walls everywhere she looked.

'One day, my cousin comes for to visit with me. He is rich. He has a car and he wears nice clothes. He told me he knows a man who can give me a job where I can make a lot of money. He said I could make enough to pay the man who lends money so he will leave us alone, and more to feed my brother. I only have to go away for a while and live with a nice Russian family in Dublin and teach their children to speak English.'

Galya lifted the coffee and drank, even though it burned her tongue. Better she burn her tongue than weep with regret in front of this kind man. Mama had always taught her to be upright and strong, never to be weak. Because the weak will always suffer.

'It didn't work out that way, did it?' Billy Crawford asked.

'No,' Galya said. She told him about Aleksander, but she said nothing about how she might have, just for a foolish moment, thought she loved the handsome young man. She stifled a yawn and took a deeper swig of coffee.

'When I come to Ireland, a man waits at the airport in a – how do you call it? Like your van, but with seats?'

'A minibus,' he said.

'Yes, a minibus. And he collected other girls, and some men. He drove us for an hour. I ask him if we go to Dublin, but he said, be quiet. We came to a place, all around it long buildings with steam coming from them, and a smell like animals, but there were no animals. He brought us to a building and put us inside. There were beds, like a prison, or an army place. He said we sleep here, he comes back in the morning.'

The thought of slumber triggered another yawn, but this time Galya could not hold it back.

'Some of the others, they say they want to go away from this place, but he closes the door and he locks it. There were no windows, and only a toilet and a sink at one end. The girls cried, and so did some of the men. Some girls said they came here to be cleaners, some of them to dance in bars. The men said they came to make houses and roads. But when the man comes back, he says we have to work in these buildings, in the heat and the bad smell, and pick the mushrooms.

'We say we don't want to do this work, but this man, he says we owe him money. He has our passports. We can't go away from this place until we pay him back this money. So we have to work. Then we . . . in the place . . .'

She did not know how much time passed as she stared at the tabletop, trying to grab at the strands of her thoughts.

'Are you tired?' Billy Crawford asked.

'Yes,' she said.

'Of course you are.'

He smiled again, and Galya smelled sour milk.

'You've been through so much,' he said. 'Do you want to sleep?'

Galya nodded.

'There's a room upstairs,' he said. 'It's not much, but you can sleep there for a while if you want. I have some calls to make, anyway. We've a lot to figure out if we're going to get you home.'

'Who will you call?' Galya asked.

'People,' he said. 'Agencies. They deal with girls like you all the time, girls who've been smuggled into the country. They arrange everything, get you a new passport, organise flights, all that. Why don't you go to sleep? By the time you wake up, it'll all be sorted, and I can take you to them.'

'Okay,' Galya said.

She might have felt hope or fear in her heart, she couldn't be sure, but her focus was on keeping her head upright and her eyes open. She swallowed. Something powdery and bitter cloyed the back of her mouth. Two thick arms slipped around her as the world fell away.

19

The man who called himself Billy Crawford removed only the mobile phone and Galya's shoes, a pair of worn trainers that were far too big for her. He winced when he saw the state of her feet, blistered and torn. He left the rest of her clothing in place, even though she was covered in a dead man's blood. It might be less comfortable for her, but he wished to protect her modesty.

Later, once she had been saved, he could look.

And touch.

And taste.

But not until then. For now, he pulled the blanket up under her chin. He would dispose of the phone later.

He had almost left her at the roadside when she'd told him what she'd done. The police would surely be searching for her. But she'd seen his face, his van, his number plates. So he could not leave her there, no matter how dangerous she was.

And she was so pretty, like a pale doll.

Now she was safe. Quiet and still, like a good girl.

He brushed the yellow hair away from her face. His finger slipped between her dry lips, pulled them back.

Good teeth.

He smiled and backed towards the door. She'd be under for four or five hours, maybe. He had many things to do between now and then.

The first being to feed the creature upstairs.

He pulled the door closed and turned the key in the lock.

20

Lennon picked Connolly up at his house near Ulsterville Avenue. Rented, he told Lennon. The housing crash had lowered prices in the Lisburn Road area of the city, but not so low that a uniformed officer could afford one, even if he could get a mortgage. Having a pair of six-month-old babies didn't help his finances, he complained as Lennon drove to the apartment building on the outskirts of Bangor. Traffic moved at a deliberate and steady pace as the snow deepened on the ground.

Connolly did his best to hide his yawns. He had changed out of his uniform and into a casual jacket and jeans. He held an overcoat on his lap.

'I haven't had much kip either,' Lennon said.

'I got an hour at most,' Connolly said. 'The wife wanted me to help her with stuff today, look after the twins, that sort of thing. She's having everyone for Christmas this year. First time she's ever done it, so it didn't go down too well when I said I had to work.'

'I can imagine,' Lennon said. 'But you'll be at home tonight. She can't complain about that.'

'She might,' Connolly said.

Lennon pulled off the Belfast Road and drove to the quiet cul-de-sac where the three-storey apartment building stood.

It was a modest place. Clean, anonymous, dull. The perfect location from which to run prostitutes. Good access from the city, just fifteen minutes by car for a lonely man, and neighbours who probably didn't pay much attention to the comings and goings. Lennon scanned the other cars parked there as he pulled up. At least half of them were old BMWs or Audis, left-hand drive with Continental licence plates: Poland, Latvia, Lithuania. Migrant workers lived here, many of them probably on short leases.

Yes, a needful businessman could come here without fear of being recognised by a neighbour. Lennon wished he didn't understand that quite so clearly.

It had been more than six months since he'd last visited such a place himself. And then two months before that. Less than half a dozen times since Ellen had been in his care. Before, he had been able to wash himself clean of the shame after leaving some hollow-eyed young woman with a hundred pounds on a bedside locker. But since Ellen took her place in his home, he had been unable to scrub the crawling feeling from his skin. It wasn't that the girls were unclean, that he feared he had contracted some vulgar infection, but that he imagined the disgrace seeped from inside him, out through his pores, sticking to anything he touched.

So he had made the decision to stop. Of course, he knew if it had been as simple as making a moral and logical choice then he never would have started in the first place. He had gone six weeks after Ellen first moved in without feeling the slightest temptation. But then one night he let her have a sleepover with Lucy and Susan, and he found himself lifting his car keys from the table, taking the lift downstairs, getting into his car and driving to a place he knew in Glengormley.

He didn't allow his conscience a voice until he came home two hours later and his better mind began to pick over the deed. The next morning, Ellen wanted to hold his hand when he went to collect her from Susan's apartment upstairs. He wouldn't allow it, fearing the sin would spread from his fingers to hers, and she punished him with silence for a full day.

Still he didn't learn the lesson, and only two weeks later he made another late-night journey to a dark corner of the city. And again a few weeks later. Each time, he promised himself, and the part of his heart that belonged to Ellen, that he would not do it again. Each time, he knew he would break that promise.

Jack Lennon knew a human soul could bear an almost infinite

amount of shame as long it remained inside, and stayed hidden from others. Many bad people survived that way. In the quietest minutes of the night, he wondered if he was one of them.

The landlord's agent and a uniformed sergeant from C District waited outside the apartment building. Lennon and Connolly got out of the car and presented their identification. The landlord's agent looked worried. The sergeant looked bored.

The agent introduced himself as Ken Lauler. He let them into the building, and they followed him up to the top floor.

'It wasn't us who let this place out originally,' Lauler said. 'There was a different agent before us. We just took over the contract for the landlord, the maintenance, all that.'

'What about the rent?' Lennon asked.

'It's paid by standing order every month, straight from a bank account.'

'Whose bank account?'

'It's under the name of Spencer,' Lauler said. 'Same name as the lease. The rent gets paid on time every month, we don't get any complaints from the neighbours, so we've no call to be coming round asking questions.'

'Until now,' Lennon said.

'Quite,' Lauler said. 'Here we are.'

He inserted a key and turned it. The door swung inward.

Lennon stepped past him. 'Looks like there was a party,' he said.

A dozen empty beer cans lay scattered on a glass coffee table along with a half-full bottle of Buckfast fortified wine, loose tobacco and cigarette papers. A poorly decorated Christmas tree stood in the corner and a few strands of tinsel clung to the fake fireplace.

Lauler tut-tutted at the mess.

'Stay there,' Lennon told him.

He walked to the kitchenette, followed by Connolly. The hob looked like it had never been used, but crumbs dusted the toaster and spilled water pooled around the kettle. A drawer stood open. A bundle of black plastic bin bags lay by the sink, a roll of adhesive tape beside them.

'Shit,' Lennon said.

'What?' Connolly asked. He looked at the items, followed Lennon's thoughts, and said, 'Ah.'

Lennon opened more drawers, all of them empty, except for one. There he found a brown envelope containing several hundred pounds in cash and an employment contract.

And a passport.

He lifted it from the drawer. The green cover said LIETUVOS RESPUBLIKA, the Republic of Lithuania. He had seen others like it. This was an older passport, not bearing the burgundy cover now required by European law, and not biometric as all new passports were. He opened it to the data page.

Issued in 2005, it said, to Niele Gimbutienė, born in 1988. He looked at the image. A pretty young woman, blonde hair, fine features. He flicked through the rest of the pages, searching for immigration stamps. There were none. It had never travelled outside the European Union.

'This might be the girl they were keeping here,' Lennon said. He held the passport up for Connolly to see.

'A prostitute?' Lauler asked from the doorway.

'Why else would they keep a place like this?'

'I can assure you,' Lauler said, 'the agency has no knowledge of any illegal—'

'So where is she now?' Connolly asked.

Lennon didn't answer. He examined the employment contract next. It bore a logo saying EUROPEAN PEOPLE MANAGEMENT. Each paragraph was printed in three languages: English, French, and what Lennon assumed to be Lithuanian. It bore two signatures, one resembling that on the passport, the other a name Lennon couldn't make out. It listed a Brussels address as the company's head office.

He returned the contract to the envelope, but tucked the passport into his pocket.

'Excuse me,' Lauler called.

Lennon stepped out of the kitchenette and looked closer at the living area's wooden laminate flooring. Lauler went to move from the doorway, but Lennon held his hand up.

'I said stay there,' he said.

'Listen, you can't take a tenant's property from—'

'I need the photograph,' Lennon said. 'It'll be returned along with everything else we gather.'

'But—'

'Shut up,' Lennon said.

He let his gaze wander the floor until he found it. There, a reddish-brown streak, running away from one of the doors. Lennon pointed.

'I see it,' Connolly said.

'See what?' Lauler asked.

Lennon said, 'Sergeant, can you please show Mr Lauler outside?'

The officer from C District took Lauler's arm and guided him to the corridor.

Lennon walked to the door, watching where he put his feet, and opened it. The metal smell, insistent, pushed him back a step. Beneath it lay something not quite rotten, something that would be foul before too long.

Connolly coughed. 'Is that . . . ?'

'Yes,' Lennon said.

He moved into the room, his shoes clicking on the linoleum-covered floor, his breathing shallow. The dark pool spread beyond the bed, touching the far wall. It had thickened in the hours since the blood had spilled. What appeared to be vomit had splashed nearby. Red footprints wandered around the room, gathered in a huddle by the pile of stained sheets where they'd cleaned their shoes. A track like a long brushstroke arced towards the foot of the bed.

'Jesus,' Connolly said. 'So Tomas Strazdas was killed here, and whoever did it took Sam Mawhinney and the foreign fella to the other side of the city?'

'Maybe,' Lennon said. 'Or maybe Sam and the foreigner killed Tomas, and someone else took exception to that and held them to account.'

'Tit-for-tat?'

88

'Just like the good old days,' Lennon said.

A glint of reflected light caught his attention. He advanced as far as he could without treading in the blood. A shard of mirrored glass lay in the red, one end wrapped in torn cloth. A makeshift dagger, perfect for opening a man's throat. He'd seen such a thing before, three years ago, when an informant behind bars had his face slashed to ribbons by another inmate. It was a prison weapon. Used by a prisoner.

Lennon's hand went to his pocket.

'You think there'll be more?' Connolly asked.

'Hmm?' He felt the hard shape of the passport.

'More killings,' Connolly said.

'I hope not. I don't know about you, but I don't fancy spending Christmas looking at shit like this. One good thing might come out of it, though.'

Connolly stepped into the room. 'What's that?'

Lennon took his phone from his pocket and began dialling DCI Ferguson's number. 'Sam Mawhinney and his mate were killed in D District. We found Tomas in our patch, B District, but he was killed in C. With a bit of luck, it'll be given to one of the other districts' MITs, and we can go home.'

Even as he spoke, Lennon held little optimism that things would work out that way. But he could hope.

21

Herkus drove to Rugby Road, near Botanic Gardens, where Rasa's flat occupied the upper floor of a terraced house. A professional couple lived below. He had learned this part of town was called the Holylands but he did not know why. He couldn't see anything holy about it, but there were some good restaurants and an excellent bookstore. Not that he read much, let alone in English, but he enjoyed the shop's warm soft light, the sight of books stacked on shelves. It reminded him of his schooldays.

Rasa looked tired and harried when she answered the front door. It was probably an early start for her. She was lucky she got any sleep at all; he'd been running the length and breadth of the city since yesterday morning with no sign of it letting up. And now this damned snow on top of everything else.

He rarely indulged, but he thought he might allow himself a little of the boss's goods for himself once he purchased them from Rasa's contact. Just enough to give him a boost and get him through the morning.

Herkus followed her upstairs and into her flat. The place smelled of cigarettes laced with the aroma of incense from a joss stick that burned on the coffee table. Clothes and fashion magazines lay strewn on the furniture and floor. A tailor's dummy stood in the corner, fabric draped around it.

'Did you have to do that to Darius?' Rasa asked as she sat at the small table by the window. Spools of thread cluttered its surface, scissors and needles scattered amongst them. A plant pot rested on the windowsill, its occupant browning with thirst. She lifted a cigarette packet and a lighter.

'Yes, I did,' Herkus said. 'Give me one of those.'

Rasa made the sign of the cross, took a cigarette for herself, and handed the packet to him. Herkus suspected she and Darius might have had something going on. It was only natural she'd be sorry for the big man's passing, but she was stony inside. She would get over it soon enough.

He sat down to face her across the table and pulled a cigarette from the packet. Rasa lit hers, then held the flame out for him.

'What a mess,' she said through the smoke.

Herkus grunted in agreement. He had filled Rasa in on developments when he'd phoned her, so he had no desire to discuss it further. But she did.

'That idiot,' Rasa said. 'Sam Mawhinney. He caused all this. I'm glad you took care of him. His brother's no better.'

Herkus did not answer. He drew on the cigarette.

'Stupid boys. And that little bitch. I knew she was trouble the second I set eyes on her.'

'Then why did you pick her to take to Belfast?' Herkus asked.

'Because she looked good,' Rasa said. 'Men will pay serious money for a girl who looks like that. She can become a good worker if you train her right, take the time. But those idiots, the brothers, they wanted to put her to work right away instead of waiting. I told them to give it a couple of weeks, give her a chance to accept it, maybe dope her up, but they wouldn't listen. Now look at the shit they caused.'

Herkus gazed out of the window, watched snow fall. Rasa had chosen a pleasant spot in which to live, close to the park and all that Botanic Avenue offered. Few students could afford to rent a place on this street. The bustle of the city seemed a world away from the peaceful scene outside.

'When did you last see the girl?' he asked.

'Yesterday afternoon,' Rasa said. 'I had to take her in hand.'

'Why?'

'Because she let a customer go without giving him anything. She had the nerve to say he just wanted to talk.'

Herkus kept his eyes on the street below. 'Talk?'

'That's what she said. But I know men. Men don't want to talk. Men only want to—'

'Who was he?'

'I don't remember his name,' Rasa said. 'But I've seen him before. A short man, but heavy.'

'Fat?'

Rasa shook her head. 'Not fat. Muscular, broad-shouldered, like my grandfather. Like a barrel on legs. He had a round face and a beard, dark hair swept back. He gave her a necklace.'

Herkus rested his chin on his hand, let his eyes unfocus, allowed his mind to follow the loose thread it had discovered among Rasa's words.

When he had been silent for a time, she asked, 'What's wrong?'

He turned his attention back to her. 'What sort of necklace?'

'A cross,' Rasa said.

Herkus stubbed the cigarette out in the plant pot's dry compost. He stood and looked around the room, found an envelope and a pen sitting on the coffee table. He brought them to her.

'Draw the man,' he said.

She stared at him, her face loose with incomprehension.

Herkus pressed the pen and paper into Rasa's hands. 'You know how to draw. I've seen it. Make a picture of him.'

She thought for a moment, then scrawled on the envelope. Her crude strokes formed a round face, thick hair, a beard just as she'd described. Herkus had no idea if it looked like the man or not, but it wasn't a bad sketch of somebody. Rasa had worked in the fashion business before she left Lithuania and had wanted to do the same here, perhaps as a designer. Instead she had become a link in a supply chain for young girls. Not a big difference in career as far as Herkus was concerned.

He took the envelope from her. 'Does it look like him?'

'From what I can remember,' she said.

He indicated the line that slashed over one of the eyebrows and asked, 'What's this?'

'He has a scar,' she said. 'He's an ugly man.'

Herkus tucked the paper into his breast pocket. 'So who's the dealer you're sending me to?' he asked.

'His name's Jim Pollock,' Rasa said. 'I always buy from him. He gives me a good price.'

'He knows I'm coming?'

'I called him straight after you phoned me. Why?'

'No reason,' Herkus said. He turned and walked to the door.

She called after him, 'How is Arturas?'

Herkus stopped. 'A little on edge,' he said.

'Is he angry?' she asked.

'Of course.'

Rasa stood and crossed the room to him. 'I mean, is he angry at me? Because I found the girl. Does he blame me?'

He studied the lines of her face, the colouring of her skin, imagined she must have been beautiful in her youth. A pang he guessed to be sadness sounded in his breast.

'Arturas is angry at everything,' he said. 'He's angry at me. He's angry at his brother. He's angry at the fucking air he breathes.'

Herkus noticed the shake in Rasa's hand as she took a long drag on her cigarette.

'Listen,' he said. 'Maybe you should take off for a while. Spend Christmas away. You might still get a flight out this afternoon if you're quick. Or you could go across the border. Either way, just get out of this place for a few days.'

She nodded and gave him a flicker of a smile. 'Yes. That's a good idea. Maybe I will.'

He let himself out, left Rasa there in her unkempt flat, alone. A woman like her, he thought, she should be married with children almost grown by now. Maybe even a young grandmother. Not living in a faraway city, selling flesh to the filth that traded in such things.

Five years ago, pity had been an alien emotion to Herkus Katilius. But he had felt it more and more often in recent times, along with the aching in his knees and the small of his back.

'I'm getting old,' he said to himself as he unlocked the Mercedes and climbed in.

*

93

Traffic thickened as Herkus drove east, across the Albert Bridge, heading for Sydenham. Motorists kept their speed low as they travelled through slush and compacted ice. He followed the instructions from the car's satnav system until he arrived at a newly built apartment block that sprawled around a small square, looking more like a school or a clinic than a place to live.

He preferred Rasa's flat on its quiet street to this series of squares and triangles. No matter. He didn't have to stay here long, just buy the goods and go.

The Merc's lights blinked as Herkus locked the car. He turned up his collar against the cold and shoved his hands down into his pockets. A trail of layered footprints in the snow gave the only indication of a path to the building's entrance.

An array of buttons studded a metal panel by the door. Frost formed a crisp coating on its surface. Herkus selected the buzzer for the flat number Rasa had given him and held his thumb against it.

No answer.

He pressed again.

A tinny voice crackled: 'What?'

'This is Pollock?' Herkus asked.

'Who wants to know?'

'Rasa sent me,' he said. 'To buy stuff.'

A pause, then, 'Who sent you to what?'

'Rasa,' Herkus said. 'She told me she buys from you before. She told me you make a good price.'

'I don't know any Rasa,' the voice said. 'Now fuck off.'

Even through the tiny speaker, Herkus knew fear when he heard it. The voice had that edge, that brittle signal of restrained panic.

But why?

The cogs of his mind turned too slowly, hindered by a lack of sleep, but they connected at last. Adrenalin followed realisation, charging his limbs. Instinct took over. Herkus spun away from the door, dropping low to the ground as the attacker came at him, a knife gripped in his hand.

The man's momentum carried him forward, his gut meeting

Herkus's shoulder, the air driven from his lungs with a strangled wheeze. Herkus rammed into the attacker's midsection, pushing him upward, and let gravity do the rest.

Snow cushioned the man's fall, and Herkus had a moment to see his upturned face before he drove his heel into it.

Mark Mawhinney fell back, his lip already swelling. The knife slipped from his fingers, a blade that looked like he'd taken it from his mother's kitchen. He spat blood, red spraying on white, and coughed.

When he tried to regain his feet, Herkus kicked him square in the groin. Mawhinney fell to his side, pulled his knees up, whined like a starving dog.

'Don't get up,' Herkus said in English. 'Your brother was a stupid man. Now he is dead. If you a smart man, you stay down, you stay alive.'

Mawhinney writhed in the snow, hissing through his torn lips. 'You bastard,' he said, the words squeezed through his teeth, tears spilling from his eyes, melting tiny pits in the snow where they fell. 'Fucking bastard . . . Sam did nothing . . . no call to . . . do that . . . bastard.'

Herkus crouched beside him and picked the knife from the snow. He pointed the blade at him. 'Sam let the whore kill Tomas,' he said. 'Arturas will forget this, you think? I don't think. You go away from here, maybe Arturas can forget you. Go now.'

Mawhinney rolled onto his belly, hoisted himself up on his hands and knees, and crawled. Crimson drool formed a line between his mouth and the ground, leaving a trail behind him.

Herkus stood. He took a handkerchief from his pocket, wiped the knife handle clean, and tossed it into the snow as he walked back to the Mercedes. As he approached the car, pain called from his shoulder. He stopped, rotated his arm, felt the tendons and muscles complain.

'I'm getting old,' he said.

Mark Mawhinney had meant to harm him, possibly kill him. Had Herkus not reacted in time, he might have succeeded.

The Irish brothers had messed it up, Rasa had said. They'd tried to put the girl to work too soon. It was their fault. And Arturas would say the same.

Herkus looked over his shoulder.

Mark had reached the wall of the building. He grabbed a window-sill, tried to pull himself to his feet.

'Fuck,' Herkus said.

He turned and marched towards the other man, his hands ready.

22

Dreams shifted from darkness to light, from joy to terror. Galya was a child again, and her grandfather held her hand in his. The old man's skin was coarse and cracked, and he smelled of tobacco. They walked along a path in the dark woods near her birthplace close to the Ukrainian-Russian border. Wild things watched from the trees.

Up ahead, she saw what might have been a little girl with yellow hair. She hastened her step, straining her eyes to focus on the shape. After a few moments, she realised the coarse skin no longer rubbed against her own: her hand was empty. She looked back along her path. Papa lay there on his back, those coarse hands folded across his chest, his face pale in what little light this place offered.

Growls came from the trees around him. A snout appeared from the undergrowth, low to the ground, sniffing the trail of the dead man. Then another, and another – dogs emerging from the woods to feast on her offering.

Galya opened her mouth to shout at them, but the earth tilted, throwing her down on the stones and rotting leaves. The ground lurched, pitching her against Papa's body. Except Papa no longer lay there, and she rolled in the stones and mud.

The dogs advanced, and she knew they had not come to feed on her grandfather. They had come for her. She tried to get to her feet, to get away from them, but the mud held her down like a warm blanket.

They pounced. She raised her hands to shield herself. Their mouths felt like hard hands on her body, their teeth like blunt, graceless fingers. As she drowned in the mud, those fingers probed her ears, her ribs, her toes, her thighs, everywhere but those secret places reserved for a lover she might never meet. Finally, they parted her lips and ran across her teeth.

Galya smelled sweat and sour milk and knew she was dreaming. She swam upward through the mire, desperate to wake, but she grew tired, the effort too much. Instead, she let the darkness take her down into its belly, swallowed by a sleep so thick she thought she might have died.

As she sank, the hands left her, summoned by another voice, an animal howl in the distance.

23

Billy Crawford left the girl and went to answer the thing upstairs. Always it called. Always wanting more. Never letting him be. One day it would take the light from his eyes, he was certain.

He climbed the stairway to the attic room, his shoulders brushing the walls as he ascended. It called again, its voice tearing at him like a claw. He stood still and quiet at the door, wincing at each screech.

'God help me,' he said, his voice not even a whisper. A private exchange between him and the Lord. 'God give me the strength to endure it.'

He opened the door and stepped inside. He breathed shallow lest its odour overcome him. Six paces took him to within its vision.

Its eyes focused, its toothless mouth opened. It cried out, claws flaying.

'Quiet,' he said.

Its voice cracked as it rose, a broken wail that scratched at his hearing like a rat's claws.

'Quiet,' he said, more forceful now.

Again it cried, its pale blue eyes wide and tearful.

He placed a hard hand over its mouth, forced it back down. It stared up at him. He felt its gums slip and slither on his callused skin.

'Quiet,' he said. 'Or I'll hurt you.'

It grew still. Its toothless mouth stopped seeking purchase on his skin.

He knelt beside it. 'Pray with me,' he said.

He brought his hands together, bowed his head, closed his eyes.

'Our Father,' he said.

He prayed that God on High would take mercy on this creature and end its suffering soon. He prayed for a time when he could sleep through the night without hearing its wounded howls. He prayed the Lord would take pity on whatever it had for a soul, festering inside its breast.

He prayed, and it wept.

24

Lennon was on his way to his office, a can of Coke in one hand, the preliminary forensic report on Tomas Strazdas in the other, when a passing sergeant asked him if he'd heard about the Sydenham killing. The victim might be of interest.

'Who?' Lennon asked.

'Mark Mawhinney.'

Lennon stopped. 'Sam Mawhinney's brother?'

'That's what I heard,' the sergeant said. 'He's well known. The first officer on the scene recognised him. They said his neck was broken. Footprints in the snow show a struggle.'

Lennon went to his desk with a heaviness at his core. He threw the report on the pile of papers already gathered there and pressed the chilled drink can against his forehead.

Four dead in twelve hours.

He'd left Connolly at the flat in Bangor along with the sergeant from C District. All they could do was wait for another forensics team to come and take over. Matching the blood to Tomas Strazdas was merely a formality, although it wouldn't be done this side of Christmas.

Lennon sat down, opened the can, and cursed as its contents fizzed over the paperwork. He pulled the Strazdas report and the passport out of harm's way and mopped up the spillage with a tissue.

The report was little more than a sketch from the Forensic Service, a private company that handled much of the scientific duties for the Police Service of Northern Ireland. They worked from former police buildings in Carrickfergus, a setting that was entirely inadequate for the work they had to do. Their old Belfast premises had been destroyed in a bomb attack in the early Nineties, and they'd been making do in the seaside town since then.

Despite the limitations of their base, they still managed to provide one of the most advanced and comprehensive forensic services in Europe, honed through decades of investigating terrorist attacks, large and small, that had taken place on their doorstep almost daily.

As far as Lennon knew, Tomas Strazdas's body still lay out by the waterside, sheltered from the snow by a white tent, waiting to be packed up and brought to the new forensic mortuary at the Royal Victoria Hospital. There, a consultant from the State Pathologist's Department would do the honours.

On Christmas Eve it would be whichever poor bastard was on call for the holiday. Bad enough they should have one corpse to examine. Now they had three more. Lennon made another silent wish that he wouldn't have to be the officer in attendance when they got the scalpels and saws out.

He had called by CI Uprichard's office and asked if the related cases would be handed to one of the other districts, but Uprichard didn't know. They were having trouble pinning anyone down on Christmas Eve but Uprichard would call around, see if he could get a decision.

Lennon was not hopeful. He took his mobile from his pocket as he leafed through the report.

The gash in Strazdas's throat smiled at him as Susan answered.

'How's Ellen?' he asked.

'She's been asking for her Daddy,' Susan said. 'Will you be long?'

'I don't know,' Lennon said. 'Have you been watching the news?'

'I've had it on in the background,' she said. 'Somebody at the docks, and another two in Newtownabbey. Which of them are you chasing after?'

'Right now, all of them,' Lennon said. 'But you never know, maybe someone will take them off my hands.'

'Is that likely?'

'Not very,' he said. 'Can you keep Ellen a while longer?'

'You know I will,' she said. 'It'll be fun for Lucy. I don't know what Ellen's going to think about it, though. They're having a nap just now.'

'Can I talk to her?'

'Jack, I only just got them settled.'

'I know,' he said. 'Just for a minute. That's all.'

'All right,' Susan said, weariness in her voice.

He turned photographs and pages while he waited. Wound to the throat the most likely cause of death, to be confirmed by the State Pathologist's Department. Piece of material and length of electrical cord removed from the scene for examination. Lack of blood at the scene suggests death occurred elsewhere and the body transported to the location of its discovery. Presence of tyre tracks further reinforces this supposition.

Forensic and pathology reports spent so much time stating the bloody obvious, Lennon thought. The details were the key. Hidden, like the points of light not at first clear when you look at the night sky but that come into view as you look away.

Details like a piece of mirror glass and a girl's passport.

He heard a soft breath against his ear, but no greeting.

'Hiya, darling,' he said.

'Hello,' Ellen said, her voice blunted by sleep.

'How's you?'

'Okay.'

'Just okay?'

'Mm.'

'You been playing with Lucy?'

'Mm-hm.'

'Are you being good?'

'Mm-hm.'

'Did you have a nice sleep?'

'It was okay. I had a bad dream.'

'What about?' Lennon asked. His daughter's dreams were seldom dull.

'About a lady,' Ellen said. 'Dogs were chasing her. They had fingers for teeth.'

'Sounds scary,' Lennon said.

'Mm-hm.'

'But you're okay now.'

'Mm-hm. When are you coming home?'

'A bit later,' Lennon said.

Ellen did not answer.

'This afternoon,' Lennon said. 'Maybe this evening.'

'Okay,' Ellen said.

The phone clicked as she hung up.

Lennon looked at the handset for a moment before returning it to his pocket.

His thoughts returned to Tomas Strazdas and the other bodies that seemed to float in his wake. From what Lennon could tell, Strazdas was a low-level thug, as were the Mawhinney brothers. Not the kind of scumbags that gang wars erupted over. There had to be something underlying the killings, a root cause. Lennon suspected – no, felt in his bones – that the girl whose passport lay before him had something to do with it.

There had to be more to Tomas than was visible on the surface. And if you needed to see below the surface, there was one branch of the police force to talk to. Lennon hesitated for a moment, then lifted the desk phone's handset and dialled the extension for the C3 Intelligence Branch office.

'DI Lennon calling for DCI Hewitt,' he said.

He listened to bland hold music and swallowed his own disgust at going to Hewitt for help. The most Lennon's former friend had suffered for his betrayals was a bullet in his leg, courtesy of a madman called Gerry Fegan.

Fegan was dead now, along with many others. Dan Hewitt had as much blood on his hands as those he investigated, and that know-ledge gave Lennon a little leverage over him. He had only used it once before, during the inquiry into the events that took Marie's life. Lennon would hold Hewitt to account one day, but for now he was useful, as much as it made his skin crawl to deal with him.

The hold music stopped.

'What do you want?' Hewitt asked.

'How are you, Dan?'

'Fuck you, that's how I am,' Hewitt said. 'What do you want?'

'Just a little guidance,' Lennon said. 'You know about the killings of Tomas Strazdas and Sam Mawhinney, along with another unidentified male.'

'We're monitoring the situation, yes.'

'And another death in Sydenham,' Lennon said. 'Mark Mawhinney. Call me crazy, but I've a notion they're related.'

'We've considered that possibility,' Hewitt said. 'But you're getting a little ahead of yourself, aren't you? Once the link between the killings has been formally acknowledged, an MIT will be assigned. Right now, Tomas Strazdas is the only case you're involved with.'

'You do keep tabs on things, don't you, Dan?'

'It's my job to be well-informed,' Hewitt said. 'For instance, I know that the man found with Sam Mawhinney will be identified as Darius Banys, an associate of young Tomas. His babysitter, really.'

'Babysitter?'

'Tomas couldn't keep himself out of trouble,' Hewitt said. 'Darius's job was mostly to keep an eye on him, stop him from doing too much damage to himself or anyone else.'

'What was the relationship between the brothers and Tomas?'

Hewitt sighed. 'Why don't you do your own detective work, Jack?'

'Because you and your mates in C3 are always one step ahead of the rest of us,' Lennon said. 'And you owe me.'

'I owe you nothing,' Hewitt said.

'You want to test that in front of the Police Ombudsman?'

'Fuck you.'

'Then call it a favour to an old friend. It's a secure line. Nobody's listening.'

Lennon heard the change in Hewitt's breathing and reached for a pen.

'All right,' Hewitt said. 'The Mawhinney brothers branched into prostitution over the last year or so, buying girls from a Lithuanian woman called Rasa Kairytė, girls she helped traffic from the Republic into the North. She worked mostly with Tomas Strazdas.'

'Spell that name,' Lennon said.

Hewitt recited the letters as Lennon scribbled on his notepad.

'What's European People Management?' Lennon asked.

Hewitt paused. 'How do you know about that?'

'I saw an employment contract,' Lennon said. 'It was in a drawer at the flat, along with a passport.'

'What passport?'

'It belongs to a Lithuanian girl,' Lennon said. 'I'm guessing she's the prostitute the Mawhinneys were keeping there.'

'Maybe,' Hewitt said.

'You haven't answered my question,' Lennon said. 'The employment contract was between the girl and this company called European People Management. You know something about it. I could tell by your voice.'

'Maybe you should put in a request through the proper channels,' Hewitt said. 'I'm sure you'll get all the info you need for your case.'

'That'll take weeks,' Lennon said. 'Why bother with that when I can go straight to the source?'

'All right,' Hewitt said. 'European People Management is the Strazdas family business.'

'Family business?'

'Tomas was the younger brother of a man called Arturas Strazdas, owner of a number of labour agencies ostensibly supplying migrant workers to factories, mushroom farms, cleaning companies – that sort of thing. But we've had an eye on him for a long time now, at the behest of our European counterparts. We believe he's been using the agencies as a way of supplying paperwork for women trafficked into prostitution all around Britain and Ireland.'

'How does that work?' Lennon asked.

'One passport will be used for travel back and forth between Dublin and places like Vilnius, or sometimes Brussels, where he's based. The same passport might be used for a return journey once every couple of weeks, but often the immigration people don't look that closely at the photograph. One dark-haired girl with an Eastern European accent is hard to tell from another dark-haired girl with an Eastern European accent if you're not paying strict attention.'

Lennon reached for the passport and opened it to the data page.

Maybe this blonde girl in the photograph wasn't the prostitute who'd worked at the flat, but rather it was someone very like her. Had she been there of her own free will? He thought of some of the women he'd visited in the night in the not-so-distant past. He swallowed.

'Tell you what,' Lennon said. 'I'll run a theory past you; you tell me if it fits with what you know about the situation.'

A pause, then Hewitt said, 'All right.'

Lennon began, sorting his thoughts as he spoke. 'I think Tomas, this Darius bloke and Sam Mawhinney were having some friendly Christmas drinks in that flat out in Bangor, possibly along with a prostitute they were running out of there, but they had a little bit of a tiff. That wound up with Tomas getting his throat cut. The other two stuck Tomas in their car and drove him down to the docks, meaning to dump him in the water, but they were disturbed by the harbour cop.

'But Tomas's people weren't best pleased about this, and they took Sam and his Lithuanian friend out to Newtownabbey, blew their brains out, and burnt the car. Sound okay so far?'

'It seems a reasonable train of thought,' Hewitt said. 'But that doesn't explain Mark Mawhinney.'

'No,' Lennon said. 'Any witnesses to that?'

'Too early to tell,' Hewitt said. 'DCI Quinn's MIT have only been down there an hour.'

'Okay,' Lennon said. 'So if I wanted to talk to someone who grieved the passing of Tomas Strazdas, where would I start?'

'You could start with the Kairytė woman. She has a flat in the Holylands. Or there's the driver, Herkus Katilius. Big lad, hard bastard, ex-military. But there's a better option.'

'What's that?' Lennon asked.

'Arturas Strazdas, Tomas's brother.'

'You said he was based in Brussels.'

'He is,' Hewitt said. 'But he flew into the International Airport last night. We – and several other organisations – keep tabs on Mr Strazdas. He always stays in the same hotel.'

Lennon scribbled down the name on his pad. An expensive place, good clientele, near the Waterfront theatre.

'That's unusually forthcoming of you, Dan. What's your angle?'

'No angle,' Hewitt said. 'You would've tracked him down anyway. It's your job to chase next of kin in a case like this, inform them of their loved one's death.'

'A good reason to call on him,' Lennon said.

'True. But Jack?'

'What?'

'Tread lightly,' Hewitt said. 'Strazdas is dangerous. I won't shed a tear if you come to harm because you got yourself in over your head, but you could balls up several live investigations in the process. I've told you more than I should, so I don't want it coming back to bite me in the arse.'

'I'll be a model of discretion,' Lennon said, not caring in the least what might bite Dan Hewitt's arse.

'I'm counting on it,' Hewitt said.

25

Arturas Strazdas lay staring at the ceiling when his mobile phone rang. The cracked display said number withheld.

He hit the answer button and asked in English, 'Who is this?'

'You know.'

'Yes,' Strazdas said. He sat upright on the bed.

'My condolences on the passing of your brother.'

'Thank you. What do you want?'

'To give you a warning. A police officer will call on you before long. Detective Inspector Jack Lennon. Be careful with him.'

'How does he know I'm here?' Strazdas asked.

'He's a smart cop, that's how. He has many sources. He might cause you some problems.'

'Might he?'

'Very likely. But I can help you out. Run interference. Keep you informed of what he's up to. But I would expect to be compensated accordingly.'

'Of course,' Strazdas said.

'Are we agreed, then?'

A knock at the hotel suite's door.

'Hold on,' Strazdas said.

He went to the living area, put his eye against the peephole, and saw the distorted shape of Herkus waiting in the corridor. His nostrils tingled in anticipation. He opened the door and Herkus rushed inside.

Strazdas brought the phone back to his ear.

Silence.

'Hello?' he said.

Nothing. He stared at the display for a second before remembering that Herkus had entered the room.

'That idiot brother of Sam's tried to take me,' Herkus said, pacing.
'What?'

'I went to get your stuff from Rasa's dealer, but Mark Mawhinney was waiting for me. He fucked it up, so I finished him. Rasa's dealer must have set me up.'

'Where's my coke?' Strazdas asked.

Herkus stopped pacing. 'Didn't you hear what I said?'

'Yes, I heard,' Strazdas said. 'Someone tried to hurt you. Where's my coke?'

Herkus stood with his mouth open, his arms wide.

Strazdas threw the phone at him, shouted, 'Where's my coke? I sent you to do one thing for me, just one—'

He would never have believed Herkus could move so fast had he not seen it before. Strazdas's feet left the floor, his throat gripped in the big man's thick fingers, his back slammed into the wall.

'Listen to me,' Herkus said, his breath hot on Strazdas's face. 'I almost got my fucking guts sliced open by one of the morons you do business with while I was trying to get your coke. Do you think it's going to stop there? Those brothers had friends. Those friends aren't going to let it go. And sooner or later someone's going to mention your name to the cops. This thing has gotten out of hand. We need to get out of this shit-hole of a city right now. You can have all the coke you can snort when we get to Brussels, but right now we need to get away from here. Do you understand?'

Strazdas tried to prise Herkus's fingers from his throat but they were too strong, like stone. He croaked, and Herkus loosened his grip.

'Get your hands off me,' Strazdas said.

Herkus let go and backed off. 'Sorry, boss, but we need to get out of here.'

Strazdas coughed and walked to the couch. 'Did you find the girl?'

'No,' Herkus said.

'Then we don't go anywhere.' Strazdas sat down. 'When she's dead, then we can go.'

'Forget about her, she's—'

'I promised my mother,' Strazdas said. 'I keep my promises. You should do the same. You promised to bring me some coke.'

Herkus shook his head. 'Christ, listen to yourself. Four people are dead and all you can think about is your coke?'

Strazdas wanted to say yes, all he could think of was the coke, but his right mind held the words back. Instead, he said, 'I'm sorry for the deaths. All the more reason to track down the girl. It's her fault. She caused all this.'

Herkus took a piece of paper from his pocket and dropped it in Strazdas's lap. It was an envelope bearing a sketch of a bearded man.

'What's this?' Strazdas asked.

'He was the last one to talk to the girl,' Herkus said, taking a vodka from the minibar. 'Rasa told me he visited her yesterday morning, but the girl said he only wanted to talk. He gave her a necklace with a cross on it.'

'You think he knows something?'

Herkus downed the vodka in one and hissed. 'Maybe. Maybe not. But he's all we've got to go on.'

'Then find him,' Strazdas said. He held out the envelope.

Herkus took the paper. 'Boss, I'll do whatever you want, you know that.'

Strazdas did not answer.

'Anything you say, I'll do it. But please, at least think about it. If the cops don't come for you, the Loyalists will. If I'm out looking for this girl I can't protect you. You've got to get out of here. I'll stay and look for her, but you go to the airport, get the first plane to Brussels you can.'

'No,' Strazdas said.

'Think about it.'

'No.'

Herkus nodded. 'All right,' he said. He studied the sketch. 'If this man visited the whorehouse in Bangor, he'll have visited others. I'll ask around, but I have to be careful. There's one man I can trust. I'll go see him.'

He turned and walked for the door.

'Herkus,' Strazdas called.

Herkus stopped, his shoulders slumped. He looked back. 'Yes, boss?'

Strazdas touched his nose.

'I'll see what I can do,' Herkus said.

26

The ache ebbed and flowed behind Galya's eyes. At times it felt like the heavy blankets held her down, at others like they carried her aloft on some warm updraught. Her consciousness came and went this way for what seemed like days. Deep in the waking part of her mind, she knew it must have been only a few hours.

When at last she could lift her eyelids, they let in a painful sliver of weak light. She closed them again, but not before she took in a little of her surroundings.

A darkened bedroom, but not the one she had been held in for almost a week. This was somewhere different. But where?

Then she remembered.

The hot blood on her hands, fleeing through the night, cold tarmac tearing at the soles of her feet, the white van and its strange, kind driver coming for her.

The coffee and the sour-sweet smell of the buttermilk shandy.

Galya's stomach flexed at the memory of the odour, and she rolled to the edge of the bed, the blankets knotting around her legs. She retched, bringing up only thin splashes of a dark and bitter liquid.

The coffee he had given her.

Had it been drugged? Or had she simply been so tired that she could remain awake no longer? She was still fully clothed, except for the shoes she had stolen, so she hoped he hadn't touched her.

Galya sat up in the bed, but the pain followed her movement, shifting inside her skull. She brought her palms to her temples.

When the pulsing in her ears abated, she held her breath and listened to the house.

Quiet, not even the ticking of a clock.

She pushed the blankets away and lowered her bare feet to the floor. The coarse fibres of the carpet tugged at her tender skin, and the sting caused her to hiss through her teeth.

In the dimness she picked out the features of the room. Decades-old floral wallpaper, peeling at the corners. A cheap chest of drawers against the wall. The air smelled of damp and something lower, something faded.

Galya pushed upward, got to her feet, and fell against the chest of drawers. She leaned against it for a time, allowing her sense of balance to return, before going to the window and pulling aside the thin curtain.

A single pane with no handle. Black paint coated the inside of the glass. Tiny gaps at the edges of the pane let in a small amount of light. Here and there, the paint had been scraped by what looked like fingernails. Without thinking, Galya touched those places, tested the paint's consistency with her own nail.

Who would paint out a window? Why?

Someone with things to hide, she thought.

Fear rose inside her, a small bubble of it, but growing.

Galya crossed the room, using the wall to support herself. She knew before she tried it that the door would be locked. It stood solid in its frame, not even a millimetre of give. She ran her fingertips along its edges, felt the scratches in the thick paint.

She put her ear to the cold, slick surface and listened again. Still and silent beyond the door.

Galya took a breath, held it for a moment of indecision, then called, 'Hello?'

Quiet like a graveyard, not even the sound of traffic in the distance.

She placed a palm against the painted wood, held it there as if she might feel the heartbeat of the house, then pulled it back and slapped the door twice.

'Hello?' she called again, more strength behind it.

Something answered.

Galya stepped back from the door.

The howl came from somewhere above, the sound of a wounded dog, or a beast awaiting its turn in the abattoir.

Galya did not call again.

Instead, she returned to the bed and sat on its edge. She chewed her thumbnail as she thought, fighting to keep the fear down in her belly, not letting it climb to her mind where it would drive all reason from her.

This man, Billy Crawford, did not mean to help her, that much was obvious. So what was his intention? The scratches on the window pane and the door – someone had been locked in here before. Someone had clawed at the paintwork trying to find a way out.

And what had happened to that person?

Galya remembered what the man had told her at the table as he gave her bitter coffee to drink.

'I am the sixth,' she said.

Her hand went to her mouth but it was too late; the idea had already escaped her.

Tears stung her eyes as the fear crept up from her breast into her throat. Five had come before her, five had scratched the door and the window, five had sat where Galya sat. Had they wept? Had they screamed?

She would not weep.

She would not scream.

Whatever this man intended for her, whatever desires made him lock her in this room, she would not submit to fear. Instead, she would act.

Galya rubbed the tears away with the heel of her hand, stood, and went to the chest of drawers. She opened the first one, looking for something, anything hard enough to break glass. It was empty save for a sheet of old newspaper lining the bottom. So were the second and third drawers.

She pulled the top drawer out as far as it would go, felt the bump as the runners reached the farthest extent of their travel. She lifted and pulled again, freeing the drawer from the chest.

It was poor quality, but solid and heavy. She went to the window. The curtain came away with one tug and fell to the floor. She gripped the drawer by the corners and held it up to shoulder height. Her body's weight behind it, she rammed it into the window pane.

The glass held.

Galya pulled the drawer back, once again slammed it into the glass. Still the window stayed intact.

The howling from above resumed, a voice cracked by pain and sorrow.

She struck the glass again and again, every bit of her strength channelled through it, until the drawer split and fell apart in her hands. The glass stood firm. The voice above rose and fell like a siren. Galya collapsed to her knees among the fragments of wood and offered up her own cries.

27

Billy Crawford sat on the threadbare couch in his living room, his back straight, his hands on his knees, listening to the muffled wails above his head. He'd been at prayer for over an hour now. He had neither a clock to tell him so, nor a watch on his wrist. He'd always had an inbuilt sense of time. He went to bed at the same hour every night, and awoke at the same time every morning, had done since he was a boy. Never been late in his life, people would say about Billy Crawford, if they ever talked about him.

The crying and howling from above continued.

It didn't worry him. No one would hear. The old three-storey semi stood well away from any other buildings, just off the Cavehill Road, on the outskirts of the city. It backed onto waste ground, and the adjoining house had been derelict for years. It had changed hands several times as property prices rose and fell, but as yet no developer had tried to turn it back into a home. With the state of the economy as it was now, it would be years before anyone would look at it again.

As well as replacing all his windows with tempered double glazing, he had insulated the wall cavities. Little or no noise could enter or leave the house.

Let the girl cry all she wanted.

The first girl had cried a lot.

They all had.

He had drowned them out by singing unto the Lord.

'What a friend we have in Jesus,' he sang, his voice resonating deep in his barrel chest, 'all our sins and griefs to bear.'

He closed his eyes and felt the shape of the words on his tongue.

'What a privilege to carry,' he sang, 'everything to God in prayer.'

The wailing from above grew stronger, but his voice swelled, filling the house, blotting out all else until it was the only sound in the whole wide world.

28

Lennon knocked on the door and waited. A *Do Not Disturb* card hung from the handle. A maid smiled as she pushed a trolley laden with sheets and towels past.

He knocked again.

A smartly dressed man of early middle age emerged from the elevator along the corridor. A briefcase in one hand, he studied the signs indicating the layout of the floor, evidently searching for a room number, before approaching the door at which Lennon waited. The suited man rapped the door twice with his knuckles. It opened instantly and he stepped inside.

'Excuse me,' Lennon said.

The door closed in his face. He didn't see who had opened it, only caught a glimpse of the suite beyond, including leather armchairs and a huge flatscreen television.

He hammered the door with his fist.

The suited man opened it. 'Can I help you?'

Lennon peered over his shoulder. 'I'm Detective Inspector Jack Lennon, PSNI. I need to speak with Mr Strazdas.'

The man blocked the doorway with his body. 'Identification.'

Lennon smelled a lawyer. He produced his wallet and showed his ID.

'I'm David Rainey,' the man said. 'I represent Mr Strazdas. Maybe I can help you?'

'It's a personal matter.' Lennon leaned forward, trying to see more of the room.

Rainey straightened his back, using what height he had to obscure Lennon's view. 'I have Mr Strazdas's complete confidence.'

'Even so, I'd like to speak to Mr Strazdas in person. I'm afraid I have some bad news for him.'

'Very well.' Rainey stood back. 'Please come in.'

Lennon stepped into the suite's living area, all high ceilings and opulent upholstery. Arturas Strazdas sat at the centre of a couch, his legs crossed, his arms draped across the back. He watched Lennon with cold blue eyes set in a pale face beneath thick eyebrows. Perspiration formed a sheen on his forehead. Dark circles weighted his eyes. Raw red skin edged his nostrils.

'Nice suite,' Lennon said. 'I don't think I've ever set foot in a place like this. In my line of work, it tends to be the dumps you get called to.'

'No one called you here,' Strazdas said, his accent thick.

'No,' Lennon said. 'Can I sit down?'

Strazdas did not reply. Lennon looked to Rainey, who extended a hand towards an armchair on the other side of the coffee table from his client.

As Lennon sat down, he said, 'I have some very bad news for you, Mr Strazdas.'

'Go on,' Strazdas said.

'Your brother is Tomas Strazdas, correct?' Lennon watched his eyes.

'Correct,' Strazdas said.

'I regret to inform you that Tomas was found dead last night at Dufferin Road, in the Harbour estate. He was identifiable by a Lithuanian driver's licence in his wallet.'

Strazdas didn't flinch, didn't draw breath, didn't react in any way.

'Pending confirmation by a post-mortem to be carried out by the State Pathologist's Department, we believe Tomas was murdered. Most likely he was killed elsewhere, we suspect at an apartment on the outskirts of Bangor, then his body was moved to where it was found. We believe his killer, or killers, intended to dump his body in the water, but they were disturbed by an officer of the Harbour Police, whom they assaulted before making their escape.'

Strazdas stared ahead. His tongue slipped from between his lips, moistened them, then retreated.

Rainey cleared his throat. 'That is indeed very sad news, Inspector. Mr Strazdas thanks you for bringing it to him. Now, if you don't mind, he would like some time to take it in.'

He took a business card from his pocket and brought it to Lennon. 'If you would like to speak to Mr Strazdas further, please call this number and I'll ensure that he cooperates fully with your investigation.'

Lennon took the card and dropped it on the coffee table. 'Thank you. I have a few questions now, if it's all the same to you.'

Rainey leaned in close and spoke in a hushed tone. 'Mr Strazdas needs some peace to absorb this terrible news. Now, I really must ask you to—'

'Mr Rainey, I'm sure you understand that in a murder investigation like this, time is of the essence. The sooner Mr Strazdas answers my questions, the sooner we can find who killed his brother. You wouldn't want you or your client to appear to have been obstructive to the investigation, would you?'

Rainey straightened and looked to Strazdas.

Strazdas gave a nod so small, Lennon wasn't sure he'd seen it at all.

'All right,' Rainey said. 'Make it quick. And when I say it's over, it's over. Agreed?'

'Okay,' Lennon said.

Rainey retreated to the corner.

Lennon took his notepad and pen from his pocket. 'Mr Strazdas, what was your brother doing in Northern Ireland at the time of his death?'

'Tomas was a citizen of the European Union,' Strazdas said. 'He was entitled to travel and reside anywhere within the EU without hindrance. As am I.'

'Of course,' Lennon said. 'But that wasn't my question. What was Tomas doing here? Work? Pleasure?'

'I have an interest in investing in this city.' Strazdas waved a hand at the window as if the buildings beyond were his for the taking. 'That's why I flew in last night. Tomas had been here for some time, looking at various properties on my behalf, some for potential development and one as a possible site for an office for my main business.'

'Your main business,' Lennon said. 'I understand that's running a labour agency. Supplying migrant workers to local businesses.'

'That's correct.'

'So, Tomas will have been in touch with commercial estate agents and so on? Who might he have been talking to?'

'I can confirm that,' Rainey said from the corner. 'I visited several properties around the city with him. I can give you a list of agents, if needed.'

Lennon ignored him. 'Did Tomas know two brothers called Sam and Mark Mawhinney?'

Strazdas shrugged. 'I don't know.'

'What was Tomas's involvement with Loyalist paramilitary groups in Belfast?'

Rainey said, 'None that we are aware of. Inspector, if this line of questioning continues, I'll have to ask you to leave.'

'Tomas had been arrested several times for public-order offences,' Lennon said. 'He was a fighter.'

'Tomas was quick-tempered.' Strazdas showed no anger at the smearing of his brother's character. 'He took after our father that way. Sometimes it got him into trouble.'

'Perhaps he picked a fight with the wrong person last night.'

'Perhaps.'

'Did Tomas work for you supplying trafficked women to the local sex trade?'

Silence for long seconds.

Rainey walked across the room, extended a hand towards the door, and smiled. 'Thank you, Inspector, that will be all.'

Lennon took the lawyer's card from the coffee table and stood. 'I'll be in touch.'

'I have no doubt of that.' Rainey stood back to allow Lennon to pass, then showed him out to the corridor.

'Inspector,' he called as Lennon was about to walk to the lift.

Lennon turned.

'I won't tolerate any harassment of my client.' Rainey gave his best, sternest glare.

Lennon walked back to him, came right up close. 'And I won't tolerate a fucking gang war on Christmas Eve. I count four dead in less than twenty-four hours. As far as I can tell, it's been nothing but scumbags going after each other, but a young police officer is in hospital over this. Whatever's going on, it better stop. One more body turns up, and your client is the first on my list for questioning. Understood?'

'If you wish to interview my client again, you'll need to do so under caution,' Rainey said, folding his arms across his shallow chest.

Lennon said, 'That can be arranged.'

29

Strazdas sat quite still while he waited for Rainey to return. He closed his eyes and listened to the blood in his ears. It did not drown out the voice of his mother's hate. A movement of air and the hissing of expensive soles on thick carpet stirred him.

'You'll have to be careful,' the lawyer said as he closed the door. 'Anything else happens, you'll be in the firing line.'

'It's under control,' Strazdas said.

He did not like lawyers, but they were an essential part of doing business. Particularly at times like these.

'Under control?' Rainey snorted. 'Four dead, he told me. You said to me there was only your brother and the two that did for him. Arturas, my friend, you pay well, but not well enough for me to stand that kind of heat.'

Strazdas said, 'Then I'll pay you more.'

'I'm not a criminal lawyer, for a start.' Rainey sat down in the armchair opposite. 'Patsy Toner would've been your man for this sort of thing, but he's dead now. If I were you, I'd be on the first flight back to Brussels: get out of the spotlight, lie low for a while.'

'You're the second person to tell me that today,' Strazdas said. 'But I'm staying here until the job is done.'

Rainey sat forward in his chair. 'Until what job is done?' Before Strazdas could answer, he held a hand up and said, 'No, don't tell me.'

The lawyer reached into his pocket and took out a small glass vial filled with white powder. A tiny silver spoon was attached to it by a fine chain.

He asked, 'Do you mind? To settle my nerves.'

Strazdas licked his lips and sniffed. 'I don't mind at all,' he said.

PART TWO: HERKUS

30

Herkus picked up one thousand pounds in cash from the safe hidden beneath the kitchen sink in his apartment before making his way to the east of the city.

Anger still churned in his gut, but he knew how to control it. Anger at Arturas for not seeing sense and getting out. Anger at the whore for cutting Tomas's throat. Anger at those idiot brothers for letting this all happen.

The Mawhinneys were low-ranking members of a Loyalist faction headed by Rodney Crozier. Crozier was still in a bad state after being knifed just over a year ago by a rival, yet he managed to keep a firm hold on his people. But Herkus doubted the attempt on his life had been sanctioned by Crozier or any of those who ran his operation while he was laid up. Men like Crozier knew the difference between business and a personal vendetta. If they'd authorised it, they would have sent someone who knew what he was doing.

And Herkus would be dead.

That thought caused Herkus's mouth to dry. Twenty, ten, or even five years ago, the idea of death had not bothered him. He'd been young, strong, quick, and brave. Perhaps even foolhardy. If life were to end, it would simply be another adventure, like stepping off the edge of the world.

But then he began to notice the deepening lines on his face, and how his muscular bulk was slowly softening and sagging. How sometimes it hurt his knees to climb stairs and his lungs had to work harder the higher he climbed.

One night he dreamed of Agne, the wife he had left behind in Lithuania. He awoke with his throat raw and hoarse from screaming. They had married not long after he came out of the army and rented a flat in Vilnius. She talked about children all the time, never stopped, always babies, what she would name them, whether they would be male or female, until it stopped him from performing properly. Every time he mounted her, every time he felt his climax approach, he would see the distant look in her eyes as she thought of the child he would give her. And then he would withdraw, shrunken and defeated, and she would weep as if the child were stillborn.

The day before Herkus boarded the plane for Brussels they talked about their new life together, away from the greyness of their own country. He promised he would send her a ticket just as soon as he had earned the money. An old friend had told him the businessman Strazdas could offer them a new start in Belgium.

To celebrate, they filled a basket with wine, beer and good things to eat, and drove out of the city to the forests that surrounded the Neris River. He'd dug the hole a week before, hidden in the dark channels between the trees. She died with a quiet acceptance, didn't even cry out when he struck her that first time, and he supposed she'd always known it would end this way.

Herkus had liked Belfast at first, but now it grated on him. The rain, the small-mindedness, the damned pompous self-importance of its people who thought their petty little war was more important than anyone else's. He cursed the city's inhabitants as he drove, watching them stream along the pavements, in and out of betting shops, pubs and run-down electrical and clothing stores. None of the big chains that had colonised the city centre had ventured out here among the flags, graffiti and painted paving stones.

The Maxie's Taxis premises stood sandwiched between Indian and Chinese takeaways on the Holywood Road. Officially, the business was owned by Brian Maxwell. In reality, his brother Gordie ran the place from an upstairs office. He also orchestrated other ventures from the tiny workspace, though none of them generated any paperwork.

Gordie Maxwell did not stand when Herkus entered. He remained on the other side of his chipboard desk, feet up, chair tipped back. His belly stretched his shirt, making it gape between the buttons. Herkus saw the wisps of greying hair, smelled the bitter tang of body odour.

'There was no call to do Sam Mawhinney,' Maxwell said. 'All right, him and his brother were stupid cunts, wee boys playing the big boys' game, but Sam didn't deserve that.'

Herkus sat down. 'He let a whore kill my boss's brother.'

'Your boss's brother was a big-mouthed ignorant fucker,' Maxwell said. 'He put one of my drivers in the hospital for no good reason. There's not many'll be sorry to see the back of him.'

'If Arturas hears you say these things, he will be very angry.'

'That's his tough shit,' Maxwell said. 'And now I hear Mark Mawhinney had a wee accident this morning.'

Herkus did not respond.

Maxwell shook his head. 'A few people were asking around, looking to know where you were. Friends of the Mawhinneys. I would've told them you were coming here, only I hate those bags of shite even more than I hate you and your fucking boss.'

'You are a kind man,' Herkus said. Sarcasm was the closest he ever came to humour. 'Do you have what I wanted?'

Maxwell picked at his teeth, studied whatever he'd retrieved. 'Aye,' he said. He opened a drawer, pulled a large padded envelope from it, and dropped it on the desktop.

Herkus reached for it and poured the contents out onto a newspaper. A dozen nine-millimetre rounds rolled across the inky paper. The plastic bag full of white powder fell between them.

'Not often I'd let anyone pick stuff up from here,' Maxwell said. 'That's what the taxis is for. And I got it quick, too. You understand why I had to charge so much.'

'Yes,' Herkus said. With a gloved hand, he took the roll of notes from his pocket and tossed it across the desk. Maxwell caught it and started counting.

Herkus took the Glock 17 from his waistband.

Maxwell stopped counting. 'Is that a cop's gun?' he asked.

'Yes,' Herkus said.

'If I'd known it was for a peeler's gun, I wouldn't have got you them bullets. Where'd you get it?'

Herkus popped the pistol's magazine and replaced the two rounds he'd used that morning.

'All right, none of my business,' Maxwell said.

Herkus scooped up the remaining loose ammunition and dropped it into his pockets, along with the bag of cocaine. He left the pistol on the desktop, its muzzle staring at Maxwell.

'I'm looking for a man,' Herkus said.

'Oh, aye?'

'He uses whores.'

'I know a lot of men uses whores,' Maxwell said. He pronounced it *hooers*.

Herkus produced the envelope with the sketch on it and passed it across. 'This man,' he said.

Maxwell held it at arm's length. He moistened his lips with his tongue. 'Who is he?'

'Just a man,' Herkus said. 'But I pay money for him.'

Maxwell shot him a look, licked his lips again. 'Chases whores, you say?'

'Yes,' Herkus said.

'You think he has something to do with this girl that did your man Tomas in?'

'Yes.'

Maxwell stood and went to a small photocopier. 'Do you mind?'

Herkus shrugged.

Maxwell slipped the envelope onto the copier's glass and made a duplicate. 'I'll pass some copies round my drivers, see if the picture rings any bells. All right?'

Herkus nodded.

'And you be careful with that gun,' Maxwell said. 'You get caught with them bullets or that coke, you didn't get them from me, right?'

'Right,' Herkus said.

He stood and went to the door, opened it, was almost through when Maxwell called after him.

'If I turn this fella up for you, how much money are we talking?'

Herkus stopped and looked back into the office. 'Good money,' he said. 'Buy you a shirt that fits.'

31

Galya had listened to him sing for at least an hour before she'd fallen asleep again. She'd heard words like *Jesus*, *saviour* and *almighty* creeping up through the floor, while occasionally the other voice, the animal voice from above, had provided a skewed harmony as it wailed.

She had crawled back into the bed, wrapped herself in the blankets, and prayed to Mama. Sleep took her as she mouthed the words against the pillow.

A sound awoke her: the slamming of a door. She sat up, listened. The metallic sound of a lock. Galya squeezed her eyes shut and strained the limits of her hearing. There, maybe, the noise of an engine first clattering into life, then dissolving into the surrounding quiet.

It had been so faint she couldn't be sure if she'd heard anything after the door being locked. It could have been her own sleep-addled imagination.

The painted-out window only allowed the thinnest slivers of light into the room, but Galya could tell by the movement of the shadows that some time had passed. Her temples pulsed, and her tongue rasped the roof of her mouth. She pushed the blankets back, and the air crept cold and damp around her. Her breath misted. She smelled the decaying blood on her clothes, like metal and ripe meat.

The wailing from above had stopped. Quiet hung over the place, the world heavy with silence. Was she alone in this house? Had Billy Crawford, if that was really his name, left her here?

She climbed out of the bed and picked her way through the remnants of the drawer she had smashed. Once more, she pressed her ear against the door and listened.

Galya leaned her forehead against the smooth paint and commanded herself to think. Not panic like before, not cry in fear, but think until she found a way out.

She stepped back from the door and surveyed the room. The bed, the chest of drawers, a closet in the far corner, and the cheap carpet. Nothing else. She went from wall to wall, tapping each with her knuckles. All solid.

The pieces of the smashed drawer lay scattered at her feet. She dropped to her knees and peered under the bed. Dust scratched at her lungs and nasal passages. She reached for the drawer front, its handle still attached. It felt solid in her hands. She got back to her feet and dropped it on the bed.

A single painted door sealed the closet. Galya opened it. Empty, save for the spiders and their webs. It was perhaps sixty centimetres wide, and the same in depth, with bare floorboards at its bottom. She stepped inside, felt the rough wood on her feet.

The smell in here was different. Cleaner.

No, not cleaner. Newer. She smelled paint, not brand new but not long applied.

She ran her fingertips over the surfaces of the walls, felt the almost imperceptible ripples left by a paintbrush. If the rest of the room was so old and worn, why paint the interior of a closet?

Galya explored further with her hands, letting them skim the walls and up into the darkness over her head. She couldn't reach the ceiling, but her fingers found something hard and cold.

A hook.

She stretched up until she found the chain it hung from, pulled, and found it fixed solid to the closet's ceiling. It was strong enough to support her weight, her toes skittering across the floorboards until her knees hit the rear wall with a hollow thud.

Hollow?

She released the hook, let her feet settle on the floor. With one knuckle, she tapped the left wall.

Solid.

The right wall.

Solid.

The back wall.

Hollow.

Again, Galya tapped, exploring the surface, listening as she went. She worked left to right, an inch at a time. Every gentle knock resonated until she got halfway. A solid part, perhaps two inches wide, then hollow again all the way across.

She stepped out of the closet and lifted the drawer front from the floor. Its corners were blunted from being rammed against the glass, but it was all she had. She moved back into the closet and raised the drawer front to shoulder height. Putting her weight behind it, she drove the wood into the rear wall.

The torn animal voice rose somewhere above. Galya closed her eyes and prayed once more to Mama's spirit.

Again, she struck the wall. A sprinkling of dust fell away. The voice called in response.

Another strike, all her strength channelled through her shoulders, and a small square of plaster fell away to reveal thin wooden slats.

'Thank you, Mama,' Galya whispered.

32

Lennon found Roscoe Patterson playing pool in a social club off Sandy Row. Roscoe didn't look up as Lennon entered. He took his shot, potted the purple stripe, and lined up his next.

'A word,' Lennon said, kicking snow from his shoes.

'Fuck off,' Roscoe said. The yellow stripe went down.

His pool opponent glared. The half-dozen fellow drinkers watched from the shaded corners of the bar.

'That's not nice,' Lennon said, keeping his tone as friendly as he could manage given the surroundings. 'C'mon, just a word. It'll only take a minute, then you can get back to beating your friend here.'

Roscoe looked up at his compatriot but didn't spare Lennon a glance. He placed the cue on the table and walked past Lennon towards the door, keeping his jaw firm and his eyes averted all the way. He grabbed a coat from a hook by the exit.

Lennon followed him out to the patch of waste ground that served as a car park.

'You know better than to come round here,' Roscoe said as he fished a packet of cigarettes from his coat pocket. 'What makes you think I've got anything to say to you? You're lucky I didn't have your fucking brains blown out after that last time you came asking questions.'

'Desperate times call for desperate measures,' Lennon said. He pointed to Roscoe's cigarettes. 'Can you spare one?'

'Not for you,' Roscoe said. He cupped his hand around the flame from his lighter until the cigarette caught.

Lennon plucked the cigarette from his lips and brought it to his own. He inhaled the heat.

'Cheeky cunt,' Roscoe said, taking another from the packet.

'Charming as ever,' Lennon said. 'This won't take long. Help me out, and I'll piss off. Don't, and I'll be round to your house for my Christmas dinner.'

Roscoe lit his cigarette and put the packet away. Snow settled on his shaven scalp. He pulled his hood up.

'Fuck, you don't want Christmas dinner at my house. My missus wouldn't know a turkey from a turd.' He took the cigarette from his mouth long enough to spit in the snow. 'So what do you want?'

'Sam and Mark Mawhinney,' Lennon said.

Roscoe smirked. 'Them two? They had it coming. Pair of scum-bags. They used to do the odd wee bit for me, but they dipped their hands one time too many. I gave them a beating and told them to fuck off. They got tied up with Rodney Crozier's lot, so they were in good company.'

'Running prostitutes?' Lennon asked.

Roscoe's smirk turned to a grin. 'You should know,' he said.

Lennon felt his face redden, hot against the icy breeze. 'Watch your mouth,' he said. He couldn't hold Roscoe's stare. 'I don't do that any more.'

Roscoe raised his eyebrows, his grin widening.

Lennon and Roscoe had once had an understanding. Lennon visited some of the apartments Roscoe ran his girls from, took advantage of the services at no charge, and in return none of them got raided. It worked out for everyone. Roscoe ran a clean business, or as clean as such an enterprise could be, and he always had an ear to the ground. Anything worth knowing was on his radar.

That understanding had ended over a year ago when Roscoe had let Dan Hewitt know that Marie and Ellen were hidden in one of his places. The betrayal earned Roscoe a beating. Had he not been so useful to Lennon, he would have gotten worse.

'A tiger can't change its spots,' Roscoe said.

'You mean a leopard.'

'Aye, whatever you say. Anyway, yeah, the Mawhinneys took to running whores.'

'What kind?' Lennon asked. 'Trafficked?'

'Aye,' Roscoe said. 'Dirty fuckers. I don't hold with that carry-on. It's a dodgy business, full of dodgy boys. Like I said, they had it coming.'

'These dodgy boys,' Lennon said. 'Would they be Lithuanians?'

'That's right.'

'One of them was Tomas Strazdas,' Lennon said. 'You ever come across him?'

'A couple of times. Mouthy bastard, quick with his fists. Not any more, though.'

'Not any more,' Lennon echoed. 'Sam Mawhinney cut his throat, so someone blew his brains out.'

'No, he didn't,' Roscoe said.

'What?'

'Sam Mawhinney didn't cut your man's throat,' Roscoe said. 'Some girl did.'

'Some girl?' Lennon leaned close. 'A prostitute?'

'Aye, some whore,' Roscoe said. 'She cut your man's throat and got away. The Liths held Sam responsible, so they popped him. Then Mark Mawhinney tries to get the Liths back for his brother. I heard he got his neck broke for his trouble.'

Roscoe stopped talking and started laughing. 'Fuck me, you really don't know shite, do you?'

'No,' Lennon said, not sharing his amusement. 'Enlighten me.'

'Mark was mouthing all round the place he was going to get even. His mate Jim Pollock let him know that big fella was going to come over to buy some gear. Seems Mark wasn't up to the job, so the big fella gave him a doing and got away.'

'Big fella?'

'Herkel or Hercules or something like that. Big fucker, looks like he could hammer you into the ground. Works for the dead fella's brother.'

'Herkus,' Lennon said, remembering his conversation with Dan Hewitt.

'Aye, maybe. Anyway, he's going mad looking for this girl. He's put the word out through Gordie Maxwell, offering money and everything.'

'Any word on where she is?'

'They think she might be with some bloke who uses whores regular.' Roscoe smiled. 'Maybe that's you.'

Lennon ignored the jibe and dropped his cigarette in the snow to fizzle out. 'I'd consider it a personal favour if you'd give me a shout as soon as you hear anything new.'

'Might do,' Roscoe said. 'What's in it for me?'

'I don't tell your missus what you said about her cooking.'

Roscoe grinned. 'Arsehole.'

'Keep in touch,' Lennon said as he trudged through the snow back to his car.

'Away and shite,' Roscoe called after him.

Lennon unlocked the Audi and climbed in. He inserted the key into the ignition, turned it, and flicked on the wipers to clear the snow that had settled on the windscreen.

The dashboard clock read coming up on one o'clock. He had intended calling back to Susan's flat for lunch so he could see Ellen. But Gordie Maxwell's office was all the way across town.

A girl, Roscoe had said. All this caused by a prostitute who escaped her captors. Lennon took the passport from his pocket and studied the photograph, even though he knew it was unlikely to be her. Was she still in the city? How close was Herkus to finding her?

He dialled the front desk at his station. Moffat answered.

'I need you to put a call out,' Lennon said. 'Tell everyone to keep an eye out for Herkus Katilius. You can scare up the registration number on his car.'

'What do I tell them it's about?' Moffat asked.

'Nothing, for the moment,' Lennon said. 'Just tell them if they spot him, find some other reason to give him a tug. If anyone detains him, give me a call and I'll go to them. And warn them he's dangerous.'

'Will do,' Moffat said. 'By the way, I heard some rumblings from the higher-ups. No press release, nothing official just yet, but they're treating all four killings as one case.'

'That's no surprise,' Lennon said.

'There's more,' Moffat said. 'Looks like it's falling to DCI Thompson's MIT.'

Lennon cursed. 'Which means it falls to me,' he said.

'Merry Christmas,' Moffat said.

Lennon hung up and started the engine.

33

Billy Crawford, wheeling a flatbed trolley, walked directly to the trade section of the Boucher Road hardware superstore where they stocked building supplies. He hadn't expected the girl to call him so quickly or he would have been better prepared. Normally it took a week or two of abuse at the hands of their captors to make them desperate enough to find a way to call him.

But this girl was different.

If he'd known, he wouldn't have made the contact so close to Christmas. Thankfully, it had occurred to him to double-check his tools before it was too late. On inspection, he realised he needed blades for his twelve-inch hacksaw, a new chisel bit for his hand-held pneumatic drill, and ballast for mixing concrete.

The cellar of his house had a linoleum-covered floor beneath the toolbox and the few pieces of furniture that lay there. If a person were to remove those items, then pull back the linoleum, he would find a concrete surface. And if that person looked carefully, he would see five patches, each roughly a metre square, that had been dug up and filled in again.

There was room for perhaps five more such excavations. Once those were filled, he always had the backyard. Plenty of room.

The cellar's concrete floor was only two to three inches thick, laid over packed earth. The first time he'd had to remove a square of the flooring, he'd used a concrete saw, but it had been difficult to work with in such an enclosed space, and far too powerful for what turned out to be a reasonably straightforward job. The second time, he simply used his pneumatic drill with a good chisel bit to cut the shape of a square, then set about breaking the layer of concrete. By the third occasion, it took less than an hour's work to clear a patch of earth. Another couple of hours' digging and he was done. All that remained was to mix the concrete, refill the hole and cover its contents.

Even allowing for all the sawing to be done, he could start at nine in the morning and be finished by early afternoon. Tiring, certainly, but no more so than a day's work on a building site would be.

Seasonal music played over the superstore's public address system, interspersed with sales messages disguised as holiday greetings. Only a few other shoppers browsed the aisles, all middle-aged men with nothing better to do over the next few days but complete some DIY project or other.

Like him.

There were smaller, friendlier stores much closer to his home but, even if they had been open on Christmas Eve, he would still have come here. He favoured the anonymity. Here they had self-service checkouts where you could scan your own goods and pay without having to engage in conversation with anyone.

He exited the trade section with a twenty-kilogram bag of ballast, a mixture of sand and aggregate to which he would add cement powder and water to make concrete.

Next he went to the tools-and-accessories aisle and found a pack of heavy-duty hacksaw blades. When he'd first begun he'd wondered if he would need a butcher's saw for this kind of work, but the blades and frames were shockingly expensive so he'd tried a regular good-quality hacksaw and found it to be perfectly adequate for the task. He dropped the pack of blades onto the trolley beside the ballast and went looking for the chisel bit.

He searched through dozens upon dozens of drill bits, all hung on pegs, an entire wall of them. Were they out of stock? This close to Christmas, it could be days before they'd have more. What would he do with the girl for all that time? He couldn't keep her in his house for three or four days. Even if he saved her tonight, as he had planned, by Boxing Day the smell would ripen. That had been the case the first time, before he had planned out his procedure properly. Four days it had sat there, festering, before he'd figured out what to do with it.

Calm, he told himself.

If they were out of stock here, they had another depot to the north of the city. He could simply drive there. The chances of their being out of stock in both places were slim.

As his heartbeat came back under control, he spotted the metallic shape in a bin of loose drill bits on the floor beneath the display. He knelt down, pulled the chisel bit from the bin, felt the heft of its thick shaft, the sharpness of its cutting edge through the thin latex skin of the surgical gloves he wore. It made a satisfying heavy clank as he dropped it on the trolley bed.

He scanned his purchases at the checkout, keeping his gaze downward, making eye contact with no one. He fed the machine paper money, waited for his receipt, and wheeled the trolley towards the exit.

As he reached his van, a voice called, 'Sir? Sir!'

He stiffened, pretended he didn't hear. He unlocked the sliding side door and heaved the bag of ballast up into the van.

The voice called again – a young woman, shrill and insistent. He tossed the hacksaw blades and the chisel bit in after the ballast.

Footsteps coming, the voice piercing.

He wheeled the trolley to the bay, wished the young woman would leave him be.

She would not.

'Sir, you forgot your change,' she said as she approached.

He feigned startlement. 'Did I?'

'Here you go,' she said, smiling, holding it out to him. She wore a bright orange bib that matched her poorly applied fake tan. Tinsel circled her neck like a snake, a Santa Claus hat on her head.

'Thank you,' he said, reaching for the coins.

She noticed the latex covering his skin.

'Eczema,' he said.

Her smile almost flickered out before she remembered the good manners her employers had taught her. She dropped the money into his palm without touching him.

'Thank you,' he said. He checked her name tag. 'Collette.'

'S'okay,' she said, backing away. 'Merry Christmas.'

'Same to you,' he said.

He watched her retreat to the store before he climbed into the van and started the engine. As he pulled onto the Boucher Road he argued and counter-argued the seriousness of what had just happened.

Yes, he had made her nervous.

Yes, she would remember him, the items he'd bought, and the surgical gloves on his hands.

Yes, she might even have noted the registration of his van.

All those things would be of concern if the police were to ask her any questions.

But what reason would the police have to question her? What crime would lead them to her door? What news item would cause her to remember the strange man in the car park and lift a telephone?

None at all.

There would be no crime.

That was why he chose them as he did. The stolen souls, the lost girls, the whores with no identities. Would the thieves of young women go to the police when in turn those same young women were stolen from them?

'I steal the stolen,' he said.

He coughed and reddened when he realised he had spoken out loud. It had been happening more often lately. At the oddest of times a thought would fall from his mind and onto his tongue before he could catch it.

Sometimes he would follow it, respond to it, begin a conversation. He had been calling himself Billy Crawford for so long now that it seemed his old self was another person entirely. This other self and Billy would exchange ideas, concepts, argue the rights and wrongs of the world.

Occasionally, not often, but enough to be worrying, the conversations became heated. These incidents had become more frequent since he'd begun his work. Once, sometime between digging the second and third holes in his concrete floor, he had even come to blows with himself.

Such foolishness had to stop. He couldn't afford to be unpredictable in his own mind. His work needed care and a steady hand. Rash actions would see him destroyed.

'Enough,' he said to himself.

Time to think of the now, the definite, not the maybes or the mights. It was afternoon already, and he still had a long day ahead of him. He had a young girl waiting for him, soft yellow hair on her pretty head, and two rows of lovely white teeth behind her lips.

He could almost feel them on his tongue.

34

Herkus cursed the traffic as he fought his way back to the hotel. Christmas shoppers flooding the city centre, too stupid to have bought their presents beforehand. He shouted at them, spittle dotting the inside of the windscreen.

Perhaps he shouldn't have taken that last hit of the cocaine he'd gotten from Maxwell. Two blasts should've been enough to shake the heavy murk from his brow, but still he took another.

He willed himself to be calm as he inched from Chichester Street onto Victoria Street. The hotel stood just a few hundred yards from one of the city's biggest shopping centres. Horns blared as cars tried to enter and exit the underground car park. Two cops did their best to direct traffic but were largely ignored by the motorists.

Herkus was stuck and could do little about it. He turned up the heat and shouted anyway. It made him feel better.

His phone rang.

'What?' he asked.

'It's me,' Arturas said. 'Where are you?'

'Not far, just down the road, but the traffic's bad.'

'How long?'

'I don't know,' Herkus said. 'Might be a while. I've moved maybe ten feet in as many minutes. Fucking shoppers.'

A pause, then Arturas asked, 'Do you have anything for me?'

'Yes, I've got something.'

'Get out and walk,' Arturas said.

'What?'

'Pull over and park,' Arturas said. 'You can walk here if you're so close.'

Herkus gave an exasperated laugh. 'No, I can't. There's nowhere to pull over. Even if there was, I couldn't get across the traffic. It's too—'

'I don't care. Just get here.'

'Listen, boss, I—'

The knock at the driver's window almost caused Herkus to drop the phone.

'Hold on,' he said to Arturas.

The traffic cop bent down and looked through the glass at him, his pudgy cheeks red and wet from the snow. He knocked again and made a winding motion with his gloved hand.

Herkus gave a polite smile and hit the down button.

'Afternoon, sir,' the cop said.

Herkus nodded.

'Any idea why I came over and knocked your window?' the cop asked, a tired flatness to his voice.

Herkus shook his head.

'I came over and knocked your window because I saw you using your phone,' the cop said. 'As I'm sure you're aware, it's an offence to operate a mobile phone when in charge of a motor vehicle.'

'Is it?' Herkus asked. He hung up, ignoring the tinny sound of Arturas's voice, and dropped the phone onto the dashboard. Watching the policeman, he placed his hands in plain view on the steering wheel. The sweat on his palms slicked the leather.

'Yes, it is,' the cop said. 'I'll not ask you to step out of the car because of the traffic, but I'll have a look at your documents, if you don't mind.'

'Dock-ment?' Herkus asked.

'Licence and insurance certificate,' the cop said, his pleasant demeanour growing more forced.

'I English no good,' Herkus said.

'Licence and insurance,' the cop said. 'Now.'

Herkus shook his head. 'No English.'

The cop opened the door, reached in and took the key from the ignition, letting the car's engine die. 'Out,' he said. He jerked his thumb in a gesture that couldn't be misunderstood, whatever the language.

Herkus let his right hand drop between his legs, his fingertips almost touching the floor of the car. The Glock and ammunition lay tucked into a compartment cut into the underside of the seat. He only needed to reach down, pull back the fabric, and grab the pistol.

'Out,' the cop said again.

'No English,' Herkus said again.

Possibilities raced through his mind, but he knew they were fuelled by the cocaine. The packet was hidden along with the Glock. He breathed deep, felt the winter air tingle in his nasal passages.

Be calm, Herkus told himself. Be good. They can't touch you. He lifted his hand from between his legs, picked up the mobile and got out of the car.

'Wasn't so hard, was it?' the cop said.

Herkus shrugged. The other cop had stayed where he was, directing traffic, but kept an eye on his partner as he waved and signalled at the motorists.

'Documents,' the cop said to Herkus. 'Licence. Insurance.'

'Okay,' Herkus said.

He reached inside the car, pulled down the sun visor, grabbed his Lithuanian licence and company insurance certificate, and handed them over.

Herkus waited while the cop examined the plastic card and the sheet of paper. 'European People Management?' he asked.

'My boss,' Herkus said. 'He pay insurance.'

'Your English has improved,' the cop said. 'Well, let's see if you can understand this: we're going to move your car to the side of the road so we can have a proper chat. Okay?'

'Okay,' Herkus said.

The cop whistled to his partner, a taller, thinner man, and beckoned him over. They huddled in conversation, agreed something, and the fat cop got into the Mercedes. He restarted the engine while the other began directing traffic around it.

'Why don't you move over to the pavement, sir?' he asked.

Herkus did as he was told, but took his time about it. He ambled

147

towards the footpath as if it was his own wish to do so. The cop resumed his directing, talking into a radio on his lapel at the same time. The Mercedes inched its way to the kerb.

The phone in Herkus's pocket rang. He pulled it out, looked at the display. Arturas, it said. He cursed and hit the reject button.

Let him wait, Herkus thought. Or he can come out here and talk to these cops.

They didn't care about him using a phone while driving. That was just an excuse to stop him. Something was going on here. What did they really want?

Wait and see, Herkus thought. Wait and see.

35

Lennon cut across the south of the city from Sandy Row, along the Lisburn Road, skirted around Queen's University, then Botanic Avenue. He pulled up at the address on Rugby Road that Dan Hewitt had given him. A light burned in the window of the flat on the upper floor.

He locked the car, went to the door and rang the bell. Stepping back, he looked up at the window. The light went out. He rang the bell again.

'Coming,' a voice called from somewhere inside.

He heard footsteps on stairs, heels on a tiled floor coming closer.

The door opened and he saw a woman with an overnight bag. She stared at him for a moment, looked over his shoulder at his car, then back to him.

'Taxi?' she asked.

'No,' Lennon said. 'Police.'

Her mouth and eyes widened, then her face hardened.

He held his identification out for her to see. She did not look at it.

'I sorry,' she said. 'No English.'

'Rasa Kairytė?' Lennon asked.

She shook her head. 'No English.'

'Can we speak inside?'

'No,' she said.

'Here, then.'

She stepped back, tried to close the door, but Lennon blocked it.

'Tomas Strazdas,' he said. 'Sam Mawhinney, Mark Mawhinney, Darius Banys.'

Her eyes brimmed. 'No English,' she said once more, her voice breaking.

'You could be next,' Lennon said.

'No,' she said. 'Not me. I did nothing.'

'I can help you,' Lennon said. 'Talk to me and I can make you safe.'

She laughed. 'Safe? With police? Arturas owns police.'

'Arturas Strazdas?'

A car pulled up, its tyres spraying grey slush. It sounded its horn.

'I go now,' she said. She stepped out, closed the door behind her.

'What do you mean, Arturas owns the police?' Lennon asked as she pushed past him.

'I go,' she said. Snowflakes settled on her hair.

The cab driver got out of the car and opened his boot. He took Rasa's bag from her and dropped it in. As Lennon followed her, the driver watched him with narrow eyes.

'Where?' Lennon asked.

'Away from here,' she said.

The cab driver asked, 'Something wrong, love?'

'No,' she said as she opened the rear door and lowered herself inside.

Lennon grabbed the handle, stopped her from closing the door behind her.

The cab driver tried to squeeze between Lennon and the woman. 'Here, mate, you can't—'

'Fuck off,' Lennon said, pushing him out of the way. He showed the driver his identification, then spoke to Rasa. 'Who does Arturas have in the police?'

'You arrest me now?' she asked.

'No,' Lennon said.

'Then I go,' she said.

She pulled the door hard from his grip, closed it, turned her eyes away from him.

The driver hurried to his side of the taxi, climbed in, and put it in gear. The wheels spun as they fought for grip before the car pulled away.

Lennon cursed and headed back to his Audi. His phone rang before he got there.

'We've found your man,' the duty officer said.

36

Plaster and wood dropped away until the first hole was big enough for Galya's shoulders. A gap of four centimetres, then more wooden slats, plaster on the other side of those. A few minutes more and she had put a fist-sized hole through that. She dropped the drawer front to the closet floor and wiped sweat from her brow.

The voice above shrilled and undulated. Galya ignored it. Her shoulders and elbows throbbed, pulsing as if she was still hammering at the wall.

She reached through the opening, her fingers finding cool air. Stretching upwards, she felt a hard, smooth surface. Downwards, coarse fabric. Towels, she thought. A closet, like this one.

Where did it open to?

She strained, splintered wood catching on her sleeve. Her fingertips found wood. She pushed. A door gave way. A breeze stroked her fingers. She withdrew her arm and put her eyes to the hole. Daylight, weak but insistent, showed the contents of the closet. Beyond, a hallway, banisters, a handrail.

Galya lifted the drawer front again. She turned it in her grip so the sharpest corner faced the hole. The slats gave more easily now that she was forcing them outward, away from the joists they were nailed to. She grunted with each blow, feeling a deep and hot satisfaction as each piece of wood and plaster fell into the closet on the other side of the wall.

The voice from above answered every strike with a wounded cry. Fevered with the exertion, Galya imagined it was the house that howled, protesting against the injuries she inflicted upon it. She howled back as the hole opened out, larger and larger until light from the hallway beyond touched her face.

Galya let the drawer front fall. She coughed as plaster dust prickled her throat and lungs. It coated the inside of her mouth, so she rolled saliva around to clean it, then spat on the floor. Mama would have scolded her for such an unladylike act. Like a beast in a field, Mama might have said.

Galya laughed, then shot a hand to her mouth. She tasted blood, realised her hands were blistered and cut. Her heart knocked hard against her breast.

'Calm,' she said to herself.

She sniffed, spat again, then snaked both arms through the hole, her head following, then her shoulders, still tender from being forced through the gates of a building site in the early hours. The splintered ends of the wooden slats scratched at her clothing. She pushed stacked towels out of the way and grabbed the forward edge of the shelf they sat upon with her hands. She pulled.

Her feet cleared the floor by no more than a few centimetres. She pulled harder. Sharp points of wood pierced her top and through to her chest. The fine chain around her neck tightened, then snapped, and she felt the cross drop away. She kicked at cool air, trying to force her weight forward. Her heel connected with the closet's door frame, and she understood. She wedged one foot at either side of the door and pushed with her legs.

Her top ripped on the wood, jagged splinters cutting stinging tracks along her stomach and sides. She pulled with her arms and kicked forward with her feet until her own weight dragged her across the shelf and through the hole. Towels tumbled around her as she fell to the floor on the other side, the jarring of her shoulder and neck cushioned by thick carpet.

Galya rolled onto her back, gasping, dust billowing in the air above her. She coughed, and burning pain flared in the muscles between her neck and shoulder. No air to scream, she drew her knees up and clenched her jaw. Black points appeared in her vision, like devilled stars.

Slowly, she pulled air into her lungs, pushed it out again, in again, until her vision cleared. She rolled to her side, holding her shoulder steady as she moved, then got to her knees. Towels lay strewn on the carpet, its pattern darkened by age, flowers interwoven across it.

The paint on the banisters was a dull brownish yellow, the wallpaper the same. It was as if someone had closed the door of this house thirty years ago and never returned. Even the air seemed tainted by decay.

Galya climbed to her feet and stretched her arm out, testing the pain in her shoulder. It eased as she moved the joint. She held her breath and listened. The voice from upstairs still rose and fell, but now it seemed to tire. At first Galya thought it might have been a dog, but now she knew it was human. A human in pain.

On the far side of the room Galya had escaped from was a narrow flight of stairs. She could only see the first few steps before they rose into darkness. The cries echoed from up there. She turned her eyes to the stairs leading downwards, out of this place of strange men and locked doors.

Did the owner of the voice need help? Of course. But Galya had to get out before the man returned. What if the voice belonged to a girl like her? Had he trapped someone else in this house?

She stood still for long seconds, the desire to flee battling the need to help whoever cried so, locked in place by indecision. What if it was she who was closed away up there, crying out like an animal?

'I will help,' Galya said.

She walked to the staircase and stared up into the dark. A cold draught swept past her and ascended as if following her gaze.

'Hello?' she called in English.

The voice stopped dead.

'Hello?' Galya called again. 'Who is there?'

The voice rose once more, louder than before, more ragged as it reached its highest pitch.

Galya looked back to the stairs leading downward, took one step in that direction. She halted, one foot in front of the other.

A thought entered her mind, hard and unforgiving: Mama would help.

Galya knew this to be true. She turned and mounted the first step. It creaked under her foot.

The voice paused, then grew to a shriek, tearing down from the blackness above. Galya put a hand on each wall, steadied herself.

'Help,' she said.

She climbed, slow and deliberate, fighting the urge to turn around. The walls felt damp against her palms. Every stair moaned as she passed. The air chilled, and a deep odour cloyed at her senses, like the smell of the animals on Mama's farm, those that were sick and dying.

The darkness thinned as she reached the top. She saw two doors, one closed, the other open. Weak light slipped through onto a small landing, no more than a metre square.

Galya pressed the open door with her fingertips, let it swing inwards, more light flowing out to her. A single bed, more like a cot from a prison cell, stood beneath one window cut into the roof. No other furniture except for a plain wooden chair and a rail with a few men's clothes hanging from it.

She looked back to the closed door. A key protruded beneath the handle. She turned it, felt metal move on metal, tumblers realigning. The door loosened in its frame. She turned the handle.

The smell hit her first. Urine and faeces layered on bile and bleach. Galya brought a hand to her mouth and nose. The howling ceased, cut off by a rasping inhalation.

A bed stood across the room, its headboard against the wall, the eaves of the roof rising up like a church steeple above it. A form lay twitching beneath the blankets.

Galya stepped across the threshold, felt cold floorboards under her feet. She moved slow, watching the bed as she approached. The shape cried out. A thin hand reached up into the shaft of light that cut the stench-ridden air.

A woman's hand, worn by age, nails long, yellowed and cracked. Scars crossed freshly scabbed cuts on the skin.

'Hello?' Galya said in English, her voice too quiet to be a whisper.

The voice answered, an ululation that died to a hiss as the woman's lungs emptied.

'Do you need help?' Galya asked.

A head rose from the pillow, a hollowed face blotched red, spidery white tendrils of hair reaching out from pink scalp. The woman's black eyes stared, a toothless mouth opening and closing. The cords of her neck trembled with the effort of holding her head upright until they could support it no longer. It dropped back to the pillow as she moaned.

Galya drew alongside the bed. The woman gaped up at her. Drool ran from one twisted corner of her mouth, her gums pink and shining behind thin lips.

'Aaaahhhh,' she said, her mouth wide.

'I can't understand,' Galya said. 'Do you need help? Do I get someone? A doctor?'

'Mwaah,' the woman said. Her arms reached up, hands like claws, but her stick-thin legs remained still beneath the blankets.

'What do you want?' Galya asked.

The old woman hissed through her gums and grabbed Galya's arm. Galya tried to pull away, but the woman's scarred fingers knotted around her wrist like hard vines. With her other hand she reached up to the top of the wooden headboard. It was chipped and splintered, dried blood staining its varnish. The old woman dragged her fingers across its surface until a new wound opened.

'Don't,' Galya said. 'You hurt yourself. Is bad.'

The old woman tightened her grip as Galya tried to back away. She brought her bleeding forefinger down to the bedclothes covering her midsection and slashed lines across it.

'Please stop,' Galya said. 'I'll get help.'

The old woman pointed at the bloody shapes she had smeared on the sheets. Galya looked down at them and felt the aged hand release her wrist. She studied the shapes, the red lines, criss-crossing the stained fabric. As she stared, they began to make sense, the lines making a connection in her mind.

Three letters.

One word.

RUN.

37

It took Lennon almost twenty minutes to walk from a side street near Queen's University to the city centre. The traffic had come to a standstill, so he'd decided to park up and trudge the rest of the way through the snow. By the time he rounded the corner of the shopping centre on to Victoria Street, his supposedly waterproof shoes had given in, socks drenched, toes going numb.

His mobile rang as he spotted the two traffic cops and the man they'd detained. Lennon moved close to the shopping centre's wall in the hope of it providing some shelter. He answered his phone.

'That child's been alone all day,' Bernie McKenna said.

'She hasn't been alone,' Lennon said. 'She's been with Susan and Lucy.'

'She should be with family, not dumped with some neighbour who's too soft to say no.'

'They aren't "some neighbour",' Lennon said. 'Lucy's her best friend.'

'That's as may be,' Bernie said, 'but the child's got no call to be on her own at Christmas. I can pick her up and have her back here before teatime. She can spend Christmas with them that wants her. You won't have to worry about it.'

'I'll be home this evening,' Lennon said. 'She'll spend Christmas with me.'

It took some effort to say those words with conviction, as if he really believed them. Family or not, he'd rather Ellen woke up in Susan's apartment than in Bernie McKenna's house.

'That Susan one told me you got called away,' Bernie said, her voice almost gleeful in the scolding. 'Something to do with them killings. She said she didn't know when you'd be back.'

'I'll be back this evening,' Lennon said. 'You'll see Ellen on Boxing Day, just like I told you. Don't ring me again.'

He hung up. The phone rang almost immediately, but he hit the reject button and stowed it away.

Up ahead, a tall broad man in a leather jacket stood scowling at the side of the road, a black Mercedes parked half on the kerb beside him, one of the cops directing traffic around it.

Lennon approached and showed the officers his ID. The big man did not react but continued to gaze into the distance, as if there were things of much greater concern than the policemen who surrounded him.

'Herkus Katilius,' Lennon said.

Herkus shrugged.

'I'm Detective Inspector Jack Lennon. I'm investigating the murder of Tomas Strazdas, an associate of yours.'

Herkus spared Lennon a glance.

'The brother of Arturas Strazdas, your employer.'

'English no good,' Herkus said.

'That's the second time I've heard that today,' Lennon said. 'I didn't believe it the first time, either.'

One of the traffic cops stepped forward. 'His English is fine.'

Herkus gave the cop a hard stare.

Lennon's mobile rang again. He took it from his pocket, saw it was Bernie McKenna, and once again rejected the call. He switched the phone to vibrate, and returned it to his pocket.

'Is there anything you want to tell me about Tomas's murder?' Lennon asked.

Herkus shook his head. He winced when his own phone rang.

'You expecting a call?' Lennon asked.

Herkus gave a sly smile. 'Were you?'

'Not from anyone I want to talk to.'

'Same,' Herkus said.

Lennon wondered for the tenth time if he should have had Herkus taken to the station. For the tenth time he decided against it. The hard environment of an interview room might soften up the average man off the street, but Lennon knew to look at Herkus that he'd seen the inside of a cell too many times for it to bother him in the slightest. A man like him would know to clam up for a formal interview and wait for his lawyer to arrive. That prick Rainey who'd been in Strazdas's hotel room, probably. He'd swoop in and demand Herkus be released or cautioned. And Lennon had nothing but a few whispers to hold over the Lithuanian, so best to do it here. Use the whispers to his advantage.

'I know about the girl,' Lennon said.

The smile fell from Herkus's face. As it crept back, he asked, 'What girl?'

Lennon took the passport from his pocket, opened it, held the photograph in front of Herkus's nose.

'The girl who travelled here on this passport,' Lennon said. 'She probably looks more than a little like the woman in this picture.'

'I don't know about any girl,' Herkus said.

'I do,' Lennon said. 'I know all about this girl. I know she killed your boss's brother. I know Darius Banys and Sam Mawhinney were killed in retaliation. I also know Mark Mawhinney got his neck broken this morning. Sooner or later, I'm going to start thinking you had something to do with all this. Then I'm going to have to take you in and question you under caution.'

Herkus returned his gaze to the distance. 'English no good,' he said.

'I'll ask you one more time,' Lennon said, not letting the frustration sharpen his voice. 'Is there anything you can tell me about Tomas Strazdas's death? Or the girl who caused it?'

'Like I say, I don't know this girl,' Herkus said.

'You look tired,' Lennon said, returning the passport to his pocket.

'You also,' Herkus said.

'Well, I had a long night. I bet you did too.'

'Yes,' Herkus said. 'Long night.'

'Probably chasing the same wild goose,' Lennon said.

Herkus's brow creased. 'Huh?'

'Never mind,' Lennon said. He leaned closer, lowered his voice. 'Listen, I heard a whisper. Maybe you can tell me if it's true or not.'

'Maybe.'

159

'The whisper said there was a man, a punter, talking to the girl before she killed poor Tomas. It said this punter might have some idea where the girl went. You hear any whispers like that?'

Herkus smiled. 'I hear many whisper.'

'I also heard there was a sketch of this man being passed around certain people, that there was a reward being offered for news of his whereabouts. What about that whisper? Did you hear that one?'

Herkus let his gaze creep away, like a lizard crawling for cover. 'Like I say, I hear many whisper.'

'I don't suppose you happen to have a copy of that sketch on your person, do you?'

Snow settled in Herkus's hair. 'What is sketch?'

'A picture,' Lennon said. Cold slipped in through the folds of his coat, bringing weariness with it. 'It's on the back of an envelope. Photocopies are being distributed amongst taxi drivers.'

'You hear this whisper?' Herkus asked.

Lennon felt his patience drain away. 'Listen, let's quit the fucking around, Mr Katilius. I know Gordie Maxwell is handing out copies to his drivers. I know you have the original. Hand it over so we can get out of this cold.'

Herkus shook his head. 'I no have picture.'

'Empty your pockets,' Lennon said.

'No,' Herkus said.

'I wasn't asking,' Lennon said.

'You no have right.' Herkus tapped the side of his nose and winked. 'I know these things.'

'You know sweet fuck all,' Lennon said. 'Stop-and-search powers. You have traces of a white powder around your nostrils and your pupils are dilated. That's grounds for a search. Empty your pockets.' Lennon slapped the roof of the Mercedes. 'On there,' he said.

Herkus stood still, his face expressionless.

'You want to come in? We can search the car too while we're at it.'

Herkus's tongue slipped from behind his teeth, wetted his lips. He cursed in Lithuanian and pulled a wad of notes, sterling and euro, from his trouser pocket, followed by keys, a wallet.

'Jacket too,' Lennon said.

Herkus cursed once more and placed folded papers, a cigarette packet and a lighter on the car roof.

Lennon looked at each page in turn: hotel receipts, a printout of flights for Brussels, a statement from a local bank showing a balance of over fifteen grand.

But no sketch.

'Arms out,' Lennon said.

Herkus kept his big hands by his sides.

Lennon raised them up himself and lifted Herkus's lapel to see the inner pocket. 'You got any sharps on you?'

'I look like junkie?' Herkus asked.

Lennon wiped his thumb under the other man's nose, showed him the white powder. 'Yes,' he said. 'You do. If I stick myself, this won't end well. You understand?'

Herkus yawned.

Lennon slipped his hand into one pocket – empty – then the other. He felt paper.

'What's this?' he asked.

'Don't know.'

Lennon withdrew the paper from Herkus's pocket. A window envelope, torn open, its contents long gone. On the reverse, a crude sketch of a man with a round face, thick dark hair and a beard. Lennon held it in front of Herkus's eyes.

'Is not mine.'

'So it just fell into your pocket?'

'Don't know.'

'And I suppose you've no idea who this is a picture of?'

'Don't know.'

'You won't mind if I keep it, then.'

Herkus held his hand out. 'Is mine now. You no right for take it.'

The bastard was quite correct. Lennon had no reason to take the envelope from him. Even under stop-and-search powers, there was no law against having a picture in your pocket. Lennon fished his mobile out of his coat and held the envelope in front of it. The phone sounded a synthetic whirr and click as he took a photograph of the drawing. He handed the envelope back, along with a business card.

'If you should happen to realise you know something about your associate's death, give us a shout.'

Herkus stowed the envelope and card away and started gathering up the rest of the scraps from the roof of the Mercedes. 'I go now?' he asked.

'All right' Lennon said. 'But remember, we'll be keeping an eye on you and your boss. I expect I'll see you soon.'

Herkus walked around to the driver's side of the car. 'Happy Christmas,' he said, a smirk on his lips.

Lennon did not reply.

38

The cops waved Herkus through the traffic. This detective smelled of trouble. Herkus had known a policeman like him in Vilnius. He was buried in the woods not far from Herkus's wife.

He dialled Arturas and said, 'I'm on my way.'

'About time,' Arturas said.

'The cops pulled me over,' Herkus said. 'They kept me there until a detective showed up. His name was Lennon.'

'Broad-shouldered, blond hair?'

'Yes,' Herkus said.

'He was here this morning.'

'He knows about the whore,' Herkus said. 'He knows she killed Tomas, and he knows we're looking for her.'

'He knows nothing,' Arturas said. 'He's just reaching.'

'He knows enough,' Herkus said. 'He has the passport she used to travel here. There are two more flights to Brussels today. One from Belfast, one from Dublin. You should be on one of them, get out of here until this blows over.'

'I promised my mother,' Arturas said. 'I promised her I'd find the whore. Do you want to tell her we ran away?'

Herkus thought about this for a moment. He had met Laima Strazdienė only once. He had been in Belgium for less than a year, struggling with the French language when in Brussels, confounded by Flemish when he set foot outside the city.

He had been working at a brothel near the Gare Bruxelles-Centrale that serviced the business and diplomatic travellers who commuted through the station. His job description was simple: man the door, refuse those who looked like bad news, and beat the shit out of anyone who caused grief inside.

It had been a busy enough night, but nothing out of the ordinary until an English client, a politician called Hargreaves if Herkus remembered correctly, kicked up hell because one of the girls had taken money from his wallet. Herkus went to the room and stood between the whore and the client. The girl denied it. Hargreaves's face reddened with anger.

'She say she not take it,' Herkus said in English.

'She bloody did,' the client said as he pulled on his trousers. 'I had seven hundred euros when I came here. When I went to get the money to pay her, there was only three hundred. That's four hundred euros gone.'

Herkus looked back to the girl. She ranted in French, the words coming hard and fast. The only one he made out was *enculer*, which he knew meant something bad. Hargreaves understood it too, going by his reaction.

A hard clearing of the throat from the doorway caused Hargreaves to pause. Herkus turned to see Laima Strazdienė enter the room. She stood no higher than his shoulder and had a thin build with elfin features. But he knew there was nothing playful about her.

It wasn't the way she wore a business suit and rings that dwarfed her fingers, or the set of her shoulders as she crossed the room, or the tightness of her mouth. It was the dark chill in her eyes, like pieces of coal embedded in the sockets.

'What seems to be the problem?' she asked in perfect English.

Herkus explained as best he could over the protestations and interruptions of both the whore and the client.

Laima nodded once and gave a polite smile. 'One moment,' she said.

Herkus, the girl and Hargreaves watched her leave the room.

'Where'd she go?' Hargreaves asked.

Before Herkus could answer, Laima returned with a roll of hundred-euro notes in her hand. She counted off four and handed them to the client.

'Of course, there will be no charge for your visit today,' she said.

'Thank you,' Hargreaves said.

Without his anger to shore him up, he was left with only the sordid nature of his business here. He dressed quickly, and thanked Laima once more.

'Please show this gentleman out,' she said to Herkus.

He obliged, guiding Hargreaves out of the room, and Laima closed the door behind them. The Englishman and Herkus exchanged no more words on the way to the front door. Their gazes did not meet as the first screams came from the room they had just left.

The client gone, Herkus lingered there by the door, no desire to hear the cries with any more clarity. The other girls gathered in the hall, exchanging fearful glances, some of them flinching with each new shriek.

Soon the screams became moans, and then faded to silence interrupted by grunts of exertion. The girls drifted back to their rooms, tears in their eyes, unable to bear what they heard.

Eventually Laima emerged. She mopped her brow with a handkerchief, her breath hitching in her chest. The lacy fabric left a red smear on her forehead. Herkus would have told her so, offered to fetch her a clean tissue, but he noticed her rings then.

The strands of hair wafted from them like wisps of candy floss. Skin clung to the diamonds.

'That young woman no longer works for us,' Laima said. 'Please escort her from my property.'

Herkus left the girl within crawling distance of the hospital's emergency entrance. It took the best part of a bottle of vodka to get him to sleep that night.

'No,' Herkus said. 'I don't want to tell her.'

'So we stay,' Arturas said. 'Besides, if this detective really had anything, he'd have formally questioned one of us by now. Keep looking.'

'All right,' Herkus said. 'But it's dangerous.'

'Don't worry. I'll be generous to you this Christmas.'

'How generous?'

A pause. Then, 'Very generous.'

'Okay,' Herkus said.

'But first, bring me what I asked for.'

The hotel came into view. 'Soon,' Herkus said.

39

Galya knew before she tried that the doors would be locked, but hope and fear made her do it anyway. She went to the front first, found it sealed tight, reinforced by a heavy padlock. She pulled inward, aware of the futility of it as she did so, but the door was solid. Wood, no glass, its surface glossed by thick paint.

She went to the kitchen, and her stomach reminded her with a growl that she hadn't eaten in . . . how long? No time to think of that. Instead, she turned her mind to the door leading to the backyard. She jerked the handle. Again no movement. A flutter of panic in her breast. She placed a hand over her heart, kept the fear in its place.

The window above the sink.

She grabbed the net curtain that covered it and pulled. It fluttered to the floor like a dying angel. She lifted one of the wooden chairs from around the small table and threw it against the glass. It clattered to the floor, the window intact, but a mug dropped from the drainer and smashed on the tiles. She looked down at the shards and saw red spreading across a yellow football shirt. She blinked the image away.

Reinforced double glazing, the same as in the room she had been locked in. She knew that to try to break it would waste what strength she had remaining. But what to do? She couldn't stand here waiting for him to return.

Galya went back to the front door and took hold of the padlock, turned it as far as its bar would allow.

Every lock has a key.

Look for it.

She opened each drawer in the kitchen, found nothing but blunt cutlery and useless junk: old batteries, plastic fittings from self-assembly furniture, rolls of tape. The kinds of things people threw away when they had no use for them. But not this man.

In the last drawer, right at the back, she found an old mobile phone. Its casing was bright pink, a shining flower sticker applied to the back of it. She wondered for a moment where he had acquired what looked like a little girl's phone, but she halted her thoughts before they went too far down that path and caused the fear in her breast to rise up and overpower her. She pressed and held the phone's power button.

The screen remained a blank grey, so she dropped it back into the drawer.

When the cupboards revealed nothing more, Galya left the kitchen. Two more rooms led off from the entrance hall. She opened the first, but the door met resistance after a few centimetres of movement. She could barely squeeze her head through the gap and see the darkened interior.

Boxes stacked almost to the ceiling, some containing papers, others holding worn tools or household items. Amongst them, bags of old clothing, blankets and sheets. One of the piles had collapsed, pushing rubbish against the door. A smell lay thick on the air, damp and dust lingering, unable to escape. Galya guessed the door hadn't been opened in months, perhaps years. She pulled it closed, returned the gathered detritus to darkness.

The second door opened onto a living room. A single couch stood at its centre, a low table in front of it, a large bible upon that. The ticking clock on the mantelpiece was the only other item she could see in the room. Another net curtain softened the already muted daylight from outside.

She crossed the floor to the table and looked down at the book. A faded and yellowed bookmark lay across the pages: a picture of Jesus kneeling, his blue-eyed gaze meeting that of a child, a verse in a complex script beneath the image. Galya read the word 'suffer' and searched her memory for its meaning in Russian. When she found it, she looked away.

She noticed another piece of furniture in the room, obscured behind the door she had entered through. An antique writing desk, its roller top open, a dozen or more small drawers arranged around a larger one, all looming like the walls of a castle over a leather mat. Drawers perfect for hiding a key.

Galya opened one after another, finding each empty save for a few scraps of paper. Finally, she pulled the handle of the larger drawer, but it did not move.

A certainty she knew to be foolish settled in her gut: the key she sought was in there. She pulled out the smaller drawers on each side of it, four in total, leaving gaps big enough for her hands. The wood felt cool and dry against her fingers as she reached in and ran them along the drawer's flanks. She twisted her hand so that her fingertips squeezed through the narrow gap at the top, hoping she could reach inside to feel the drawer's contents.

Something was there, something soft, like a velvet cloth. She pushed harder, the wood digging into her flesh, until her knuckles jammed in the small space. It hurt, but she ignored that sensation, concentrated on another. Something hard – no, several somethings – beneath the velvet, their presence barely perceptible to her touch.

Galya pulled her hands free, skin tearing from her knuckles, red beads appearing in the tiny channels the wood had cut. She sucked at them, tasted salty metal, and remembered the Lithuanian, his eyes wide, the bubbling in his throat.

Nausea came in a warm wave. She rode it out while she thought.

The kitchen. Find something to prise open the drawer.

She went as fast as her stinging soles would allow and found a knife – heavy stainless steel, an ivory hilt. The kind of knife Mama would have used to cut hard butter, passed on to her by her own grandmother.

Galya returned to the desk and slid the knife into the gap at the top of the drawer, close to the lock. She pushed up and back, but the desk rocked against the wall, its movement stealing most of her force. She braced it with her hip and tried again.

This time all her strength was applied to the thin panel of wood.

It bowed, but did not break. She crouched down, wedged herself against the desk, pushed up with her legs.

The wood cracked. Galya giggled. Pressure pulsed against her temples.

Once again, she pushed with all the power in her body, and the wood gave way, the drawer's face splitting in two, leaving the lock clinging to a few splintered scraps. Galya breathed hard, her cheeks hot. She pulled the wood away and reached inside.

The velvet bag snagged on the splinters. She slipped her fingers inside the red circle and felt the hard things inside. She knew immediately they weren't keys, or anything like keys, even before they spilled out onto the cracked leather desktop.

Her mind stumbled over the objects, trying to match them to some context from her experience. Jewels, she thought, creamy white pearls with jagged ends like plant roots.

Roots.

Not jewels.

Her stomach turned on itself. She pulled her hand away from the small hard things, scattering them across the leather. They formed a loose circle, arranging themselves prettily for her, a chorus line of enamel and blood flecks.

A row of teeth smiling up at her.

The dizziness might have dragged her to the floor if not for the faint sound of an engine outside.

40

Billy Crawford applied the handbrake and removed the key from the ignition. The old Toyota Hiace van shuddered and rattled as the engine died. He sat silent, thinking about the day ahead.

If he got everything done that needed doing, he might have time to attend the late carol service at his church. He enjoyed the event every year, along with the Christmas Morning service, and he would have been disappointed to miss them. But the girl had been delivered unto him unexpectedly, and who was he to question the Lord's will? If he couldn't attend church, then so be it, God would pardon his absence.

He climbed out of the van's cabin and walked to the back gate, his boots crunching in the snow. It swung closed with a tired creak and he refastened the padlock. He returned to the van, opened the sliding side door, and retrieved the chisel bit and hacksaw blades he'd purchased. The sack of ballast would wait until later.

Trudging to the back door, he sorted through his keys, his breath misting as he hummed 'Silent Night' to himself. He remembered how, as a boy, he had seethed at the other children in assembly mocking the sacred tune. When they sang the line 'sleep in heavenly peace', they would whoop through the last word, making it *peeeee-eeeace*, and giggling among themselves. He imagined Jesus on high, weeping at their disrespect, and he had to fight to stop himself from screaming, '*Enough! Don't laugh at our Saviour!*'

Once, his lip bled from biting it so hard and he had to go to the school nurse. He sat in her room amid the smell of antiseptic and sweat, a wad of tissue pressed to his mouth, anger boiling in his gut.

'Are you feeling all right?' she asked.

He did not answer.

'You're breathing awful hard,' she said.

He spat blood on her dress. She stepped back, her mouth wide. Then she bent down and slapped him hard across the cheek. He walked home with a stiffness in his trousers, heat in places he'd never felt it before.

Thirty years ago, and Billy Crawford still felt the sting of her palm when he reached for himself in the night.

As he inserted the key in the deadlock, he glanced up at the kitchen window.

He froze, his heart thudding against his breastbone.

Something was very wrong.

The net curtain no longer hung on the other side of the glass, the room beyond clearly visible.

'No,' he said aloud.

Stop, he thought. Don't panic.

Forcing steadiness into his hand, he undid both locks and pushed the back door open. From the threshold he saw the upended chair, the shattered mug, the net curtain lying bunched on the floor.

Slowly, he stepped inside and lowered the pieces of hardware to the floor. He closed the door without a sound, sealing out the cold, locked it, put the keys in his pocket. He listened.

Silence. Not even the thing upstairs raised its voice.

He scanned the kitchen, saw the open drawers, cutlery and hoarded objects glittering within.

Odours on the still air caught his attention. Mould and damp, laced with girl-scent. He moved to the hall, and knew the dining room had been opened by the stale smell that lingered there. The living room door stood ajar, and he wondered if it had been so when he'd left. He entered the room. His bible where he'd left it, the couch undisturbed.

He turned to the writing desk, saw the opened drawers, the broken wood.

His treasures, scattered like rubbish on the leather.

He moistened his lips and left the room.

He climbed the stairs and stepped onto the landing. The closet door lay open. He saw the scattered towels, the fragments of wood, the plaster dust, and he understood.

Rage tore up from his belly, and he roared.

41

Galya flinched as the sound reached her. She made herself small in the darkness and listened. His footsteps hard and slow on the uncarpeted stairs, then scuffling on the hall floor above her head.

The cellar's damp cold crept beneath her skin, bleeding into her muscles, reminding them of their fatigue.

'I know you're still in the house,' he called, his voice dulled by the closed door at the top of the cellar stairs. 'I can smell you. I know you can hear me.'

She retreated further into the corner, behind an old freezer that hummed low and steady.

'There's no need to be afraid,' he said. His footsteps creaked along the hallway. 'I only want to help you. That's all.'

Galya felt around the linoleum flooring for anything heavy, anything sharp, anything that could be used as a weapon. She found only ridges and dips in the surface, as if the concrete beneath had cracked and been filled in.

'I know you found some . . . things.' The footsteps stopped at the door above. 'I know it seems strange. To keep those things. But I don't want you to worry. Everything's going to be all right.'

Galya inched along the wall, moving away from the freezer. She felt something hard, wooden, blocking her way. A cabinet. Doors, unlocked. They swung open.

'Those people I told you about,' he said, his voice at the top of the stairway, only a door between him and her. 'I spoke to them when I was out. I went to see them, that's why I was away. They're coming for you.'

She explored the cabinet's innards, reaching into the corners, up into its roof, her fingers clasping at nothing but dust and paint flecks.

'But not today. It's Christmas Eve. They don't have any staff. It'll be the day after tomorrow. But they're coming. Then you can go home. I promise.'

A thin slash of light cut across the floor as the door above opened.

'I promise,' he said.

42

Lennon sent the image to Connolly's phone as soon as he was back in his car, along with instructions on what to do with it.

While he waited, he thought about his next act. Logically, he should have gone straight to Maxie's Taxis to see what he could find out there, but he couldn't help but think about Ellen. Less than ten minutes would get him over to Susan's flat, with traffic thinning away from the city centre. Then he could cut across the river towards Holywood Road.

His phone rang. The display said 'Number Blocked', just as it would from the station.

Lennon thumbed the button and asked, 'Did you get the picture?'

'How're ya, Jack?'

Lennon stopped breathing.

'You there, Jack?'

The voice, its thick southern accent a mockery of sweetness.

'I'm here,' Lennon said.

'You get my card?'

Lennon's fingers still felt dirty where he'd touched it. 'Yes.'

'What'd you think? Did you put it up?'

'No,' Lennon said. 'I tore it up and threw it away.'

'That's not nice, Jack. There's me all thoughtful, and you just throw it away. I'm sure your mother raised you better.'

'I don't—'

'Is that how you're raising that wee girl?'

'Shut your mouth.'

'She's a pretty wee thing. Pity her ma didn't get out like you and me did.'

'Stay away from my daughter.'

'Or what?'

'Or I'll kill you.'

'You killed me already, Jack. Remember? In that big house near Drogheda. You put a bullet in me and left me to burn. You don't get a second go. Not with me, you don't.'

'Stay away from—'

'Next time you see me, Jack, it'll be too late for anything. All you can do is pray I make it easier for you and your wee girl than you made it for me.'

'You fucking—'

'Or maybe I'll burn that child, leave her all scarred and twisted like me. Then I'll give you a year or two to watch her suffer before I put you out of your misery. How's that sound, Jack?'

'I'll kill you.'

'So you said. Merry Christmas, Jack.'

The phone died.

Lennon dropped it on the passenger seat, wiped the heat from his eyes, and started the engine. He ignored the blaring of horns as he accelerated into the traffic, visions of Ellen in flame behind his tearful eyes.

43

Billy Crawford reached for the light switch at the top of the stairs. The cellar stayed dark.

Smart girl, he thought.

Was there a torch out in the van? He was almost sure he had stashed one under the driver's seat in case of emergencies, but the batteries had run out. There was another down there in the dark, sitting in or near his toolbox. So he could go down there and get it, but then he might as well just take care of her in the dark.

He held his breath and listened, heard nothing but his own heartbeat. Hard in his chest, like when he lay down to sleep at night and he was all alone in the world. Even God couldn't see him then, when he was at the mercy of the beasts that roamed his mind.

'Are you hungry?' he asked the darkness.

It did not answer. He took two steps inside.

'I can make us something to eat,' he said. 'I have bread and soup. Or maybe a baked potato. And coffee. What do you think?'

The stairs creaked as he descended until he felt the hard floor beneath his feet. He stood still and silent as his eyes adjusted to the gloom, the light from above allowing vague shapes to emerge from the black. Glass crunched under his boot as he took a step towards the workbench. The light bulb.

He ran his hands over the smooth wooden surface, felt nothing but the dust and swarf from the tasks performed there. To his right, the cabinet. He could see in the dimness that its doors had been closed, even though he was sure he had left them open.

His tongue toured the inside of his mouth as he thought. Yes, he *had* left it open. He crossed to it, gripped the handles.

'I only want to help you,' he said.

He jerked the doors open. No waft of girl-smell rose from its innards. He reached inside, not trusting his eyes. Empty.

'Will you let me help you?' he asked, turning to face the dark space around him. 'Will you, ple—'

A sun exploded in his vision, then died again, leaving bright green contrails in its wake. He raised his hands, trying to swat the glare's residue away.

Another light exploded, but not in front of his eyes. He had a moment to wonder at its source before another blow rocked his head sideways and the floor slammed into his shoulder.

44

Galya reached the stairs, the torch still in her right hand, the force of the blow still ringing in her elbow and wrist, light-bulb fragments embedded in her feet. She mounted the steps, took them two at a time, the open door above her, the light falling through.

Keys.

She stopped, one foot above the other, the door in touching distance. He would have the keys on him. Had she heard them jangle when he hit the floor? Yes, she believed so.

If she tried the front door she would likely find it locked, and she would only have given him time to recover. Better to go back, find the keys, while he was still reeling.

Galya offered a short and silent prayer to Mama and turned around. She descended slowly, her left hand on the rail, her right holding the torch. It didn't cross her mind to switch it on until she reached the cellar floor and felt more tiny pieces of glass pierce her already torn skin.

She turned the torch in her hand until she found the switch. A circle of pale light opened on the linoleum, found nothing but white sparkling glass and a single drop of red.

A sour-milk smell, warm air on the back of her neck.

Galya spun, the torch arcing up and out, but a hard hand grabbed her wrist.

His moon face came close, his teeth bared.

'Please don't,' he said.

Galya tried to pull her arm away, but it might as well have been nailed to a wall. Anger flared in her heart, anger at herself for allowing him to reclaim her so easily. She jerked her arm again, throwing the weight of her body behind it.

His grip hardened. A red line crept from his temple to his cheek, slipping between the thick hairs of his beard.

'Let me help you,' he said.

Galya turned her rage on him and growled as she slashed at his pale skin with her free hand, leaving a red welt beneath his right eye, mirroring the scar that ran above it. Small beads of blood broke on its surface.

He pushed her back and down. She landed hard, sending a spike of pain up her spine. Before she could cry out, he bent down and grabbed a handful of her hair.

'I only want to help you,' he said. 'To save you.'

'Let me go,' she said.

'Shut up,' he said, yanking her head back. 'Don't fight me. Don't make me do something . . . bad.'

'I want to go home,' Galya said, more to herself than to him. 'Please let me go home, I won't tell anyone about you, about this place, please, I—'

'Shut up,' he said, his face close to hers, his sour-milk breath hot on her cheeks. 'I don't understand what you're saying.'

She realised she'd been speaking in Russian. Her mind raced to find the words in English, but they would not come.

He let go of her hair, let her fall back on the floor. The torch flicked on, and she shielded her eyes from its burning glare.

'You can stay down here,' he said, backing away. 'In the dark.'

He reached the steps. 'Think things over. Calm down. Try to understand I don't want to hurt you.'

He climbed, keeping the torch trained on her, watching her over his shoulder. When he reached the top step, he turned and stared down at her.

Galya crawled away from the weak pool of light on the floor, found the darkness.

'Go on,' he said. 'Hide. It won't be long now. You'll see. I have a few things to do, some things to get ready, and then we'll begin. I promised I'd save you, and I will. Just you wait. It'll be beautiful. You'll thank God I found you. They all thanked God I found them. All of them. In the end.'

The door closed, and the air grew thick with darkness. Galya found a corner and wept.

45

Lennon exited the lift and rapped his knuckles hard on Susan's door. It had only been a few hours since he'd left her flat but it felt like days. He had his hand raised to knock again when she answered it.

'Jesus, don't kick my door in,' she scolded. 'What's wrong?'

Lennon looked past her into the flat. He heard the girls' voices, a disagreement of some kind.

'Nothing,' he said.

'You're lying,' she said, stepping back. 'But come in, anyway. You might remember you have a daughter.'

Lennon closed the door behind him. 'Yeah, I'm sorry. It's been a bad day.'

'It's been worse for some people, going by the news. Any closer to getting it wrapped up?'

'A little,' he said.

Susan went to enter the living room, but Lennon took her elbow.

'What?' she asked, a line of concern at the centre of her forehead. 'What is it?'

'Nothing, it's just—'

She pulled away from him. 'For Christ's sake, don't string me along. I'm not one of those slappers you used to trawl the bars for. Tell me what's wrong.'

'All right,' he said, putting his hands on her upper arms. 'Has there been anyone around today? Anyone looking for me? Or anyone unusual, anyone you wouldn't expect to see around the apartments?'

'No,' she said, shaking her head. 'No one. Why?'

'Any phone calls?'

'Just Ellen's aunt about five times.' She folded her arms across her chest. 'Tell me why you're so worried about visitors and phone calls.'

'It's probably nothing,' Lennon said.

'But it might be something.'

'I don't know,' he said. 'Maybe.'

Susan took a step away, her face hardening against him. 'Look, Jack, I do a lot for you. I've never once complained, I've never said no unless I couldn't help it. I've helped you raise that wee girl for more than a year now, and all the thanks I ever got were a kiss and a fumble. I did it because I like you, and I like Ellen.'

Lennon reached for her arms again, but she slapped his hands away.

'Now listen to me, Jack. If there's the slightest possibility that you've brought trouble to my door, then you bloody well tell me. If there's reason for me to fear for the safety of my daughter, then I want to know right now, or you can fuck off.'

He put his hands in his pockets, leaned his back against the wall, and let the air and anger out of his lungs.

'There might be someone out there with a grudge against me,' Lennon said.

'Who?'

'I don't know his name. I don't know anything about him. He's the one who took Ellen and her mother.'

'Christ,' she said, the anger leaving her.

'I was sure he was dead. I thought the fire had got him. Then I got a card this morning. Signed with just one letter: a T. I tore it up and threw it away.'

'Where was it sent from?'

'The postmark said Finglas, but he probably had someone else send it for him. He could be anywhere – abroad, most likely – but he must have contacts, people he can send messages through.'

'So he might not even be in Ireland,' Susan said.

Lennon studied the tasteful pattern on her carpet. 'I got a phone call from him a few minutes ago. He made some threats, nothing specific, but he mentioned Ellen.'

Susan bit on her fingernail. 'You think he'll come for her?'

'No, not now,' Lennon said. 'I don't think so. If he was going to make a move, he'd just make it. He wouldn't give me advance warning. He just wants to make me squirm. To scare me.'

'Did he succeed?'

Lennon looked through the crack in the door to see Ellen grab a crayon from Lucy's hand.

'Yes,' he said.

Susan's fingertips brushed his cheek. Lennon shivered.

'It's okay to be scared,' she said. 'You might be Big Bad Jack to all the scum you lock up, but I know you better than you think.'

She followed his gaze into the living room. 'It's only when you have something of real value that you know what fear really feels like. They're so fragile. I've always got this little ball of terror inside me, that I'm going to lose my Lucy. I don't think it'll ever go away.'

Susan put her palm flat on Lennon's chest, over his heart. 'Welcome to humanity,' she said. 'Now, why don't you go and say hello to your daughter?'

Lennon did as he was told.

Ellen looked up from her drawing, went to speak, then changed her mind. She turned her attention back to the sheet of paper on the coffee table. Lucy, apparently affronted by the loss of her crayon, had flounced off and was busy pulling toys from the box they'd been tidied into.

'Hiya, sweetheart,' he said.

'Mm,' she said.

'What you doing?' he asked, sitting on the couch opposite her.

'Drawing,' she said. 'Where've you been?'

'At work,' he said.

'You said you'd be off today,' Ellen said without looking up.

'I know. I'm sorry. But there's been lots of stuff happening.'

'Are you going back to work?'

Lennon scratched his chin, realised he needed a shave. 'Yes,' he said.

Ellen did not reply.

'But I'll be back tonight,' he said. 'Maybe in time to tuck you in. If not, then I'll be here when you get up in the morning. When you see what Santa's brought you.'

'Auntie Bernie's been phoning,' Ellen said.

Lennon brought his hands together, wrapped the fingers of his left hand tight around the fist of his right. 'I know,' he said.

'She wants me to go to her house for Christmas.'

He swallowed. 'Do you want to go to Auntie Bernie's? Or do you want to stay here with me and Susan and Lucy?'

Ellen thought about it for a few seconds. 'Will you be here for Santa coming?'

'Yes,' Lennon said.

'Promise?'

'Cross my heart,' Lennon said, making two slashes across his chest.

'Say the rest.'

'And hope to die.'

'Okay,' Ellen said. 'I'll stay here.'

'Thank you,' Lennon said.

He slipped off the couch and onto the floor, crawled around the table to Ellen's side.

'What are you drawing?' he asked.

'My dreams,' Ellen said.

He pointed to the picture of a girl with yellow hair. 'Is that you?' he asked.

Ellen shook her head.

He traced the line of reddish-brown footprints across the page. 'Did she walk in mud?'

'No,' Ellen said.

The image of the girl stood at one side of the page. At the other stood what looked like an elderly lady with her arms outstretched, as if beckoning the girl to her. Between them stood a dark figure, drawn in mad swirls and jagged angles.

'Who's he?' Lennon asked.

'Don't know,' Ellen said. 'He smells like milk.'

He looked again at the figure of the girl. For some reason he couldn't quite grasp, he thought of the passport in his pocket, and the picture of a young woman who looked something like the one he sought.

Before he could question Ellen further, his phone rang. He looked up and saw Susan watching him from the kitchenette. The display said the number was blocked, just as it had before. He pressed the green button, brought the phone to his ear, and said nothing.

After a while, a confused voice said, 'Hello?'

'Connolly?' Lennon asked.

'Sir?'

'Sorry, I thought you might be . . . someone else. You got anything for me?'

'Might have,' Connolly said. 'I've been through the ViSOR database, like you said.'

'Okay,' Lennon said. The Violent and Sex Offender Register listed all those convicted of a sexual offence for anything from five years to life, and some who were merely suspected of being a risk.

'I didn't find anyone local,' Connolly said. 'Nobody that looked anything like that sketch you sent, and nothing for assaults involving prostitutes. But there was one bloke stood out.'

Lennon smoothed Ellen's hair, bent down and kissed the crown of her head, and moved out of her hearing. 'Go on,' he said.

'A fella called Edwin Paynter, P-A-Y-N-T-E-R, from Salford, Greater Manchester. He was done seven years ago for assault and imprisonment of a street girl, served about eighteen months. Seems he was caught with this woman tied up in the back of his van during a routine traffic stop. God knows what he was going to do with her.'

'Jesus,' Lennon said.

'Anyway, going by the database, he registered in Salford and the local police kept tabs on him for two years, then he decided he was moving to Belfast to live with an aunt of his, make a new start, I suppose.'

Susan handed Lennon a steaming mug of tea. He nodded his thanks and took a sip.

'So he registers over here,' Connolly continued. 'But after about a year he drops off the radar. He's not been heard of for more than two years now.'

'You got a photo of him? And an address for the aunt?' Lennon asked.

'Yes, but—'

'Email all the info to me. I can pick it up on my phone.'

'But I don't think we're supposed to send any data from ViSOR outside the network.'

'Just do it,' Lennon said. 'I'll take responsibility.'

As he hung up, Susan asked, 'Did something come up?'

'Possibly,' Lennon said. 'We'll see.'

'Do you have time for something to eat? A sandwich?'

'Okay,' he said, taking a seat on the couch. 'Thanks.'

She set about gathering the ingredients, layering bread, freshly cooked ham and salad. His stomach rumbled as he watched her work. To distract himself, he took the envelope from his pocket and studied the sketch. He noted the flow of the pen strokes, the way they cut and slashed the paper until they took the form of a rounded face. His gaze went to the jumbled lines at the centre of Ellen's drawing, the madness of the shape.

An idea edged into his mind, but he swept it away before it could take root.

Susan brought a plate to the coffee table and set it next to his mug of tea.

Lennon's phone chimed as he took the first bite of his sandwich.

46

Through heavy eyes, Herkus watched his boss snort up another line of cocaine from the hotel suite's glass-topped desk.

'Do you want some?' Arturas asked.

Herkus leaned back in the armchair and let his eyelids drop. 'No, I had some already. Let me rest my eyes for a few minutes.'

Arturas kicked his foot, jerking him awake.

'When you track down that whore, then you can sleep.' Arturas paced the room. 'I haven't slept either. You don't hear me complaining.'

Herkus straightened in the chair. 'Of course you haven't slept. You've snorted enough of that stuff to keep an army on its feet. You know, you should—'

'*You* should remember who pays your wages,' Arturas said, stabbing a finger at him.

Herkus considered countering the argument, but the fog across his mind made it seem like too much effort. Instead, he held his hands up in acquiescence.

'Give me some,' he said, rising from the chair.

Arturas laid out a line and Herkus leaned over the desk. It blasted the murk from behind his eyes, left a chill at the back of his throat. He coughed.

Herkus recognised addict behaviour: encouraging others to join in your weakness. He shouldn't have indulged, but the weariness had been chipping away at him all day long.

Arturas smiled.

Herkus didn't know why, but he straightened and returned the gesture anyway.

'I don't miss Tomas,' Arturas said.

Unsure how to answer, Herkus said, 'Oh?'

'I think . . .'

'You think what?'

'I think I'm glad he's gone,' Arturas said. His eyes made darting movements, like insects trapped in a jar.

'You don't mean that,' Herkus said.

'I think I do,' Arturas said. 'Tomas was . . . a problem.'

Herkus took a step away. 'Well, he kept things interesting.'

Arturas snorted with laughter. 'He was a fucking chain around my neck, choking me.'

'You feeling all right, boss?' Herkus asked.

'No,' Arturas said. 'My brother's dead. How the hell do you think I feel?'

'You said—'

'Shut up.' Arturas pressed the heels of his hands against his temples. 'I wasn't thinking straight. Forget what I said.'

Herkus shrugged. 'Okay.'

'Good,' Arturas said. 'Now get out of here and do what I asked you. Don't come back until you've found that whore.'

'Fine,' Herkus said. 'But lay off that stuff. Get some rest.'

'Just go,' Arturas said.

Herkus stretched, walked to the door, and let himself out without saying goodbye to Arturas. He ground the heels of his hands against his eyes as he made his way to the lifts.

Arturas had been a good boss for a long time, and Herkus had been glad of the work. But lately, maybe the last year or so, the cracks had been appearing. Had the decline coincided with the boss's advance into Belfast? Herkus believed so. There was something about this place, the grey and the rain and the hate, that got under your skin. Made you resent the very air you breathed.

He hit the elevator's down button and waited.

What could he do now? Nothing, except wait for Gordie Maxwell to phone with some information. Until then, he'd go down to the car and sleep. He stepped into the lift and hit the G button. The doors swished closed. He leaned against the mirrored wall and let his mind drift.

The phone chimed just as his eyelids sagged closed.

47

Strazdas watched the closed door as he listened to his own blood in his ears.

He knew Herkus was right. He'd die before he'd ever admit it out loud, but he knew the hulking mass of knuckle and belly spoke the truth.

'Fucking peasant,' he said, not caring that he was alone. 'I gave him everything. If it wasn't for me, he'd still be rolling around Vilnius, making a pittance from the loan sharks for beating the shit out of any poor bastard that was a day behind.'

He caught the metallic edge to his voice, like a blunt and rusted knife, and bit down on the back of his hand to silence himself. Once the pain had flushed the madness from his head, he returned to pacing.

Could he rely on Herkus to do what was necessary?

Up until a day ago, Strazdas would have thought yes, absolutely. But then everything had gone to hell and Tomas had died. Herkus's fists could only get him so far. But there was still one other who could help.

Strazdas retrieved his phone from the desk, blew away the white powder that dusted it, and dialled.

'Who is this?' the contact asked.

'Me,' Strazdas said in English. 'Arturas.'

'Why are you calling me? You don't call me. I call you. Understand?'

'Have you found the whore I'm looking for?' he asked.

'No,' the contact said. 'I've got better things to do. But Jack Lennon knows about her, and he's working on it. If he comes up with anything, and I get wind of it, I'll let you know.'

'Do I pay you well?'

'What?'

'Do I pay you well?'

'Yes, but I give you good service.'

'Give better service,' Strazdas said. 'Find this girl, or you will not be my friend.'

'I've never been your friend,' the contact said. 'If I hear anything, I'll pass it on. That's the best I can do for you. Now fuck off and don't call me again.'

The phone died. Strazdas dropped it back on the desk, letting it clatter and bounce on the glass, scattering the powder. He pointed at it.

'I will not be your friend,' he said.

48

The thing upstairs had been howling for an hour or more when Billy Crawford finally climbed the stairs to quiet it.

His preparations were done and he was ready to start, but the incessant crying from above could not be tolerated while he set about his work. No, not at all. So he climbed to its room and opened the door.

It gaped at him from the bed, its pale and wizened face raised to him.

'Quiet, now,' he said as he approached it.

Still it wailed.

'If you won't be quiet, then I'll make you quiet,' he said.

No good, it would not listen to reason, so he took the syringe from his pocket. The thing shook its head, tried to shrink from his grasp, but it could not. He gripped its hair and pressed the needle-less syringe between its lips. With no teeth to block its path, the plastic point slipped between the gums. He pushed until he felt the thing try to resist with its tongue, then he pushed harder. It gagged as the syringe reached the back of its throat.

He depressed the plunger and listened to the gargle of the liquid in the thing's throat. When the syringe was empty he dropped it on the pillow and placed his hand over the thing's mouth. Its body bucked, claws dragging across his shoulders, but eventually it weakened. Its pupils dilated, eyelids fluttering as its body went soft and pliant.

He returned its head to the pillow and wiped the drool from his hand onto the blankets. The silence slipped over him like a cloak, and he relished it for a few seconds before leaving the thing to its slumber.

He knew that one day the thing would not wake, that its body would no longer be able to cope with the sedative, but he did not mind. Sometimes he wondered why he kept it alive. Perhaps, in an odd way, he regarded it as a pet that has lost favour in a household. Like a hamster or a fish that has long since ceased to amuse the children of the family but the parents continue to feed it, quietly hoping for its demise.

Returning to the kitchen, he began preparations for his work. A large bowl for hot water, a kettle, washcloths, soap, a toothbrush, a box of sodium bicarbonate, several cable ties, his torch, and another syringe full of sedative.

But this one had a needle.

He had secured a good supply of barbiturates by breaking into a veterinary clinic almost three years ago. The place stood in the country-side between Lisburn and Moira. It smelled of disinfectant and dog faeces. He had walked through its corridors and rooms, gathering the things he needed, until he found a room lined with cages.

Dogs stared at him from their prisons. Three of them, their tongues lolling as they panted. He put his fingers against one of the cages, let the animal lap at his glove. It was an odd sensation, the wetness once-removed by a thin membrane of rubber. It triggered an image in his mind that launched up from the black depths like a shark. He recoiled, closed his eyes against the memory, before it could fully take form.

Some things were best left forgotten to the waking world. They would come at him in his dreams, he couldn't help that, but he found it best to keep a wall between his old self and his new self while he was in the present moment.

He left the dogs there in their dark cages, made one last tour of the building to make sure he'd left no trace of his presence, and then let himself out.

The police had made an appeal on the news about the missing drugs, said they were dangerous in the wrong hands. But his were exactly the right hands, so no need to worry. He had put them to good use in his work, and would do so again this evening.

God willing.

He carried a chair, the same one he had found toppled when he'd returned home earlier, into the hall and left it by the door to the cellar, then went back to the kitchen to fetch the other items. When everything was in place, he put the syringe, its needle protected by a plastic cap, into his pocket. He took the torch in his right hand and put his left on the door handle.

The door swung inward, and he felt the dark reach up to him. He flicked the torch on and shone its beam on the steps so that he could see his way down. Listening as he descended, he heard the girl's panicked breathing somewhere below.

Clearly she knew the time had come. He had to be ready for her to try something. But she was small and light while he was solid and heavy. She would not get the better of him again.

He stopped at the midway point of the stairs and moved the beam around the cellar, touring its corners and crevices. To his surprise, he found her crouched by the open cabinet. She had not tried to hide, perhaps realising it would be futile. Instead, she had spent her time attempting to open his toolbox, which lay on its side as her fingers worked at the lock.

'Leave it,' he said.

She looked up, baring her teeth like an animal caught feeding on a carcass. But she had such pretty teeth, and he immediately regretted the association.

'Stand up,' he said, taking two more steps down towards her.

She pulled at the toolbox's lid, a low growl from her throat, the cords of her neck standing out. She turned the box on end, gripped it with both hands, strained to lift it from the floor as the weight of the tools shifted inside. She let it drop to the linoleum-covered concrete, trying to somehow break open the lid.

'That won't do any good,' he said as he neared the bottom step. 'It's a good box. You won't break it.'

As he stepped onto the linoleum she hauled the toolbox from the floor again and tried to hurl it at him. It travelled only inches before it slammed and clattered on the ground.

She hunkered down, curling herself into a ball balanced on tattered feet, covered her head with her hands. She muttered something in her foreign tongue and he wondered if it was a prayer. The only word he could pick out was 'Mama', whispered over and over again.

'Please stand up,' he said.

Still she crouched, rocking on her feet, her head clutched between her hands, her mouth moving against her knees.

As he moved behind her, he switched the torch to his left hand and took the syringe from his pocket with his right. He prised the plastic cap from the needle with his teeth and spat it onto the floor. 'Please,' he said. 'One last time. Stand up. Don't make this any harder.'

She wrapped her arms tighter around her head.

He bent down and placed the torch upon the concrete, soft so as to make no noise, then straightened. The torch rolled a few inches, sending her shadow fleeing across the wall. He reached down, grabbed her hair, and pulled her upright.

She screamed as the needle pierced the flesh of her buttock. He pressed the plunger before she could squirm away from him, then pushed her across the cellar. She hit the far wall and dropped to the floor, still crying.

'Quiet,' he said. 'It didn't hurt, did it?'

She spoke only to herself, her rambling prayer continuing in that strange language of hers.

'You could've had it with some coffee, maybe a bite to eat, if you'd listened to me earlier. And now look.'

Her speech slowed and her head dipped towards the floor.

'But it works quicker like this,' he said, taking a step closer. 'You'll be under in no time. You can sleep, let me take care of everything. Don't worry, it'll be all right. You'll be home soon.'

She lay still and quiet before he'd finished speaking, so the man who called himself Billy Crawford set about his work. He did not anticipate any interruptions.

It was Christmas Eve, after all.

49

Lennon parked outside the red-brick house, three storeys, with a small unkempt garden. The sort of house that, just three years ago, would have been snapped up by a property developer and split into rented apartments, or renovated to make a luxurious family home. Most of the houses in the area seemed to have gone that way, but not this one.

He took his phone from his pocket and opened the email. Connolly had copied and pasted the information into the message and attached an image from the ViSOR system. Lennon could see why this profile had rung alarm bells for Connolly: flipping between the photo and the image of the sketch, the similarity was undeniable. The same round face, the same broad nose. No beard, but that didn't mean anything. It was the slash of pink above the eyebrow that clinched it. The sketch had the scar above the wrong eye – the photograph showed it over the left – but that was clearly a trick of the artist's memory. This was the man the Lithuanians were looking for, no question.

Lennon read through the rest of the message, though there was little to add to what Connolly had told him over the phone. The prostitute had been picked up on Sackville Street in Manchester city centre at around ten o'clock on a Saturday night and had been found tied up in the back of Paynter's van by traffic police on a routine drink-driving spot-check at seven the following morning somewhere near Salford Precinct.

Paynter had offered no explanation as to why the young woman was being held captive. She had received only minor injuries during her ordeal, and when interviewed had stated that her captor had washed her feet while preaching, comparing his actions to those of

Jesus. He had then tried to rape her, but was unable to achieve a sufficient state of arousal to carry the assault through.

Another odd side note was that Paynter had spent some time examining, then cleaning, her teeth.

When it went to trial, Paynter pleaded guilty and did not appear on the stand. The proceedings were wrapped up in a day and a half.

After his release, Paynter had gone back to his mother's home off the Eccles Old Road and registered as a sex offender. He'd kept his head down until his mother had died two years later. Days after burying her, he'd notified Greater Manchester Police that he intended to move to Northern Ireland and live with his aunt in Belfast. He was a builder by trade, so the peace-fuelled housing boom would have provided him with plenty of work.

He dutifully registered as a sex offender with the Police Service of Northern Ireland, reporting in when he was required to do so for the next year.

And then he vanished.

The investigating officers had done as much as they could, questioning everyone who knew him – and there weren't many who did – and had come up with nothing. Paynter had behaved himself since his release, and resources were tight, so his disappearance was not given a great deal of attention after a few weeks.

The aunt had sworn blind she'd no idea where he'd gone, the accountant who'd filed his last tax return had died of a heart attack, and the building contractor who gave him most of his work had upped sticks and moved to Spain as soon as the housing market started to deflate.

Which left Lennon back at the start of the trail, at the home of Sissy Reid, Paynter's aunt, with whom he had lived when he first came to Belfast.

He stashed his phone away and opened the car door. A blast of cold made him curse and shiver. He climbed out, his feet crunching in snow that had not yet turned to the greyish-brown slush he was more familiar with, and locked the car.

No footprints blemished the white covering on the garden path.

He was the first to call here since the snow had begun in earnest that morning, and it looked like no one had exited by the front door in that time either. The windows showed no light.

Was there even anyone here? The notes had said the aunt had no other family, but perhaps she was spending Christmas with a friend.

'I guess we'll find out,' Lennon said to himself, his lone voice sounding hard and dry in the winter air.

He opened the gate and trudged up to the door.

No bell.

He knocked and waited.

50

Herkus found the cab driver playing a quiz machine in a chip shop on the Antrim Road. The drive there had been quick now that the Christmas shoppers were deserting the city for their warm homes. Even so, Herkus's patience had worn so thin it had almost disappeared. It wasn't helped by the throbbing that had developed behind his eyes.

Gordie Maxwell had said the driver's name was Mackenzie, that he'd be recognisable by the crude UVF tattoo on the back of his hand.

When Mackenzie realised he was being watched, he turned to Herkus, raised his eyebrows, and said, 'Jesus, Gordie said you were a big fucker. He wasn't joking.'

Herkus took the envelope from his pocket and showed it to Mackenzie. 'This man. Who is he?'

Mackenzie turned back to his game. 'Gordie said there'd be a couple of quid in it for me.'

'Depend what you tell me,' Herkus said.

Mackenzie smirked. 'And what I tell you depends on what the money's like. Christmas costs an awful lot these days, and these is hard times and all.'

The pain scratched at the inside of Herkus's skull. He cleared his throat. 'I ask one time more. Who is he?'

Mackenzie faced him. 'Listen, you Polish cunt, I'm not some hood you can fuck about. You ask anyone around here about me, they'll tell you—'

Herkus punched him in the balls. Hard.

Mackenzie collapsed in a breathless red-faced heap.

The girl behind the counter squealed. Herkus pointed a scowl and a thick finger at her, and she became quiet and still.

He crouched down over Mackenzie, who lay in a foetal position, his hands cupping his groin.

'I am not Polish,' he said. 'Now tell me who is this man.'

Mackenzie started to argue, but Herkus seized his face in one huge hand.

'I am bad mood,' he said. 'Very tired. Don't make fight with me or I hurt you very bad. You understand?'

Mackenzie nodded.

Herkus released his face from his grip. 'Okay. So tell me.'

'All right,' Mackenzie said. 'I don't know for sure if it's him or not, but there was this fella I used to pick up from some of Roscoe Patterson's places. You know, where he runs the girls out of. He never used to say nothing, he was always quiet.

'One of the girls told me he never wanted to do nothing with them, he just wanted to talk to them about religion and stuff, you know, try to convert them. I never thought much of it. There's some people's just odd, like.

'Thing is, he always used to get me to drop him somewhere different. Always somewhere round the Cavehill Road, but never at the one place. Like he didn't want me to know where he lived.'

Herkus pushed the envelope with the drawing into Mackenzie's face. 'This man? This is him?'

'I think so,' Mackenzie said. 'Looks like him, anyway, with that scar and all. But this one time, I picked him up from somewhere out near Newtownards and brought him back to the Cavehill Road. The fare was like twelve pound or something, and he gave me the money and got out. But then after I drove off I sees, fuck, he only gave me a fiver and two ones.'

Mackenzie raised himself to a sitting position, keeping his knees apart so as to avoid aggravating his already tender groin.

'So I turned round to see if I could find the cheeky bastard,' he said. 'I saw him cutting up an entryway to the next street over, one of them as faces onto the waste ground, and I caught up to him outside this house just as he was about to go inside. The way he looked at me when I called after him, I thought he was going to go for me. I swear to God, I thought this fella's a nut job.'

Herkus stood upright and hauled Mackenzie to his feet.

'Where is this house?' he asked.

51

'I told you lot before, I don't know where he is.'

Sissy Reid peered through a six-inch gap at Lennon, keeping the door between them. A Pomeranian barked at him from behind her legs. She kicked it back with her heel.

'I didn't know two years ago, and I don't know now,' she said, and went to close the door.

Lennon blocked it with his hand. 'Even so, I'd like to have a quick chat with you about Edwin. Inside might be better.'

She scowled. 'On Christmas Eve? Have you nothing better to be doing?'

'Yes, I do,' Lennon said. 'But I'm doing this instead. The sooner you let me in, the sooner I'll leave you in peace.'

She sighed and stepped back.

He followed her through her hallway and into the living room. She sat down on an armchair facing the television on which an old Doris Day film played. Coloured lights blinked on a small Christmas tree that sat on the hearth, an open tin of Quality Street chocolates beside it. Half a dozen Christmas cards stood on the mantelpiece.

When none was offered, Lennon took a seat anyway, facing her from the couch. A puff of stale urine odour escaped from the cushion, displaced by his weight. The dog yipped at him all the while, dashing in circles.

'Shut up, Dixie,' she snapped.

The dog whined and settled by her slippered feet. It continued to glare at him, low growls coming from its throat.

Sissy reached for the remote control, muted the sound, but continued to stare at Doris's flirtations with Rock Hudson.

'Go on, then,' she said.

'When was the last time you saw him?' Lennon asked.

'I couldn't tell you exactly, but it was more than two years ago.'

'What was the weather like?'

'What's that got to do with anything?'

'Was it warm and sunny? Cold and wet?'

She shrugged. 'There was a wee nip in the air.'

'Was it dark or light outside?'

'Just getting dark,' Sissy said. 'I was still working at the time, and I'd just got home when he was setting off.'

'You'd just got home. So around six o'clock, then?'

'No, more like seven that night, I think.'

'What did you do?' he asked.

'I was a home help,' she said. 'You know, getting tea for them that can't do it for themselves, lighting their fires, putting out their rubbish, that kind of thing.'

'And it was getting dark, so maybe October time?'

'Maybe,' she said.

'Did he have any friends?'

'No, not Edwin,' she said. 'Not really. He knew people, like, but no one he really socialised with. He kept himself to himself. Quiet, but chatty when he wanted to be. He could be awful nice at times, then other times he could be crooked as anything.

'He got that from his mother. My sister. She always had a wee bit of a lacking in her. I knew she'd wind up in the state she did.'

'What state was that?' Lennon asked.

'In a mental home, screaming at the walls. I sometimes think Edwin couldn't help turning out the way he did, being raised by the likes of that.'

'Was he born here?' Lennon asked.

'No, over the water. Cora was a wild wee girl. Always chasing after the boys. Always thinking they'd like her better if she let them have their way with her. No sense in her at all. She got worse when the soldiers came. Throwing herself at them, she was. And she was a pretty enough wee thing, so she had plenty of soldiers wanted to take her out. Course, she didn't have the wit to keep her legs closed, so they got what they wanted and that was that until she chased after another one. She had our poor Ma's heart broke. There was more than one time she had to get herself sorted, and not by a doctor, if you know what I mean.'

The corners of her mouth turned down in distaste at the idea.

'Then there was this one soldier, he was near for coming out of the army when he took up with her. He mustn't have been wise himself, 'cause next thing you know, they're going together. Like boyfriend and girlfriend, I mean. So when he finishes his tour, they get married.'

Sissy's eyes grew distant as she spoke, memories playing out behind them, the flickering light of the television reflected in their sheen.

'I remember it well. A registry-office do, not even a church. She was starting to show then. Our Ma took us both into town to get new dresses for it, and she near died when she saw the belly on Cora in the fitting rooms. She slapped the head off her right there in the shop. Jesus, I can still hear the screams of her.

'It was a disgrace in them days to get pregnant out of wedlock, not like today. These days the wee girls pop out babies left, right and centre, doesn't matter if there's a daddy for them or not.

'Anyway, thank God yous're getting married, my Ma says, and that was that. There was no reception to speak of, just five of us in the pub with a plate of sandwiches. Cora and her fella, some mate of his, me and our Ma. Cora and the two boys got pissed as farts. Girls didn't worry about drinking when they were pregnant in them days. Me and our Ma drank a half a Guinness each and left them to it.'

She paused, eyed Lennon. 'You have any youngsters?'

'A little girl,' Lennon said.

Sissy clucked and shook her head. 'Wee girls are the worst. They'll break your heart.'

Lennon did not answer, so she sighed and continued.

'So off they went to England. Salford, to be exact, that's part of Manchester.'

'I know,' Lennon said.

'Well, I didn't. Not until I went over to see them one Easter. Awful auld hole they lived in. Top floor of a house, one bedroom, a sink in the corner of the living room, and a toilet they had to share with some darkies that lived downstairs. Three days I was there, and I never saw the husband once. He was out drinking all the time, chasing other women, any sort of badness he could get himself into.

'And Cora was going downhill by then. She did her best to let on nothing was wrong, but you could tell she was coming apart. You know when someone drops in on you unexpected, and you tidy the place in a panic? You know, shoving magazines behind the couch, throwing dirty dishes in the sink, that kind of thing? That's what she was like. Not the house, I mean, but in herself. Like she'd scraped up all the madness and tidied it away. But you could see it there, behind her eyes.

'And wee Edwin. He was maybe five or six at the time. Hardly the clothes to stand up in. I brought him an Easter egg and you'd have thought it was the last bit of chocolate on earth the way he took into it. But I didn't see much of him that weekend either. Cora used to lock him in the bedroom with a bible. Hours and hours in there.

'Aye, she got religion while she was away. Of a sort, anyway. All weekend, she kept trying to convert me. I told her, I says, I go to the Church of Ireland every Sunday morning with our Ma, and that's enough God and Jesus to see me through to the next Sunday. I didn't need no preaching off the likes of her. But still she kept at it, non-stop.

'In the end up I lost my patience with her and said a few things that needed saying. She didn't take too kindly to that, so she put me out. I remember waiting for a taxi out in the rain, wee Edwin watching me from the bedroom window, that round face of his up against the glass. I waved at him the once but he didn't wave back. Just kept staring.

'We didn't hear a peep from her for another year till our Ma got a letter saying the husband had died. Fell piss-drunk into the canal and drowned. Our Ma wrote back, said Cora could come home to us if she wanted, but we never heard anything more. Not until she finally lost the head altogether and got put away.

'Edwin was twelve or thirteen by then. When they found him he'd been locked in the bedroom for more than a week, nothing but the bible to keep him from going mad himself. He was lucky there was a washbasin in the bedroom, or he'd have died in there.

'We wanted him to come to Belfast to stay with me and our Ma – he was her only grandchild, and she'd never set eyes on him – but the granny on the father's side objected. She said she didn't want him coming to this place, with all the killings going on. Can't say I blamed her. You look old enough to remember what this place was like in the Eighties.'

'I remember,' Lennon said.

'Aye, well, not many of us had it easy. As far as I know, when he turned eighteen he took Cora into his care. I didn't hear anything more from them until she died. I never went to the funeral, it was over there somewhere.

'But not long after that I got a phone call from him, asking if he could come and stay with me. I was a bit wary, I'll be honest with you, seeing as I didn't really know him from Adam. But our Ma had passed on a year before and I was finding it lonely here by myself, so I thought, what harm could it do?'

Sissy wagged a finger at Lennon.

'I'll tell you something, though. If I'd known about the other, the prison and the sex-offender business, I wouldn't have let him come near me. But by the time I found out about all that, sure it was too late.'

When Sissy finished speaking she appeared deflated, as if the words had taken all the air out of her. Lennon considered ending the questioning, but knew she was the only connection to the man he sought.

'What about women?' he asked. 'Did he have any girlfriends here? Anyone he brought back? Anyone he visited?'

'God, no,' she said. 'Not unless you count wee Mrs Crawford.'

'Mrs Crawford?'

'Och, God love her, she lived in this big house off the Cavehill Road. An awful auld tumbledown place, stood on the corner, nothing but weeds all around it. I did her home help, and then Edwin did the odd bit of work around the house for her. He got to be pretty friendly with her. Wee cratur had a stroke.'

'Was there anyone else he did regular work for?'

'No, just that auld git who pissed off to Spain.'

'Is Mrs Crawford still alive?' Lennon asked.

'I couldn't tell you,' she said. 'She had another turn just before Edwin went off, and she went into hospital. I never got a call to go back to her, so I assumed she went to a home or something.'

'So where's this house?' Lennon asked.

PART THREE: EDWIN

52

Galya felt as if she was held in a hard embrace, arms like stone wrapped around her, as she lingered in the dim place between waking and dreaming. She journeyed to waking through a heavy fog, a light ahead that at first seemed friendly and welcoming but became more harsh and painful the closer she drew to it.

The first firm slap to her cheek brought only confusion. The second brought anger, and she tried to raise her arms to defend herself, but found her wrists were pinned behind her.

She dragged her eyelids open, struggling to think through the rush of sensations that threatened to overpower her mind. The light sent a spike of pain straight to the centre of her head. She blinked against it, again wanted to raise a hand to defend herself from it, again could not.

A voice said something, somewhere.

'What? Where am I?' she asked in Russian.

The voice came again, but Galya couldn't understand the words. Then she recognised them as English, and played them back, slowly grasping their meaning.

'You're all right,' the voice had said. 'Sit still, now.'

The owner of the voice moved into her vision, his moon face looming over her, lit from above by a single light bulb. She remembered breaking a light bulb, the tiny fragments raining down on her like brittle snow. Then she had been in the dark, alone and waiting. Waiting for the owner of the voice to come.

Come and do what?

Come and hurt her, she thought.

A little of the dark fog lifted and she smelled something warm and damp: steam from hot water. She turned her head as far as she could and saw him lift a large plastic bowl from a workbench. He brought it in front of her and placed it on the floor, at her feet.

She remembered him now, the sour-milk smell, the calming words, the knowing in his eyes, and fear broke through the fog. Her body jerked with the realisation, but she couldn't move her limbs. She twisted around, tried to see what bound her wrists to the chair, could barely make out a tail of plastic: a cable tie. It cut into her flesh as she tried to pull her hand away.

'Don't,' he said. 'You'll hurt yourself.'

Galya began to speak in Russian but corrected herself. 'What are you doing?' she asked.

He smiled at her. 'You'll see. Don't worry, it's something nice.'

As he walked behind her, she followed him with her eyes until the muscles of her neck protested. He took a small bottle and a sponge from the workbench.

'Please,' she said. 'What are those?'

He smiled once more and lowered himself to his knees in front of her. The linoleum covering had been rolled back to reveal the concrete beneath. Galya saw rectangular shapes in its surface where it had been dug up and filled in again. And she knew what for.

'Back home, did you ever read the Bible?' he asked.

She understood the words, but could make no sense of the question. 'Bible?'

'The Bible,' he said. 'About Jesus.'

'Yes,' she said. 'I go to church.'

'Then you know about Mary Magdalene?'

'Yes,' she said.

He took a pair of wire-cutters from his pocket and she tried to recoil.

'It's all right,' he said, his voice low and soft.

Galya felt a pressure at her ankle, heard a hard snipping noise, and her foot was free for a moment before his hard hand gripped it. Her leg tensed.

'Don't struggle,' he said. 'Relax.'

She let her leg go loose, allowed him to take her foot and bring it to his lap. He examined her sole, blowing on the torn skin, wincing with her as he touched it with his fingertips.

'And do you know about Mary Magdalene anointing His feet?' He picked at fragments of broken light bulb as he spoke. 'And, behold, a woman in the city, which was a sinner, when she knew that Jesus sat at meat in the Pharisee's house, brought an alabaster box of ointment.'

With his free hand, he poured a golden viscous fluid onto the sponge before dipping it into the steaming water. He worked the sponge between his fingers, forming a lather.

'And stood at His feet behind him weeping,' he continued, 'and began to wash His feet with tears, and did wipe them with the hairs of her head, and kissed His feet, and anointed them with the ointment.'

He brought the sponge to her sole. The lather stung, and her leg jerked. He shushed and clucked.

'Now when the Pharisee which had bidden Him saw it, he spake within himself, saying, This man, if he were a prophet, would have known who and what manner of woman this is that toucheth him: for she is a sinner.'

He worked the sponge harder against Galya's raw flesh and she cried out, her voice ringing hollow in the cellar.

'You see, Jesus was humble,' he said. 'Even though she was a whore and a sinner, He let her anoint His feet. And then, at the Last Supper, He washed His disciples' feet. And Peter said no, Lord, I won't let You wash my feet. But Jesus did. Even though it was beneath Him, He did it anyway. So even though you're a whore and a sinner I will anoint *your* feet.'

He lowered her foot to rest in the water. She gritted her teeth as the scalding heat blotted out the pain of her tattered skin. He lifted the wire-cutters from the floor and freed her other foot.

'And so you'll be saved,' he said. 'I will deliver you unto Him cleansed and anointed.'

He reached up and placed his fingers beneath her chin, his thumb against her lips. Galya tasted soap and hot water. The thumb moved across the opening of her mouth, burrowed between and in, until it met the hardness of her teeth.

'So clean,' he said. 'I'll make you so clean.'

53

Herkus stepped back onto the road and looked up at the house. In the orange glow of a street light, the place next door looked derelict, but this one was well kept. The windows looked odd, though. An old house like this should have had sash windows with wooden frames, but instead it had modern PVC frames and double glazing.

He looked around.

A strange place, two houses standing together away from all the others, at the apex of a bend. They faced no other buildings, front or back. Probably very few people ever came this way.

A cold feeling swamped Herkus's gut to match the icy wind that blew snowflakes all around him. He knew many things that no man should know. Things that can't be forgotten, no matter how much you might want to.

And Herkus knew this was a killing place.

So he would be careful. He went back to the Mercedes and fetched the Glock 17. Its weight in his pocket reassured him.

A lane cut along one side of the house, leading to the back. Herkus followed it, noting the snowed-over tyre tracks, and came to the rear of a walled yard.

The tracks formed two sides of a triangle where the vehicle had turned and reversed through the wooden gates that now stood closed. They would be locked, of course, but he tried them anyway.

He crouched down and put his eyes to the opening through which the padlock and chain were visible. Like the front, the back of the house showed no sign of life. A van stood parked in the yard, however. Its owner was in there somewhere, Herkus was certain of that.

If he stretched he could just reach the top of the gate. He grabbed hold. The toe of his boot barely fitted in the opening, but enough to get some purchase. He hauled upwards, his arms straining to lift his bulk.

Balancing there for a moment, he caught his breath while taking in the whole of the yard. It was dark, but he could make out the vague shapes of things under the snow. A wheelbarrow, what looked like a cement mixer, and other white-covered forms.

He pulled once more, threw his leg over the top of the gate, and let his body follow. Herkus was not a graceful man and he landed heavily, jarring his ankles and knees. He steadied himself against the gate for a moment before crossing the yard to the van.

He placed his hand against its bonnet. Cool. He looked at the ground. Footprints led to and from the gate, then back to the house, all covered with a fresh layer of snow. No new tracks except his own.

Herkus walked to the back door. He tried the handle, found it locked solid, then went to the window.

Cupping his hands around his eyes, he could make out a kitchen beyond the glass and, deeper inside, a hint of light. He scoured the yard until he found a pile of bricks submerged in snow, neatly stacked to form a cube. He tested the heft of one, then returned to the window.

Putting his weight behind it, he threw the brick at the centre of the window. He had to make a hurried sidestep to avoid being struck as it bounced back. A scuff on the glass was the only evidence of the blow.

Tempered glass, he thought. Whoever lived here wanted to keep those on the outside where they were – and perhaps those on the inside, too. But Herkus knew how to break tempered glass. He could use the Glock to do it, certainly, but the sound of the shot would carry across the streets and draw attention.

All he needed was a stout screwdriver, the point of which he would place at the very corner of the pane, and something substantial to strike the other end with. The brick would do, and he had a screwdriver back in the car.

'One minute,' he said to the glass.

54

Billy Crawford stood quite still, listening.

What had he heard?

It had been loud enough to be audible above the girl's choked cries. He had been working for some time with the toothbrush and bicarbonate of soda, her head pushed back, her mouth forced open.

Ideally, he would have liked to brush her teeth several times over the course of a day or two. But circumstances were not entirely under his control. Given that extra bit of time, he might have been able to whiten her teeth even more. Besides, they were already exceptionally pretty teeth, so he couldn't be too disappointed.

She had fought him at first. That was only to be expected. They always fought him until they found out the powder was harmless. She had sealed her lips shut, clenched her jaw tight, keeping the toothbrush out until he'd yanked on her hair. Then she'd opened her mouth to yell in pain, and the toothbrush had slipped in like a cat through a neglected doorway.

She had squirmed, but he'd maintained his grip on her hair, peering in, guiding the brush back over her molars and up to her incisors. Her spittle made cool points on his skin when she coughed.

Then the noise: a ringing, hollow bang from somewhere above.

He froze, his head cocked to one side. The toothbrush remained in the girl's mouth, and she gagged.

'Quiet,' he said, pulling the brush free.

She coughed hard, bucking in the chair.

He reached down, lifted the towel from the floor by the bowl. She tried to bite his fingers as he forced it between her teeth but the material got in the way. Her muffled cries continued.

'Quiet,' he said again.

She would not obey.

Anger flared in him and he raised a hand to strike her. She shrank from him, suddenly silent, her eyes screwed shut.

'Good,' he said. 'Now stay that way.'

She breathed hard through her nose, her shoulders rising and falling. He stepped away, his attention directed to the top of the stairs.

Had the noise come from the back of the house? It had sounded like something striking a window. At Halloween, children from the nearby estate ventured over and threw things at the house. He watched them from the top floor, little demons sneaking through the laneway, thinking themselves invisible. But he saw them, and he imagined the punishments he would have inflicted upon them if it had not been for fear of drawing attention to himself.

Billy Crawford went to the bottom of the stairs, straining to hear anything above the sound of the girl's whimpering and his own thundering heartbeat. He had given the thing upstairs a second dose of barbiturate; it would remain silent, not stirring until tomorrow. He considered telling the girl to be quiet again, but decided it was pointless. It was no good, he would have to go up there, find out what the noise had been. He climbed.

The house stood in darkness, just as he'd left it. The place had a stillness about it that he'd loved since he'd first set foot in it three years ago. The thing upstairs had been human then. Before it had changed. Before the Lord had gifted this place to him.

He walked to the kitchen, slow and careful, placing each foot before him like a tightrope walker. The world outside glowed orange on black, the street light on the path to the rear coating the snow. He approached the window, his breath held tight in his chest.

Footprints on the snow.

A scuff at the centre of the glass.

He released the air from his lungs as his head went light. Someone had been here. Someone had tried to break his window. Someone wanted in. Maybe a teenager from the estate, a hooligan seeking valuables to steal.

The tempered glass had been expensive, but it had saved the life of whoever had tried to gain entry. If the trespasser had succeeded in breaking the glass, it would have—

He inhaled, held his breath again.

A figure appeared at the top of the gate, silhouetted by the street light. A big man, hauling his weight over, dropping to the other side. Not a teenager, not a hooligan out for some easy thieving. This man wore good clothes. This man had broad shoulders and big hands.

Why had he come here?

The man who called himself Billy Crawford did not panic. Instead, he dissolved back into the darkness of his own house and watched.

And waited.

55

Herkus stooped to pick up the brick with his right hand and returned to the window. With his left hand he placed the point of the screwdriver against the glass at the lower corner of the pane.

He looked through the window one more time, letting his gaze wander over the variations of darkness beyond. Was there a disruption in the shadows that hadn't been there before? Probably a trick of his fatigued mind. Either way, it was too late now. He had set his course of action and he would stick to it.

The window held at the first attempt. Herkus cursed and drew his right hand back once more. He struck the butt of the screwdriver harder this time and in an instant the glass transformed from a solid pane into thousands of tiny crystals showering down to the ground. It sounded like a waterfall.

He scraped fragments away with the point of the screwdriver, then lined it up on the second pane. The glass gave with the first blow, and as the pieces glittered around him he felt a wall of warm air fall from the house.

Once the tinkling and clattering of the glass fragments had ceased, he stood still and listened. There could be no surprises. Whoever dwelled here would have heard the window shattering. Herkus did not believe he would call the police. The man whose home this was had gone to great lengths to secure it. Clearly there were things in here he did not want others to see.

Herkus put one foot on the windowsill, gripped the frame, and hauled himself up. Glass crunched beneath his feet as he stepped on the draining board on the other side and lowered himself to the floor. He grunted as he straightened his back. A man of his size was not built for climbing over gates or through windows.

He shivered. A sweat had formed on his body, and now it chilled him.

In the dark interior he could make out the door to a hallway. He crossed to it, his footsteps as light as his bulk would allow, his breathing slow and shallow, his hearing strained for any movement around him.

A crack of light caught his eye as he left the kitchen. It formed a rectangle in the black. He went to it, ran his fingers over its surface until he found a handle. The door opened with a hard creak to reveal a wooden staircase. Below, a muffled voice.

A girl's voice.

56

Galya's throat tightened against the sickly salt tang. She coughed, but couldn't expel the towel from her mouth. For a few moments she thought she might vomit, and the idea of choking here in this cellar terrified her as much as anything she had experienced in the previous twenty-four hours.

She forced herself to breathe deep through her nose, letting the oxygen flood her mind, dampening the panic enough to allow her to think. She thought she had endured all the fear she could, more than she would ever have thought possible. It might have been easier had sanity deserted her but her mind had clung on, even though it seemed it could do her no good.

But then the madman left her, and hope stole back in. For a moment she cursed it, wished she could banish it from her consciousness, but still it came.

Once more, Galya prayed to her grandmother's departed soul. She screwed her eyes shut and begged Mama for some miracle, some way out, anything. Her prayers had gone unheeded up to now, but she offered them regardless.

Tears stole her vision as she opened her eyes. She blinked hard and felt the hot lines on her cheeks. The haze cleared, but only for a moment, because what she saw caused yet more tears to fill her sight.

A man, tall and broad, coming down the steps, his big hands ready to free her.

Galya Petrova wept for joy, thanked Mama's soul, and offered one last prayer.

Please, Mama, let him be real.

57

The man who had once been Edwin Paynter watched from the top of the stairs. He had flattened himself against the kitchen wall, become part of the darkness, when the big man broke the window and entered. He had remained there unseen until the big man left the room.

Back when he was Edwin Paynter he had worked hard on not being seen. He had often enjoyed following people, observing them from only a few feet away, while they were oblivious to his interest in them. Particularly women. He had taken tremendous pleasure in stalking young mothers as they toured the aisles of supermarkets, unaware that he followed their every move. Now and then the woman would pause, bring her fingers to the back of her neck as if trying to brush away some irritant, and he would have to suppress a giggle.

Once, he had tailed a woman in a business suit from the first aisle all the way through the store to the checkout, and out to her car. It had been one of those new Volkswagen Beetles. Many things crossed his mind when he realised she and he were alone in that corner of the car park. A dozen impulses fought for release as he watched her pack away her shopping, none stronger than the urge to save her, show her the way of the Lord. But his higher mind, the part that concerned itself with his own preservation, reminded him that, if he acted in such a rash manner, then all would be lost.

That woman had no idea how thin a wall stood between her and the beast he held caged in his heart. Had he not been so strong, she would have felt the blessing of its rage.

These people, he thought later that night, these aimless animals, they don't know what watches them from the dark corners of their world. They only live because I – and the Lord I serve – allow it.

He had taken three by that time, but they had been messy, risky enterprises. The second had been better than the first, and the third better yet, but the spell in prison had taught him to restrain himself until he could carry out his work with the skill it demanded. Then the Lord had guided him to this city, and this house, and he knew then that he could begin his journey.

But that was all over now.

The big man was no burglar. He had not chosen this house at random. And if the big man had sought this place out, then there would be others.

In the time it took for a window to shatter, Billy Crawford ceased to be. Edwin Paynter was reborn. And Edwin Paynter had prepared for a time such as this. A time when he would have to run.

But first, the big man.

And the girl.

He switched the screwdriver from his left hand to his right and raised his fingertips to the light switch.

58

Herkus struggled to comprehend what he saw. It was the whore, all right, exactly as Darius had described her, and almost the woman in the passport photo the cop had shown him. But she was bruised and cut, like she'd been kicked from here to Ukraine and back again. Blood caked her clothes. A towel had been rammed into her mouth, and her feet rested in a bowl of bloody water. Cable ties bound her hands to the chair, and a toothbrush and a pair of wire-cutters lay on the floor by the bowl.

And, in spite of it all, he had never seen a girl look so joyous. God help her, did she think he had come to rescue her? He almost laughed, but closed his mouth tight lest anyone else hear.

Who had done this to her? The man Rasa had drawn? If so, he was clearly sick in the head.

And probably still in this house.

Herkus considered his best course of action. The priorities were straightforward: Arturas wanted the whore dead, and he would want proof of such. The simplest option would be to use the Glock to put a bullet in her head and then take a picture with his phone to show to the boss.

Simple was always best. Herkus did not believe in complicating matters unnecessarily. He drew the Glock from his waistband, chambered a round, and pressed the muzzle to her forehead.

He had a second to watch the hope and joy in the whore's eyes die away before the light went out and darkness fell upon him.

59

Lennon recognised the Mercedes as he pulled up behind it. He climbed out of his Audi and walked in a circle around the Merc. Footprints led to and from its driver's door, leaving a trail that ran around the side of the house.

'Shit,' he said, leaving a puff of mist to hang in the air.

The snow had stopped, but the cold bit harder and deeper than it had all day. He turned in a circle. How could a house in the city feel so isolated? What lay inside? What was Strazdas's thug doing here?

Lennon had no intention of going into this place alone. He grabbed his mobile from his pocket and called the Duty Officer at the station.

'Have you got a car available near the Cavehill Road?' he asked. 'I've got a suspected break-in, but I don't fancy tackling this by myself.'

'Most patrols are in the city centre,' the Duty Officer said. 'Keeping tabs on the drinkers. Shouldn't be too busy yet, though. You want me to send one your way?'

'Yes,' Lennon said, and gave him the address. 'I'll sit tight until—'

The icy quiet shattered with a gunshot from inside the house, the echoes of it deadened by the snow that shrouded everything. Dogs barked their alarm in the surrounding streets.

'Shot fired,' Lennon said. 'Get that car here now. Tell them I'm in trouble.'

60

Herkus had hit the concrete floor hard, the air knocked from his lungs. He had tried to roll away but the weight had settled on his chest, depriving him of air. The Glock almost slipped from his fingers, but he tightened his grip, brought it up, squeezed the trigger blind.

The muzzle flashed on a round moon face, its teeth bared, its eyes wide. Then the weight was gone and he could breathe again.

He scrambled backwards until he hit a wall. A high whine and a sensation of pressure in his ears disoriented him. His mind scrambled to piece together his surroundings from the fragments he'd noticed as he entered and found the whore. The madman's hearing would be as dulled as his own, but he would be more familiar with the layout of the cellar.

Herkus felt something as close to panic as he'd ever experienced. Should he move? Stay still? He swallowed hard to clear some of the pressure in his ears.

He could tell the madman he only wanted the whore, that he'd take her and be on his way, and no harm need come to him. But how to reason with madness?

Through the whine, he heard the whore's choked breathing. It sounded close to the floor. Had she fallen?

Herkus commanded himself to think, forced his mind to find some sort of order. True, the madman had the advantage of knowing his own dark cellar, but Herkus was armed. If the madman wanted Herkus, he would have to come to him.

He crawled towards the sound, feeling the rough floor ahead until he touched the whore's soft skin. Exploring with his fingertips, he found her cheek, her nose, the rag forced into her mouth. His free hand gripped her throat while the other pressed the pistol's muzzle to her temple.

'You want the whore?' he demanded of the darkness. 'You want me? You come.'

He grabbed the chair's back and dragged it away from the centre of the room. She kicked and mewled as he hauled her across the floor. He stopped when he felt the cold hardness against his back once more.

'You come,' he said.

'No,' a small voice said.

Herkus spun to his right, aimed the Glock in the direction of the word.

'How did you find me?' the voice asked, now to the left.

Herkus re-aimed, squeezed the trigger. The flash illuminated the madman watching from the opposite corner. Herkus swung the Glock in that direction, fired again into the darkness, the second flash showing nothing but empty air.

The whore screamed, the sound muted by the rag in her mouth and the new layer of interference in Herkus's hearing. He shook his head, swallowed, tried to shake the whistling away.

'That gun is very loud,' the madman said, his accent odd to Herkus's hearing, not like the other people from this city. 'It hurts my ears. Don't shoot it again or I'll do something bad to you. How did you find me?'

'I only come for the whore,' Herkus said.

'She's mine,' the madman said.

'No,' Herkus said. 'You steal her.'

'The Lord delivered her to me.'

Herkus laughed. 'My boss buy her. Aleksander deliver her. She not yours. She is ours.'

'Do you doubt me?'

The voice so close. Herkus swiped the Glock through the air, sure it would make contact with the madman's head. It found nothing.

Herkus blinked. His eyes began to distinguish shapes in the black, but none of them had the form of a man. He returned his free hand to the whore's throat and squeezed until she gagged.

'I'll kill her,' he said.

'That would be a waste,' the madman said. 'But if you must. There'll be another. There's always another. People like you bring them here to sell. No one knows who they are. They can't be traced. If one of them disappears, who'll report them missing? So the Lord brings them to me.'

'You're crazy,' Herkus said.

'It might appear that way. But you're wrong.'

'You're not crazy? Then listen to me. This whore belong to a bad man. She killed his brother. Now he want her dead. I take her away, it's over. I don't, this bad man, he come for you. Understand?'

The madman laughed. 'You can't scare me. Don't you see? I have the Lord Jesus Christ on my side. If an enemy comes to do me harm, He will strike them down.'

'No,' Herkus said. 'Jesus will not help you. He won't strike my boss down.'

'Yes, He will,' the madman said. 'Like this.'

Something punched Herkus hard in his side, below his ribs. Then a weight fell on him again. He tried to bring the Glock around to fire at whatever was pushing him to the ground, but the gun was so heavy, his fingers unable to hold it any more. It clattered on the concrete.

He smelled sour milk, felt a warmth spread across his abdomen.

'Like this,' the madman said.

The spike of burning heat withdrew from his side, leaving a deeper pain behind, but it struck again in a new place.

And again.

And again.

Herkus reached for it, felt something long and thin and hard, slippery with wetness.

Lips soft against his ear, teeth hard behind them.

'Like this,' they said.

61

Lennon heard the second shot as he lowered his feet from the kitchen sink to the tiled flooring. The third followed moments later.

'You're a fucking idiot,' he told himself again.

An idiot for going in alone after he'd heard the first shot. An idiot for not turning around and getting out when he heard the next two. He had advised himself of his own stupidity several times in the last few minutes, yet his higher mind seemed unwilling or unable to accept guidance from his gut instincts.

Jack Lennon was an idiot when he joined the police. He was an idiot when he refused to accept a commendation for saving the life of a fellow officer under fire. He was an idiot when he left his unborn daughter when she was still in the womb. He was an idiot when he drove a killer called Gerry Fegan across the border to settle a score.

Lennon knew he had been an idiot all his life, but it had never stopped him.

He drew his pistol and made his way deeper into the house.

62

The man who was now, as he was sure he always had been, Edwin Paynter applied upward pressure to the screwdriver's handle, forcing the blade to dig its way through the foreigner's innards. The foreigner screamed.

Paynter eased the pressure on the handle and waited for the foreigner to stop writhing.

'How did you find me?' he asked.

'Taxi company,' the foreigner said, forcing the words between his teeth.

'What taxi company?'

'Maxie's Taxis,' the foreigner said. 'Rasa made a picture. I show it to the taxi boss. He find you for me.'

'What picture?'

'Rasa made it,' the foreigner said.

'Who's Rasa? Who made it?'

'Rasa works for my boss. Looks after girls. She sees you with the whore, she makes a picture.'

Paynter's mind spun, searching for possibilities, answers, ways out. But all was lost. A picture of him had been circulated. There was nothing left now but to run.

No, there was one more thing, and she lay beside him, choking on the towel he'd shoved in her mouth.

Anger, white-hot and glorious, burst in his chest.

She had caused this. She had brought this intruder here, her girl-scent drawing him like a bitch brings dogs from miles around.

'Bitch,' he said.

'Fucking bitch.'

He clamped one wet hand to his mouth. Had he said that? Had he ever uttered such words before?

She made him do it. She made him spew these hateful consonants and vowels. She was a devil, and before he could flee he would have to cast her down with the rest of her kind beneath the cellar floor.

He reached for the screwdriver's handle, ready to pierce her temple with the blade, but the foreigner moaned as he withdrew it from his belly.

Edwin Paynter took a breath, cooling himself from the heat of revelation. Calm, he thought. He knew what he had to do.

'First things first,' he said.

Paynter pushed the foreigner's head back, felt for his exposed throat. He switched his grip on the screwdriver to overhand and raised it above his head.

'There's a cop,' the foreigner said.

63

Herkus sucked air and leaked blood.

'The cop, he knows about you,' he said.

His mind grasped at this last shred of logic. Anything to make the madman stop, to buy him some time. It worked. The blade, whatever it was, did not penetrate his body again.

'What cop?' the madman asked.

Herkus searched the pain and fog for a name. 'Lennon,' he said. 'Lennon. He knows your face.'

A stinging mix of bile and blood bubbled up into his throat. He coughed, screamed at the fire that ignited in his belly.

'How?' the madman asked.

Herkus kicked out, tried to crawl away. The madman placed a knee on his stomach. Herkus screamed again.

'Tell me how he knows my face.'

'The picture,' Herkus said, squeezing out the words between tortured gasps.

'The same picture? What are you talking about?'

Herkus wanted to answer, hoped to save his life with the knowledge, but the pain dragged his mind down, robbing him of speech.

'Tell me,' the madman said, his breath hot on Herkus's face.

The darkness grew darker still. Herkus willed his tongue to move, air to charge his vocal cords, but there was nothing left but the fire that spread from his stomach to swallow his being.

And the faces.

So many faces, all of them waiting for him.

Oh God, he thought, the words forming in his mind like bright stars above him.

Oh God, forgive me.

And then something brighter pierced his throat, and he knew there was no forgiveness, only fire.

64

Galya lay on her side, feeling the heat spread beneath her, the same metallic smell that had overwhelmed her just a day ago. She writhed, trying to pull her body away from the blood, but the chair held her in place. She worked her jaw and tongue until the towel fell from her lips.

Behind her, the sound of something hard piercing flesh. One man breathed hard with each thrust, the other gurgled and gasped, until only animal grunts remained.

She tried to force her weight forward. If she could turn on her front, onto her knees, maybe she could crawl away. The chair leaned and fell back again. She pulled once more, using her shoulders to twist the chair around. Again, it fell back.

Galya shrieked with the effort. This time, the chair followed her and her knees hit the concrete. She swallowed the cry and pushed forward.

Something pulled the chair back.

'You did this,' he said.

He turned the chair on its back, wrenching Galya's arms. Her head struck the floor and sparks ignited in her vision. She heard him step away, then return, his breathing coming in hard rasps.

A light exploded in front of her eyes, and she turned her head away.

'Look at me,' he said.

The torch beam found its way beneath her eyelids no matter how hard she squeezed them shut.

His wet palm struck her cheek. 'Look at me.'

Galya opened her eyes a fraction, saw the vague outline of his moon face by the burning light.

'You caused this,' he said. 'You brought him here. You made me kill him. Everything's ruined because of you. I have to run because of you.'

Galya could think of only a few words to say, all of them Russian, so she spoke them.

'English,' he said.

She repeated the words, the only sounds that meant anything to her.

'I don't know what you're saying,' he said. He shook his head. 'Doesn't matter.'

He pointed the stained red blade of the screwdriver at her. 'The Lord delivered you to me. So I will finish His work. I promised Him that. But you will suffer for what you've done. Beg forgiveness for your soul, for I will not spare you from the hell that's waiting for you. But not here. It's not safe here any more, because of you.'

She heard the screwdriver drop to the floor, felt the cold bite of the wire-cutters working at the cable tie that held her left wrist to the chair.

Again, Galya spoke. Again, she said the only words that she could form.

She said, 'Please, Mama, take me home.'

65

Fragments of shattered glass crunched under Lennon's feet as he made his way across the darkened kitchen, his Glock 17 drawn and ready. His breath misted as heat left the house through the empty window frame.

As he moved into the hallway, a thin streak of light moved across the wall ahead of him. He tensed, brought his left hand up to support his right, pressure on the pistol's trigger.

A door revealed a wooden staircase leading downwards to a cellar. Shadows shifted and twisted in the opening like demons wrestling over souls. He reached the top step and saw a torch beam moving in the black pit below.

A voice, low and hoarse, rose up to Lennon. He could make out only a few words among the rambling. *Your fault. Will suffer. All lost. Run.*

Another voice, soft, a girl's voice, worked below the other, reciting the same few words over and over again, words Lennon did not understand.

Lennon peered into the darkness and saw the torch shone on a young woman, bloodied and semi-conscious. Its halo revealed only a hint of the man who held it. The light weakened as it reached the top of the stairs where Lennon stood, but it was enough to show the switch. He hit it with his elbow and steadied his aim.

'Police!' he called.

The man stared up, wide-eyed, his mouth open like a hole torn in the pale disc of his face.

Lennon took it all in at once – the body of the Lithuanian he had questioned earlier, the blood pooling on the floor, the scattered tools, the pitiful form of the girl bound to the upended chair – and aimed the Glock.

'Edwin Paynter,' he said. 'Move away from the girl.'

Paynter's eyes widened further at the sound of his own name. He fell back, pulling the chair and the girl with him.

'Stay back!' he shouted, bringing something red to the girl's throat.

For a moment, Lennon thought Paynter wore a shining glove. When the fabric dripped onto the girl, he knew it was not a glove but the dead man's blood coating Paynter's hand and the screwdriver it gripped.

He tried to steady the Glock's aim on Paynter's forehead, but neither his hand nor the crazy man below would stay still.

'Let her go,' Lennon said, taking a step down.

'Don't come down here,' Paynter said.

'I'm coming down, Edwin,' Lennon said. 'I'm going to come down and get the girl. You let her go and you won't get hurt.'

The sane part of Lennon's mind shrieked at him to get out of there. But the girl's eyes fixed on his and he knew he had no choice.

'You hear me, Edwin? Move away from her, and I promise you won't get hurt.'

Paynter laughed and reached for something by the Lithuanian's body.

Lennon's reflexes understood before his consciousness did, and he dropped low as the cellar boomed with the discharge and the wall by his head exploded in a spray of red dust and brick fragments.

His balance gone, Lennon tumbled head first down the rest of the stairs, the wood slamming into his shoulders, his elbows, his knees as he turned end over end. The concrete floor struck his chin, and he tasted blood as his vision blackened.

The world skipped a beat and he was on his back, staring at a bare light bulb, his hands empty by his sides. A broad shape moved into his line of sight, blotting out the bulb's painful glow. A moon face smiled down at him.

'When will you people ever learn?' Paynter asked.

Lennon blinked up at him, coughed as he swallowed his own blood.

Paynter hunkered down and pressed the pistol's muzzle to Lennon's forehead.

'You can't beat me,' he said. 'Not when I've got the Lord on my side.'

66

Edwin Paynter had never held a gun before. When he'd grabbed it from the floor, he wasn't sure if firing it was as simple as pulling the trigger or if there was some trick he wasn't aware of. For all he knew, he might have ended up having to throw it at the policeman.

But it was indeed as simple as pulling the trigger. The recoil had sent a shock up through his elbow and into his shoulder, and his arm tingled. And his ears whistled. And it had caused a heat and a hardness in his groin.

Now Paynter had the policeman at his mercy, blinking stupidly up at him like the dog he had owned as a teenager, the dog that had continued to gaze at him with witless adoration even as he'd calmly kicked it over and over again until its eyes dimmed and its tongue sagged in its reddened sputum.

Paynter liked this gun. It was noisy and it hurt his arm, but it felt good to use it. He looked at the policeman's gun lying a few feet away and wondered if it had the same kind of bullets. It appeared identical to the one he now pressed against the policeman's forehead.

'Have you ever shot anyone?' Paynter asked.

The policeman hesitated. 'No.'

'I don't believe you. Have you ever been shot?'

'Yes,' the policeman said.

'Did it hurt?'

'Yes.'

'Were you scared?'

'Yes.'

'Are you scared now?'

'Yes.'

'Good,' Paynter said. 'I am an instrument of the Lord, and fear is the only proper response. It took me years to learn that. When people looked at me strange, when girls didn't want to talk to me, I thought there was something wrong with me. But there wasn't. They were acting like they were *supposed* to act. Afraid.'

He stood upright, keeping the pistol aimed at the policeman's head.

'What did he say your name was? Lennon, I think. Well, Mr Lennon, it's time I was going.'

The policeman's breathing quickened, his chest rising and falling. Paynter tightened his finger on the trigger, feeling the pressure, the hair's breadth between terror and for ever silent. The policeman screwed his eyes shut and raised his hands in some pointless effort to shield himself.

Enough, Paynter thought, just—

The floor rushed up at him and the pistol boomed, sending the bullet into the concrete. He had a moment to wonder what had slammed into him, sending him sprawling on the floor, before something hard struck the back of his head.

67

Lennon felt rather than saw the girl slam into Paynter. He'd seen her coming, covered his head with his forearms, and weathered the battering of elbows, knees and feet.

The girl let out an animal shriek as she set about her captor with the chair that was still bound to one of her wrists. Lennon scrambled back as she raised it and brought it down on Paynter's head. He kicked to untangle his feet from the other man's and rolled to his side to reclaim his Glock.

Paynter groaned and tried to deflect the blows with his hands, but the girl's determination got the better of him. For a few seconds it seemed he had given in, but then he turned and struck out with his boot. He caught the chair, throwing the girl's balance.

Lennon got to his feet and raised the Glock. 'Don't move,' he said. 'I'll put one in you, I swear to Christ.'

Paynter stared up at him for a moment, incredulity on his face, before a high peal of laughter escaped him.

The girl went to swing the chair at him again, but Lennon forced himself between her and Paynter.

'What's so bloody funny?' he asked.

'You swear to Christ? You think the Lord Jesus cares what promises you make?'

Lennon struggled for an answer. When one wouldn't come, he did the only other thing he could think of: he kicked Paynter hard in the balls.

Paynter doubled up and rolled onto his side, his face turning first red, then purple.

The girl lay curled against the wall, muttering something.

Somewhere outside, in the cold night, sirens rose and fell. Lennon crouched beside her, said, 'It's all right. Help's coming.'

Paynter groaned and squirmed.

'You move, and I'll shoot,' Lennon said. 'Understand?'

Paynter did not respond. Instead, he retched and spat on the floor.

Lennon kept an eye on him as he listened to the girl. Her words came tumbling one after the other, thick with her Slavic accent, a language he didn't understand or even recognise. Lithuanian? Latvian? Polish?

Whatever she said, she repeated it over and over until it sounded like some mantra, a deranged prayer to an ignorant god.

Lennon spared her a glance. 'Do you speak English?'

The sirens drew close, along with the sound of engines pushed into anger.

'What's your name?' Lennon asked.

Still she repeated the words, blurring and smearing them until he couldn't tell where the prayer ended and began again. It climbed in pitch, punctuated by desperate inhalations.

Lennon grabbed her wrist. 'What are you saying?'

She gasped and stared as if woken from a nightmare. For a moment, Lennon thought he was looking at Ellen stirred from her night terrors.

The girl blinked and said, 'Please, sir, I want to go home.'

68

Strazdas had been sitting slumped on the floor for so long, his back against the base of the couch, he'd lost track of time. His head jerked up when his phone rang. He decided to ignore it for the moment. Instead, he focused on the suite's large flatscreen television, unnaturally bright in the darkened room, the colours jarring his retinas with their intensity.

It seemed to be some old comedy show, with two men, one small and old, the other middle-aged but trying to play younger, both of them scruffy, arguing over Christmas decorations in a wretched house.

Was this what people here found funny? Pathetic men with miserable lives? Did it make them feel better about themselves to laugh at the poor souls who were unhappier than them?

The elderly wretch on the television screeched while the younger one scowled and grumbled, called the other a dirty old man.

Strazdas laughed, but he wasn't sure why.

The phone fell silent, and in the absence of noise Strazdas noticed the pain that nestled inside his skull, curled above his eyes.

What had he been doing sitting here?

Oh, yes. Drinking.

He had taken a bottle of wine from the minibar an hour ago. His nerves had been jangling more and more as this damned city fell into darkness, a heavy quiet settling on the street outside as it emptied. The silence had been so thick he imagined he could hear the blood in his veins charging around his body. A less sane man than him might have believed that the cold and the dark, borne on soundless air, were invading the hotel, creeping up its stairs, stalking its corridors.

But he was a sane man, and he believed no such thing.

Not really.

More cocaine did not make him feel better, and he began to suspect that it might even be the cause of his anxiety. So he had opened the little fridge that was hidden inside a cabinet and chosen a bottle of white wine. He had tried to read the label but his eyes seemed unable to pin the words down. He unscrewed the cap, put the bottle to his lips, and swallowed.

Arturas Strazdas did not drink alcohol often so he did not find the taste or, more specifically, the sensation of the liquid in his throat at all pleasant. But still, he persevered.

Going by the throbbing weight in his forehead, he supposed he had gotten drunk. A line or two would lift the fog.

His heart stuttered at the thought. No matter: it was the only appropriate medicine under the circumstances.

He wedged his elbows against the couch and pushed himself up onto his feet. The room felt lopsided for a moment until he extended his arms for balance.

A fine sprinkling of powder still lay on the glass desktop, the hotel key card dusted with it, a fifty-euro note rolled and ready. Plenty for a line, he thought. Best be careful. He had some left in the bag, enough to see him through to the next day if he controlled himself. Herkus could fetch some more in the morning.

Herkus.

Had that been him calling? Had he found the whore?

First, the line.

Strazdas took the card between his thumb and forefinger. He swept it across the desktop, back and forth, up and down, shepherding the powder like a dog herding sheep until he had a thin streak of white.

Not much. But sufficient for now.

He took the fifty-euro note and inserted it into his right nostril, blocked the left with a finger, inhaled the line, and all was beauty and wonder for ever and ever until eternity and beyond.

And then he coughed at the chilled snot running down the back of his throat, and his stomach groaned and cramped because he hadn't eaten since yesterday.

Maybe he should phone room service and get some—

Phone.

His memory caught up with him, and he reached for his mobile to see who had been calling. The display said the number had been blocked.

Why would his contact call at this time on Christmas Eve? If indeed it was Christmas Eve and the clock had not laboured past midnight and into Christmas Day.

As if in answer, the phone rang, the vibration in his palm jolting him more than the sound. He brought it to his ear.

'Yes?'

'Your driver is dead,' the voice said.

Strazdas stared out of his window at the street below, his mind unscrambling what he'd just been told.

'What?'

'Your driver, the man who's been charging around Belfast, searching for that girl you're so desperate to find.'

'Yes?'

'He's dead. Killed in a cellar in the west of the city. Gutted by some crazy bastard, from what I've been told.'

'Herkus?'

'We have the girl.'

Strazdas retreated to the couch and sat down. 'The girl,' he said.

'The one you've been looking for. She's been taken to A&E, but in due course she'll be in our care.'

'Your care,' Strazdas said.

'Listen, are you all right? Are you taking in what I'm telling you?'

Strazdas placed a knuckle between his teeth and bit down hard. The pain pressed against the confusion in his mind but did not push it away. He tightened his jaw, felt something sinewy between his teeth. The fog cleared. He inhaled through his nose and released his knuckle. Deep red indentations lined his skin. He rubbed it against his thigh.

'You're certain she will be in your hands?' he asked.

'Soon,' the voice said. 'She's receiving treatment now, but she'll

248

be released from hospital soon. She has to go somewhere, and all the agencies for dealing with her sort will be closed for the holiday. Besides, she's a witness to at least one murder and possibly a suspect in another. She won't go anywhere but to a police station. My station. I'll figure out how to deal with her. Don't worry.'

'Thank you,' Strazdas said. 'My mother thanks you.'

'One thing,' the voice said. 'Your driver is a known associate of yours. Expect questions. Unless you can get out of the country.'

'Out of the country?'

'Go back to Brussels,' the voice said. 'You won't get a flight until Boxing Day but if you get across the border you'll be okay until then.'

'I want to stay,' Strazdas said. 'Until the whore is taken care of. I can't go to Brussels until then.'

'Why not?'

Strazdas thought of his mother's hard eyes, and her hard hands. 'I can't, that's all,' he said.

'All right,' the voice said. 'I'll deal with her as quickly as I can. But have your bags packed, sort out whatever transport you need for the airport, and be ready to go. Christmas Day might buy you some time but after that you'll be questioned, there's no doubt.'

'All right,' Strazdas said.

'Good,' the voice said. 'And about recompense.'

'What?'

'Payment. Things have gone well beyond the remit of our arrangement. I expect to be compensated accordingly.'

'Don't worry,' Strazdas said. 'You will be. But tell me this one thing.'

'What?'

'Who is this crazy man?' Strazdas asked. 'The one who killed Herkus?'

69

There was no doubt in the mind of Edwin Paynter that he would escape. From the moment the first officers stumbled down the cellar stairs, their guns drawn, to his lying down on a trolley in a hospital corridor, he knew they could not hold him for a single second longer than he chose to be held.

It was simply a matter of biding his time, not resisting, being calm and compliant. Sooner or later, the two policemen who guarded him would slip up, and Edwin Paynter would be gone before they knew his name.

They had no choice but to bring him to the hospital. The girl had opened his scalp with the chair, but Paynter knew that scalp wounds bled heavily, meaning there was no way to be sure if the injury was more serious without a proper examination.

He held a wad of gauze to his temple with his free hand, pressing it hard against the cut to staunch the flow. A pair of cuffs fixed his other hand to the trolley. If he wanted to, he could simply throw his legs off the edge of the bed and walk away, dragging the trolley behind him.

But he did not want to. His exit would be better thought-out than that.

The hospital's Accident and Emergency ward was understaffed and overpopulated. It never failed to astound Edwin Paynter that most people marked the Lord's birthday by refusing to work and drinking too much. It was no wonder, then, that so many of Belfast's drunks wound up in an emergency ward with not enough doctors or nurses to treat them.

So Edwin Paynter found himself bound to a trolley in a corridor, listening to the moans and cries of the city's lowest while the handful of medical staff on duty ran themselves ragged trying to look after the sorry lot of them.

He had always found hospitals strange and frightful places to be, especially the A&E departments. The sounds and the smells. The things occurring behind drawn curtains, the swishes and footsteps that were none of your business. The gatherings of families waiting to be bereaved. The empty-faced geriatrics staring at you from the other side of the ward.

This place was no different. Drunks called out, challenging their demons as they sobered. Young children screamed as their parents fretted. Others checked their watches and cursed their taxes, furious at waiting so long to have their small hurts addressed. All of it meaningless bustle and noise.

Most of it Paynter could only guess at, limited as he was to this narrow bed. Let them suffer, he thought.

A nurse appeared at the foot of the trolley, an orderly close behind her.

'Mr Paynter?' she said.

'My name's Crawford,' he said. 'Billy Crawford.'

She looked at the policemen, confused.

The nearest of them shrugged. 'They told me he's Edwin Paynter. I don't care what you call him, so long as I can get home soon.'

The nurse turned her wavering smile back to Paynter. 'Mr, er . . .'

'Crawford,' Paynter said.

'Mr Crawford, there's no bays available yet but we'll get you into one as soon as we can. We're going to move you off the corridor, though. There's space in the orthopaedic room. All right?'

He did not answer.

The ceiling moved above him as he laid his head back on the thin paper-covered pillow. Wheels and feet squeaked on the vinyl-tiled floor until he rolled through a doorway into a room with beds and curtains, a light box on the wall, rows of drawers, and boxes of bandages.

'You'll be all right here for now,' the nurse said as the orderly pushed the trolley into an empty space. 'How's that bleeding coming along?'

She lifted Paynter's hand away and examined the side of his head. 'You'll live,' she said. 'Right, you sit tight here. It won't be much longer.'

The nurse whisked out of the room, the orderly trudging behind her, leaving the two policemen standing over the trolley.

One of them sat on the edge of the nearest bed while the other paced, moving in and out of Paynter's vision. He noted that their guns looked very like the one he had taken from the foreigner, and the one the policeman Lennon had aimed at him earlier in the night.

The policeman who sat on the bed checked his watch and raised his eyebrows. 'Merry fucking Christmas,' he said.

70

Lennon sat on the edge of the bed while the nurse applied two butterfly strips to the cut on his chin, then covered them with a sticking plaster. CI Uprichard entered the bay as she left. He wore an anorak over a patterned sweater and corduroy slacks. Lennon wondered if he'd ever seen Uprichard in civvies before and realised he hadn't. It made him look every one of his sixty years.

'You pick your moments,' Uprichard said. 'Happy flipping Christmas.'

Lennon smiled at his superior's inability to swear. 'Thanks for coming out,' he said. 'You didn't have to.'

'No, but best to clear up what I can tonight so there's less to fight with when I come back after the holiday.' He lifted Lennon's jacket. 'Come on, they'll want the bay for the next eejit in line.'

Lennon followed Uprichard out through the ward and into the corridor beyond.

'What do we know so far?' he asked.

Uprichard took one of a row of seats lined up outside a consultant's office. 'We're positive he's this Edwin Paynter chap young Connolly found in the ViSOR database. A quick search of the house didn't turn up any identification, but there's no doubt. There'll be a proper search after the holiday.'

'What about the woman upstairs?' Lennon asked, taking the seat next to Uprichard. She'd been found after one of the officers who arrived in the second car had heard moaning from above.

'She can't speak, but we're assuming she's the owner of the house. Looks like this Paynter character had been keeping her prisoner there. Probably for the two years he's been missing.'

'Jesus,' Lennon said.

'One thing turned up in the preliminary search that's . . . well, worrying.'

'What?'

'A bag of teeth,' Uprichard said. 'It's been left *in situ*, but I'm told they're human teeth. Molars, incisors, all in a little red velvet purse.'

'The floor of the cellar,' Lennon said.

'What about it?'

'There were rough patches, different textures, like parts of it had been dug up and filled back in again.'

Uprichard chewed his lip as he thought. 'Of course, this chap has a previous conviction for kidnapping a prostitute.'

'Girls like this one he had in Belfast,' Lennon said. 'Trafficked in, no trace of them if they disappear, no one to call the police for them.'

'It'll be a first for Belfast,' Uprichard said. 'We've never had a serial killer.'

'No, anyone with the inclination to kill for laughs had plenty of outlets until recently. What about the girl?'

'She's still in the ward,' Uprichard said. 'A lady from Care NI's talking to her.'

Care NI was a Christian charity that, among other things, assisted trafficked women in the days following their rescue. Often the women were terrified of the authorities into whose hands they had been thrust, and counsellors from the charity helped them communicate with the police officers, social workers and immigration bureaucrats with whom they were faced.

'She's in a bad way,' Uprichard said. 'But she's a tough wee girl. She'll need to be. This isn't a straight trafficking case. She'll have to answer for the man she killed.'

'We've no real evidence that she killed anyone,' Lennon said. 'Only what Roscoe Patterson told me, and that's hardly gospel.'

'Once forensics are in, there'll be plenty of evidence,' Uprichard said. 'But we can recommend leniency if she can show it was done in self-defence.'

'So where does she go?' Lennon asked. 'The Victim Care Suite, or a cell?'

'It's Christmas,' Uprichard said. 'There's no staff in the care unit to look after her. It'll have to be a cell.'

'No,' Lennon said. 'What she's just been through, we can't lock her up.'

'We might not have much choice if she's a suspect in a murder case.'

Lennon stood up. 'Are you going to arrest her?'

'No, not yet, but—'

'Are you going to interview her under caution?'

'It's not up to me to—'

'Then there's no call for that girl to spend a single minute in a cell until she has to.'

'Then what do you suggest?' Uprichard asked.

Lennon wiped his tired dry eyes as he thought. There was only one answer that would allow him any peace.

'I'm a fucking idiot,' he said.

71

Galya watched the nice woman's lips move, heard the words they formed, but little of it registered with her conscious mind. The woman talked about agencies, police, immigration, women's rights. Sometimes she held Galya's hand.

Sleep edged in, and Galya had to shake it away.

The woman was very kind, and was here to help, she said so over and over.

But the bed was so comfortable, even if every part of Galya ached or stung to some degree, and sleep was an insistent intruder.

Galya's eyes had slipped closed when a cough stirred her. She opened them and saw the policeman lean in through the drawn plastic curtain that surrounded the bed. He said something to the kind woman, and she excused herself and left with him.

On her own, the bustle of the hospital became a soothing murmur, like the sound of a stream in summer. Galya thought of Mama and Papa, the small house she had grown up in, the smell of baking bread, Mama's coarse skin, the road that led to her door. As she drifted deeper into the warmth of slumber, she saw the man with the moon face, the teeth in his hand, showing them to her, counting them out one by one, pointing out those that he'd taken from her mouth, and her finger exploring there, finding the gaps where they'd been, and then he wanted to show her something else, something bright and shining, something sharp, something—

A choked cry escaped her when the kind woman's hand brought her back to waking.

'It's all right, darling,' the kind woman said. 'You're safe. No one's going to hurt you.'

Galya slipped a finger between her lips, ran the tip over her teeth.

When she found none were missing, she gave a silent thank-you to Mama.

She looked from the kind woman to the policeman who stood behind her. He seemed exhausted. A sticking plaster covered the cut on his chin.

'This is Detective Inspector Jack Lennon of the Police Service of Northern Ireland,' the kind woman said. 'He's the one who found you.'

Galya was not sure if she was expected to respond in some way, so she nodded.

'He's been trying to sort out somewhere for you to stay once you're discharged from here,' the kind woman said. 'The police, they have special places for victims to stay, comfortable places. But it's Christmas, and they've no staff to look after you there. The only other place they have is the cells in the police station. You can stay there until after the holiday. You'll be safe, but it won't be very comfortable.'

'Cell?' Galya asked. 'Like prison?'

'Or there's another choice,' the kind woman said. 'This police officer, he has a friend, a very nice lady, and you can stay with her. She'll get you something to eat and there'll be somewhere to have a wash. What do you think?'

Galya remembered accepting another man's offer of help and the terror that had followed. But one desire came to her mind and overrode all fears.

'A bath?' she asked, imagining warm water on her body, the cleansing of it, the heat.

'I don't know about a bath with those dressings on your feet,' the kind woman said.

'Yes, a bath,' the policeman said. 'We'll keep your bandages dry somehow.'

Galya didn't think about it for long.

'Please, I want to go to this place,' she said.

72

Edwin Paynter lay quite still as they wheeled him from room to room, through scans and examinations, while nurses wiped away blood and doctors examined images of his skull. The policemen grumbled about having to stay here instead of going home to their families. They were reminded that a head injury required patient observation and they would have to wait for other officers to come and take their places.

Paynter listened to it all while he kept his gaze on the ceiling. He passed the time by mentally going through the steps that he'd practised for such an occasion. The few minutes of confusion and disorient- ation, then the eyes rolling back, the tongue going to the back of the mouth, concentrating movement on the stomach muscles, keeping the neck loose, the legs kicking out.

He had used this technique once when a young woman had challenged him in a shopping centre, accusing him of following her. It had worked wonderfully, turning her anger to fear and concern.

When the time came he would summon a seizure again, send them into a panic, and let chaos be his saviour.

But not yet.

The two officers who guarded him stiffened when the detective named Lennon entered the room. They stepped back as he approached and sat on the edge of the bed next to Paynter. Dark circles under- scored his eyes.

'Edwin Paynter,' Lennon said.

Paynter kept his mouth shut and returned his gaze to the ceiling.

'The girl's fine,' Lennon said. 'She's being discharged right now. The lady you were keeping upstairs, she'll be all right too. I'm sure you're glad to hear that.'

If Paynter concentrated, he could make out shapes in the pattern of the ceiling tiles. Heads, arms, legs, human and animal figures capering in white and grey.

'You're going to face quite a list of charges,' Lennon said. 'Abduction, probably, or false imprisonment at best. Assault. Then there's the man with a few holes in his gut, you'll have to answer for him. You might argue self-defence, say he was an intruder, but that won't hold up.'

Paynter held his breath when he picked out a face directly above. A kind and loving face, eyes staring back down at him. He smiled back.

'But there's something I'm especially curious about,' Lennon said. 'Those teeth that were found. Where did they come from?'

Paynter turned his attention back to the detective.

'And what's underneath the concrete floor in that cellar?'

The face in the ceiling whispered something, a prompt. Paynter repeated it.

'The Lord will be my judge,' he said.

Lennon smiled, stretching the sticking plaster on his chin. 'Eventually,' he said. 'Before that, you've got the courts to deal with.'

A nurse rolled a tea trolley past the room, its rattles and clanks forming vowels and consonants. Paynter spoke them word for word.

'I'll never see a courtroom,' he said. 'The Lord won't allow it.'

'The Lord has no say in the matter.'

Paynter snorted. The pain in his temple pulsed with his laughter. All around him the hospital whispered, God's word delivered to him on every draught.

'The Angel of the Lord will set me free,' he said. 'Just as Peter was freed from prison, so will I be freed.'

Lennon asked, 'You don't think the Angel of the Lord has better things to do at Christmas?'

Paynter felt the smile fade from his lips. 'It's a foolish man who mocks the Lord,' he said. 'Or his messenger.'

'Is that what you are?' Lennon asked. 'His messenger?'

Paynter looked back to the ceiling. 'There's no name for what I am,' he said.

73

Fresh snow settled on the Audi's windscreen as Lennon parked outside the apartment building in Stranmillis. The girl, Galya, had said little as he drove. She stared out the window, her face blank, his coat wrapped tight around her.

'Here we are,' he said.

Galya did not reply.

Lennon got out and walked around the car to the boot. He opened it and pulled out the foldable transit wheelchair the hospital had provided on loan. It took only a few seconds to open and lock its frame, then lower the footrests. Its small wheels left tracks in the snow as he brought it around to the passenger side.

He opened the door and Galya looked up at him for a few seconds, as if she was unsure of were she was. She took his hand when he offered it, and winced as she stood. He guided her into the chair, supporting her as she sat down. She weighed hardly anything.

On the journey here, Lennon had thought about the women whose company he had paid for. How many times over the last few years? Scores, maybe, even if he had resisted the urge for the last six months. He had always felt shame during and afterwards, but it had never stopped him. They were willing to take his money, he told himself, they had not been coerced. They got paid while he scratched the itch. Nobody got hurt. Nobody suffered.

As far as Lennon knew, none of the girls had been trafficked. Some of them were foreign, of course, with delicate features and Slavic accents. But, in his mind, they were free women. He would never go with a girl who'd been forced into it.

But how could he be sure?

He forced himself to stop thinking about it as he wheeled Galya through the entrance and into the lift. The silence lingered as they ascended. He watched her reflection in the lift's polished walls. Her eyes focused on something many miles away.

Lennon had dealt with enough assault victims to know they were not the same people they had once been. Their lives had been split in two, the Before Person and the After Person. Anything that had ever mattered to the Before Person no longer existed for the After Person.

He wondered what the Before Galya had looked like. He wondered if the After Galya would ever fill that hollowness in her countenance.

The elevator pinged as they reached Susan's floor, and the doors slid open. Susan waited for them in her doorway. She smiled at Galya, but not at Lennon.

'Thanks for this,' he said as he wheeled Galya through the door.

Susan did not answer. She led them through to the living room where wrapped presents were stacked beneath the Christmas tree, the silvery paper reflecting the blinking lights.

A moment of panic gripped Lennon. 'Did you . . . ?'

'Yes,' Susan said. 'I sneaked up to your place when they went to bed. I wrapped them for you too.'

'Thank you,' he said.

'I didn't do it for you,' Susan said. 'I did it for Ellen.'

'All the same, thank—'

'Jack,' she said, looking him hard in the eye. 'Stop talking.'

She crouched down by Galya. 'Now, sweetheart, what can I get you? Something hot to drink? Tea? Coffee? How about some toast?'

'Yes,' Galya said, her voice small like a bird's.

'Okay,' Susan said. She stroked Galya's hand and stood.

Lennon pretended not to notice that Susan had offered him nothing. He wheeled Galya to the seats. After she allowed him to help her onto the sofa, he found himself unsure what to do next. Eventually, he gave in to his own fatigue and settled into an armchair. He let his head fall back on to the cushions and closed his eyes.

What seemed like an instant later, the sound of a cup and plate being set on the coffee table jarred him awake. He lifted his head to see Galya reach for a steaming mug of tea. Susan set another in front of him.

'Not that you deserve it,' she said.

She did not return Lennon's smile.

He took the mug from the table and sipped the hot sweet tea, felt the warmth in his throat and chest as he swallowed. Susan disappeared for a few minutes, then reappeared carrying a bundle of clothes. She set them on the couch beside Galya.

'They'll be a little big for you,' she said, 'but they're warm. Better than those hospital things, anyway.'

Galya returned her mug to the coffee table and placed a hand on the pile of clothing. Lennon smelled the comforting scent of warmed fabric conditioner and had a sudden memory of being a boy in his mother's house, pulling on socks fresh from the hotpress on a cold morning. He smiled and curled his toes at the remembered sensation.

Then Galya crumbled before his eyes, and he felt his smile dissolve.

One moment she sat with her hand on the bundle of clothes, the next she seemed to fold in two, her shoulders hitching, and she wept. A low moan that sounded as if it started in her belly worked its way up through her torso and escaped her throat as a strangled whine. Heavy tears dripped from her cheeks into her lap. She opened her hands beneath them, as if trying to save them from being lost to the fabric of the dressing gown she wore.

Lennon stood, though he had no idea what to do next.

Instead, Susan did it for him. She pushed the coffee table out of the way, kneeled in front of the girl, and opened her arms. Galya fell into them, buried her head between Susan's shoulder and neck.

'It's all right, darling,' Susan said, her breath stirring the fine blonde hairs on Galya's head. 'You're safe here. No one's going to hurt you any more.'

Lennon and Susan's eyes met. Hers brimmed, a deep understanding in them, and he wondered how she knew about this kind of pain. He wanted to say something – thank you, anything – perhaps to touch her, but he could only stand with his arms at his sides, his tongue useless behind his teeth.

A movement on the other side of the room saved him from his own inadequacy. He turned his gaze there and saw Ellen and Lucy peek from the hall that led to the bedrooms.

'Merry Christmas,' he said.

The girls slipped in, unease on their faces as they saw the strange guest.

'You came back,' Ellen said.

'Course I did,' Lennon said, knowing it had been anything but certain that he would keep his promise.

Ellen didn't reply, but crossed the room and hugged his thigh.

'Has Santa been?' Lucy asked.

Lennon cleared his throat, smiled, and pointed. 'Have a look and see,' he said.

He followed the girls to the Christmas tree, brushed Susan's neck with his fingertips as he passed. She brought her hand up to meet his and allowed him a weary smile.

The girls had already begun sorting through the gifts as he lowered himself to the floor between them. Ellen wormed into his lap and set about unwrapping the packages she'd found. She and Lucy giggled and squealed and compared their presents, showing each other the bright boxes and cooing over the contents.

They each found Barbie dolls with various outfits – Lennon and Susan had colluded on this point – and they set about freeing the plastic figures from their packaging.

As Ellen adjusted her doll's arms into a satisfactory pose, Lennon remembered the one she'd had when she first came back from Birmingham with her mother, more than a year ago. It had been naked, its hair straggly, but she loved it anyway. He wondered what had happened to it.

Ellen leaned back into his chest and whispered, 'Who is she?'

'She's someone Daddy needs to help,' Lennon said. 'She's had a bad time, so we're going to look after her just for today.'

'I dreamed about her,' Ellen said.

'Did you?'

'There was a bad man,' Ellen said. 'He wanted to hurt her.'

At one time, Lennon would have been shocked at Ellen's understanding of things that should not concern her. But he had learned over the last year or so that she had a way of knowing things that she should not.

'He's going to jail,' Lennon said. 'He can't hurt anyone.'

Satisfied at his answer, Ellen got to her feet and crossed the room to where Susan dabbed Galya's cheeks with a tissue. Ellen took Galya's hand.

'Come on,' she said.

Without a word, Galya stood and allowed Ellen to lead her back to the tree, taking tiny shuffling steps on her tattered feet. She sat down on the floor between the two girls as Lennon looked on.

Ellen pressed the doll into Galya's hands. 'Lookit,' she said. 'You can change her clothes.' She selected a dress and showed it to the visitor.

Galya smiled and said, 'It is very pretty.'

Ellen chose a trouser suit. 'What about this one?'

'Is pretty also,' Galya said.

'But which one's nicer?' Ellen asked.

'The dress,' Galya said.

Ellen handed her the outfit and Galya began undoing the clasps, her tongue between her teeth, a child's concentration on her face.

Lennon left them to play.

74

Arturas Strazdas dialled the number again.

Still no answer.

'Bastard,' he said after the tone. 'Call me back, you fucking bastard.'

He dropped the phone on the bed. The room felt much smaller than it had yesterday. He had slept for perhaps an hour and dreamt of Tomas lying on a slab, his blank eyes staring upwards for ever, and no one to bury him but Herkus. Except Herkus couldn't do anything for Tomas because he too was dead.

Strazdas had woken with a feeling of weight on his chest, and he had lain there unable to scream for long minutes. When he could move, he rushed to the desk in the living room and pressed his nose to the glass top, inhaling whatever traces of powder still lay there.

He'd been trying to phone his contact ever since, and the bastard would not answer. Two hours had passed, and now the sun cast a milky white light through the clouds that covered the city.

Strazdas opened the window and gritted his teeth against the icy air that flooded in and around his naked body. He stood still and upright, goose pimples spreading over his skin, until he convulsed with the cold.

The phone rang. He grabbed it.

'Where have you been? Why haven't you answered, you fucking—'

'Arturas,' she said.

He sat on the edge of the bed, his legs weakened by her voice. 'Mother.'

'Have you forgotten me?'

'No,' he said.

'Have you forgotten what you promised me?'

'No,' he said.

'Then talk to me.'

Strazdas tried to find the words, but could not.

'Talk to me,' she said again, a hardness in her voice that dislodged a memory he preferred to keep nailed down, not free to roam his mind, crashing into the things he thought he knew. He covered his genitals with his free hand and brought his knees together.

'My driver is dead,' he said. 'A madman killed him.'

'Your driver does not concern me,' she said. 'I am only concerned with the whore who killed my son.'

Strazdas felt pressure in his bladder. 'The police have her,' he said.

He listened to silence for a few seconds before she said, 'You will take her from them.'

'My contact will deal with it,' he said.

'I don't care how you do it,' she said. 'Just know this: you will not return to me until you have done what I have asked. Do you understand?'

A deep itching heat gnawed at his groin, his bladder burning for release. 'I understand.'

'Good,' she said, and hung up.

He dropped the phone and ran to the bathroom, the first drops escaping from him before he could reach the toilet bowl. A shiver coursed through him as he closed his eyes and listened to the sound of water on water.

When his bladder was empty, he showered, the tap set as hot as he could stand it. He returned to the bedroom and retrieved his phone. Daylight had taken hold outside while he'd been gone. He dialled the contact's number one more time and waited for the answering machine.

'One hundred thousand for the whore,' he said.

Less than a minute later, the contact called back.

'It's difficult today,' he said.

'My offer lasts until noon tomorrow,' Strazdas said. 'After that, it's half. The day after, half again.'

'Leave it with me,' the contact said.

266

75

Galya woke from a dense and dreamless sleep and wondered for a few seconds where she was. The memory of where she had been came first, crushing the air from her lungs, followed by the realisation that she was safe.

She lay still for a time, trying not to think about anything but the long bath she had taken before she had come in here to sleep. She had lain in the water for almost an hour, her bandaged feet wrapped in plastic bags and propped on the rim. Songs had come to her mind, songs from her childhood that she sang with her friends. She had hummed them to herself, listening to her voice resonate between the tiled walls.

How long had she been asleep? It seemed as if she had closed her eyes only moments ago, burrowing into the warmth of Susan's bed, but when she opened them the light had changed. She listened to the activity beyond the bedroom door. The two girls laughed in unison. Dishes and pots clanked and clattered. The woman, Susan, cooking. She seemed like a good person, but tired, as if something pained her from within. Galya imagined some of that pain was the fault of Lennon, the police officer who had brought her here.

He was a curious man. A decent man, Galya thought. She wondered if he had brought her to this woman's home, instead of putting her in a cell, as some way of trying to prove his own value to himself. He smiled sometimes, and laughed, and talked, but now and then his thoughts would be elsewhere, his eyes vacant.

Did Galya trust him? She wasn't sure yet, but Susan clearly did, and that would have to do.

She pushed the quilt back and sat up, lowering her feet to the floor as softly as she could. Her soles burned on contact, even with the dressings to shield them. The pain crept up through her ankles and into her calves. Aches and stings nagged at every part of her body.

The clean clothes had been left in a small pile next to the bed. Her own had been taken by the police. Evidence, they had said.

The kind woman who spoke to Galya in the hospital had told her she had nothing to fear from the police. The killing was clearly self-defence, she had said, they would understand that. The man who died had been a criminal. The police would not mourn his passing.

But still, there were procedures, questions to answer. Courtrooms and lawyers. Months in this city, no prospect of going home.

Galya felt tears returning, but she fought them back. She would have no more of that. Not now. There would be plenty of time to weep in the days and weeks ahead.

She dressed in the jeans and T-shirt, both too big for her small shoulders and hips, and leaned on the wall as she eased her feet into the slippers. They provided a little cushioning for her feet as she walked to the door and opened it.

Galya stood for a few seconds, watching. From here she could see through the short hallway to the living room where the girls continued to play beneath the tree. The policeman talked on his mobile phone while Susan arranged plates and cutlery on a table.

Warm food smells caused Galya's tongue to moisten, and her stomach to growl. Cooked meat, hot oil, boiled vegetables. Above it all, the sweetness of sugary things. Galya imagined chocolate and caramel, and had to suppress a joyful giggle with a hand over her mouth. A wave of dizziness swept across her mind, and she steadied herself against the door frame.

Susan looked up from her preparations and smiled. 'Come on,' she said. 'Don't be shy.'

Galya walked slowly to the table, using any surface she could reach for balance. Her stomach burbled again, loud enough for Susan to raise her eyebrows.

'Sit down,' she said. 'You can get a little head start on everyone else.'

Galya lowered herself into one of the chairs, an empty plate in front of her. Susan reached into a tin and scooped up a handful of brightly wrapped sweets. She opened her hand above the plate, the sweets spilling from her fingers like pirates' treasure. Galya unwrapped a green-coloured jewel and took a bite, closed her eyes and let the chocolate melt on her tongue, exhaled through her nose as the corners of her mouth turned upward.

When she opened her eyes, the policeman sat facing her.

'They want you in tonight, ready for interview in the morning,' he said.

The fledgling smile died on her lips.

'We can eat first,' he said. 'But I have to take you in later. I asked if we could hold off until tomorrow, but the head of my MIT, my boss, he wants you in. He's not happy I didn't bring you straight from the hospital.'

Galya asked, 'After, will I come back here?'

The policeman shook his head. 'No,' he said. 'They want you in custody.'

She felt heat in her eyes.

'Don't worry,' Lennon said. 'They should have the Victim Care Suite available by tomorrow. You'll only be in the cells for one night. I'll make sure of it, I promise.'

Galya smiled, though she had a feeling Jack Lennon, like most men, seldom kept his promises.

76

They ate in near silence, the occasional whispering between Ellen and Lucy the only conversation. Lennon watched Galya as she put away more food than he would ever have thought she could manage. She cleared one plate, then simply held it out to Susan who dutifully reloaded it with turkey, ham and roast potatoes. When the dessert came – trifle and ice cream – she devoured a bowlful, one heaped spoon after another. She burped when she had finished, and the girls erupted in laughter.

'Please excuse,' she said.

'Don't worry,' Susan said as she set about gathering up the plates. 'Why don't you go and get some more sleep?'

'Thank you,' Galya said. She looked at them each in turn as she stood. 'All of you.'

Lennon smiled and nodded. 'I think I'll try for a nap too,' he said.

'No, you won't,' Susan said. 'You'll help me clear up.'

Lennon knew protesting would do him no good, so he sighed and collected cutlery and soiled napkins.

As he and Susan piled dishes in the sink, she asked, 'What'll happen to her?'

'She'll be looked after,' Lennon said. 'Even if the Public Prosecution Service goes after her for the killing, she'll hardly do any time. Most likely Care NI will house her while the case is dealt with, then she'll go home when it's all done.'

'And after that?' Susan asked. 'What she's been through, the trauma of it. How is she supposed to cope with that?'

'That's not for us to deal with,' he said, knowing how callous it sounded as he spoke.

'Christ,' Susan said. 'It's like she's just rubbish to be thrown away when you lot are done with her.'

'It's not like that,' Lennon said, even though he knew it was. 'She'll be cared for as well as we can manage. If she was an EU citizen – Polish or Latvian, anything – then she could stay here and get whatever treatment she needs. Counselling, medical care, all of that. But she's Ukrainian. That means as soon as the system's done with her, she has to get out of the country. We can't do any more for her.'

'It's a shitty way to treat a human being,' she said. 'But I know you'll do your best for her.'

Susan slipped an arm around Lennon's waist. He put his around her shoulder and pulled her close.

'Dishes will do till the morning,' she said. 'Fancy a lie-down?'

Lennon looked over his shoulder to the children who now lay in front of the television watching a Harry Potter movie.

'They'll be fine,' Susan said.

Lennon watched his daughter as she rested her chin on her hands, her feet kicking idly in the air. He thought of every girl like Galya he'd used, and remembered they had all once been small and full of wonder.

'I hope so,' he said.

77

The contact said, 'It's in hand. Lennon will leave for the station with the girl. They won't get there.'

'Good,' Strazdas said.

He sat on the floor at the foot of the bed, naked, his knees up to his chin. An icy draught explored his body. He had opened and closed the window a hundred times today. Boiling or freezing, there was no in-between.

'Then I want you on a plane out of here,' the contact said. 'There's a flight from the International Airport to Brussels at eleven in the morning. I'll arrange a taxi for you.'

'All right,' Strazdas said.

'And I want paid,' the contact said.

'Just do what I asked you to do,' Strazdas said. 'Then you will be paid.'

'It'll be done,' the contact said.

Strazdas shivered. 'One more thing,' he said.

'What?'

'I need something.'

'Like what?'

'Herkus would get it for me, but he's dead.'

'What do you need?'

'Coke,' Strazdas said.

He listened to seconds of silence before the contact said, 'Fuck off.'

78

Lennon walked Galya to the car, the warmth of Susan's kiss still lingering on his cheek. A dense fog doused the world in a sickly grey-white, masking the dark sky above. Snow, now freezing as the temperature dropped, crunched under their feet. Galya wore a pair of Susan's old trainers, at least one size too big for her, padded out by thick socks to protect her feet. She held a hooded duffel coat tight around her thin body.

He removed the sheets of cardboard he'd placed over the front and rear windscreens to shield them from the frost and dumped them in the Audi's boot, then held the door for Galya. She thanked him in her soft voice as she settled into the passenger seat.

Lennon checked the time as he fired the ignition. Almost ten. He'd been told they wanted her in before the shift change. Well, they would have to wait a few minutes, he thought. It would be slow going in this weather, and besides, it was Christmas.

The traction-control light flickered on the dashboard as he pulled out from the car park and made the right turn towards the round-about at the bottom of Stranmillis Embankment. Galya sat in silence, buried in the coat, nose and eyes visible in the opening of the hood.

'It'll be all right,' he said, though he wasn't sure if he believed it himself.

She did not answer, staring ahead as he drove along the embankment, the river lost in the fog to their right. The frozen air weighed down on the empty streets around them, exaggerating the quiet. Lennon saw no other cars, no pedestrians braving the cold.

Why had the Duty Officer insisted the girl be brought in tonight? Who was going to come in to question her? When pressed, the Duty Officer said he'd been told to make it happen, and that was that.

Lennon had asked who was doing the telling, and the Duty Officer said DCI Thompson didn't want the girl out in the wild. But a man as lazy as Thompson didn't get worked up about such things unless he was instructed to do so by someone else. Lennon wondered if the 'someone else' might be an old friend from C3 Intelligence Branch trying to make his life difficult.

He slowed the car by shifting down gears, only dabbing the brake pedal, to avoid skidding on the ice and snow. The Audi juddered and groaned as he stopped for the red light south of King's Bridge. Even though there was no one to see it, he flicked his indicator on to cross the river.

The traffic light went from red to amber, and Lennon half-clutched until the Audi started to pull. He released the handbrake on green and eased the car away without skidding, taking his time to reach the second set of lights just a few yards ahead.

'It won't be long till we're there,' he said. He turned his head to Galya, but she did not return his gaze.

'I swear,' he said. 'It'll be all right. They'll look—'

Noise erupted from somewhere out in the fog: the roar of an engine and spinning of wheels. He looked for lights but saw none. A car burst from the grey shroud, an old four-wheel-drive Nissan, its front end lurching from side to side as the driver fought the ice. For a brief second, Lennon thought someone had lost control as their car rolled down the slope from Ridgeway Street. But it gathered speed, and he knew the collision would be no accident.

He stamped on the accelerator and felt the Audi jerk beneath him as its tyres lost their grip on the ice-covered road. The rear end arced outward, turning the nose away from the river. Galya gasped as she realised what was happening. She covered her head with her arms as the other car slammed into the Audi's rear quarter.

Lennon felt rather than heard the bang of the passenger-side airbags deploying as his neck jerked sideways. His head connected with the driver's-side window, and lightning flashed behind his eyes.

He blinked – no idea if seconds or minutes had passed since the impact. His vision blurred and hardened. He listened. The Audi's engine still idled, and some warning signal pinged. He looked around the car. The rear passenger-side window had shattered, the door buckled inward, but the front remained intact. Galya still sat with her head buried in her hands, her breath coming in jagged gulps.

The damage would have been greater if the Nissan had been able to hold a straight and steady course, but the ice had robbed it of grip and speed. On the far side, hazed by the thickening fog and smoke from its engine, Lennon saw the driver's door open. A man emerged, a hood over his head, a scarf around his face. Lennon squinted through the mist as the man raised his hand.

Lennon threw the Audi into first and floored the accelerator. The tyres churned ice before the car hauled away, its rear end sweeping to the right, as the back window cracked and something tore into the roof lining. Galya screamed.

The Audi fishtailed as it fought for traction, and Lennon struggled to remember the driver training he'd received years ago when he'd joined the force. He steered into the slide, eased off the accelerator, and felt the car straighten. Every instinct screamed at him to jam the pedal into the carpet, but he kept control, concentrated on maintaining his course, not sacrificing grip for speed.

He guided the car onto King's Bridge, used the straight to gain momentum, eased back when he felt the rear wheels skitter. As he neared the junction at the far end, he glanced in his rear-view mirror. Through the reflection of the back window's splintered glass he saw headlights pierce the fog, one burning bright, the other dimmed by damage.

The lights turned red as he crossed the junction onto Sunnyside Street, but Lennon ignored them. The Nissan's lights drew closer, its four-wheel-drive clinging to the road better than the Audi could manage.

Lennon thought hard. Streets branched off Sunnyside to form warrens of residential roads, narrow and twisting. The Nissan might have better grip, but its advantage would be lost to the bulk its big wheels had to haul around the corners. Lennon pushed the accelerator as hard as he dared and climbed the shallow incline. The Nissan kept pace, and gained ground.

He slowed as he approached the corner of Deramore Avenue and turned the steering wheel, allowing the Audi to drift a little before straightening and reapplying power. He barely missed the parked cars on either side of the avenue as he guided the Audi into the channel that ran between them. In the mirror he saw the Nissan follow behind, its body leaning as it skidded into the corner. It swiped one parked car, bounced across the street to glance off another before righting itself. Alarms wailed in the night.

Only a few feet separated the Nissan's damaged front grille from the Audi's rear bumper. Lennon pushed the car harder, fought the steering wheel as the back wheels danced on the ice. Up ahead, he saw the corner of Ailesbury Drive as vague shapes in the grey. Beyond that, he knew the hard right into Deramore Gardens would be near impossible, but he had to try.

Lennon offered a silent prayer that no one else would be stupid enough to be on the road on a night like this. He shifted down to third, then second, feeling the car lurch as the engine struggled against the chassis, slowing the Audi with its own weight instead of its brakes. The car juddered as its wheels lost and remade contact with the ice.

He let the Audi coast through the tight left bend under its own momentum, guiding it as best he could with the steering wheel. The nose wouldn't turn in enough, and the wall at the other side of the narrow street loomed in the beam of his headlights. He sucked in air, ready to cry out, but instead the impact came from the rear where the Nissan nudged the back bumper, causing the Audi to veer away from the brickwork and towards the sharp right turn onto Deramore Gardens.

Again, Lennon quashed the urge to jerk the wheel to correct his course, and allowed the car to float until its nose pointed where he wanted it to go. Then he gave the engine more fuel and felt its rear hunker down. He let the air out of his lungs as he made the corner and checked the mirror. The Nissan lurched and swayed as its driver battled the ice until it skidded into Lennon's wake. It bounced from one kerb to the other, teetering as it swerved. Its front left quarter collided with a parked Toyota Celica, the sports car's low bonnet crushed beneath its wheel, and the Nissan pitched to the side, its passenger-side wheels spinning freely in the air.

Lennon watched as the gap between his Audi and the pursuer widened. The Nissan rolled on a few yards, its two earthbound wheels travelling in a drunken arc before it slammed down. Its weight continued to roll with the motion as it swerved on the ice, and its driver's-side wheels left the ground. The darkened windows erupted as it toppled onto its side. It screeched and skidded until a stationary Transit van halted it.

No one emerged as Lennon slowed and watched in his mirror. He decided against hanging around and turned off the avenue to find safety.

79

Edwin Paynter felt the time had come. When he closed his eyes he heard the Angel of the Lord speak to him in whispers that would sound to anyone else like soft footsteps on the hospital floor, or water in the pipes, or the swishing of doors opening and closing. But to Paynter they were commands, holy words, divine instructions.

Just as for the Apostle Peter two thousand years before him, the Angel of the Lord would guide his hand.

Almost twenty-four hours they'd kept him. Observation, the doctors had said, to ensure there were no complications caused by concussion. Paynter had lain there quietly throughout, first in triage, then in the corridor, then in the orthopaedic room, then in the A&E bay, then in the admissions ward, hidden behind a thin plastic curtain from the miserable specimens who occupied the other beds.

But now they were releasing him from the hospital, and now was the time to free himself from the fools who believed they held him captive.

One of the police officers set about undoing the handcuffs that bound his left wrist to the bed. The other, at least ten years younger than his sour-faced partner, watched from the foot of the bed, one hand on the butt of his pistol. Paynter had been studying the weapons all day long, through three different pairs of policemen as they changed shifts. He was certain it was the same kind of gun he had fired the night before, and that he would be able to operate it. That would be the key to his freedom, the Angel of the Lord had told him: to seize the pistol and use it.

And after? That was a question only God above could answer.

The Angel of the Lord said, *Begin.*

'I don't feel well,' Paynter said.

The policeman did not acknowledge the statement. 'Sit up,' he said.

Paynter coughed and grimaced.

'I said sit up,' the policeman repeated, keeping a grip on the bracelet he'd removed from the bed frame. The other remained on Paynter's wrist.

Paynter heaved his torso up from the bed. 'I don't feel well,' he said again. 'Really, I don't.'

He let his feet drop to the floor. He quickened his breathing. He swallowed hard.

'Don't start,' the policeman said. 'You can pish and whine all you want, but you're coming with us.'

'Please,' Paynter said. 'I need a doctor.'

'Shut your mouth and stand up.'

Paynter struggled to his feet, stumbled against the officer, groaned. The policeman pushed him away, said, 'Get to fuck.'

Paynter fell back against the bed but kept his footing. He grabbed the officer's arm with his free hand.

'I'm sick,' he said. 'I need—'

'Turn around,' the officer said, jerking Paynter's other wrist with the still-attached handcuff. He spoke to his colleague. 'Give us a hand here, will you?'

The other policeman approached and took Paynter's free arm in his hard hands.

Now, the Angel of the Lord said.

Paynter rolled his eyes back, let his legs go loose, his weight taking the policemen by surprise. The bed rolled away on its castors, pushing aside the curtain that surrounded it. Paynter's body followed as it sagged to the floor. The policemen's hands grabbed at his clothing, slowing his fall until he lay at their feet.

A nurse, alerted by the commotion, whipped aside the curtain and approached the scuffle.

The key to faking a seizure, Paynter had learned, was to concentrate the spasms on the stomach area, with all other movements radiating from that point. He ground his teeth together, forced his tongue to the back of his mouth, and bucked, his abdominal muscles tensing and relaxing, his legs kicking out.

'He's taking the piss,' the older officer said.

'I don't know,' the younger man said, crouching down beside Paynter. 'He looks bad.'

The nurse tried to work her way between them. 'Let me see,' she said. 'Give me some room.'

Paynter intensified his movements, forcing air hard between his teeth, growling from deep in his throat. He kept his hands in front of his chest, the fingers hooked like claws. The older officer held on to the bracelet, tried to grab the other wrist, but lost his balance as Paynter rolled away from him.

Neither policeman realised the younger officer had lost his pistol until Paynter's seizure stopped dead and he shoved the older man back. He stood, the weapon held at his side, aimed at the floor.

The nurse screamed.

The younger officer scrambled back. 'Jesus, he's got my gun!'

The older officer hauled himself to his feet and snatched his own pistol from its holster. He raised it, aimed square at Paynter's chest.

Patients and their visitors gasped and shrieked.

Paynter kept the gun aimed downward. They wouldn't shoot if he didn't point it at them. He had to gamble on that, if he was to be free.

'Fucking drop it,' the officer said.

Tell him no, the Angel of the Lord said.

'No,' Paynter said.

The officer realigned his aim on Paynter's forehead. 'Drop it or I'll shoot.'

Tell him no.

'No,' Paynter said.

Slowly, bending his arm at the elbow, he raised the pistol, keeping its muzzle away from the policeman facing him until it aimed at the ceiling.

'I'll fucking shoot you,' the officer said.

No, he won't.

'No, you won't,' Paynter said.

Freedom was his, whether or not the policemen or any of the onlookers realised it. He had rehearsed this moment in his mind for almost twenty-four hours, practised every movement, every word, guided by the whispering voices.

A warmth settled on his heart, something he perceived to be peace, as he remembered the words he had prepared.

Speak now, the Angel of the Lord said.

'My name is Edwin Alan Paynter,' he said. 'I have delivered eight women to the Lord: three in Salford, five in Belfast.'

'For Christ's sake, drop the gun,' the officer said.

Paynter ignored him, remembering what he'd watched the foreigner in his cellar do just hours ago. He brought his free hand to the pistol's slide assembly, pulled it back, felt metal parts move and click into place, and said, 'They will thank me when I see them in His arms.'

The officer took a step closer. 'I will shoot you dead, do you hear me?'

'You cannot hold me,' Paynter said. 'Your prisons cannot hold me. The Angel of the Lord will set me free.'

He did not hear the screams of those around him as he brought the muzzle to his lips, slipped it between his teeth, pressed it to the roof of his mouth.

He tasted oil and metal, felt the Angel of the Lord's kiss upon his cheek.

He squeezed the trigger.

PART FOUR: JACK

80

Galya waited in the passenger seat as Lennon examined the car's rear. Even with the coat wrapped tight around her, she felt the night's cold dark fingers creep in through the broken window behind her. She shivered through the fatigue that racked her body. Too exhausted to be afraid, all she wanted now was sleep.

Lennon opened the driver's door and lowered himself in. 'It's not that bad,' he said, his breath misting. 'It'll drive, anyway.'

They had toured the streets for half an hour, winding from one row of darkened houses to another, the policeman constantly watching his rear-view mirror until he was certain they were not being followed. Only then did he stop to check the damage.

He restarted the engine and pulled away from the kerb, once more picking his way through the frozen streets.

After several minutes of silence, Galya asked, 'Who was that?'

'I don't know,' Lennon said. 'But I know who sent him.'

'Who?'

'Arturas Strazdas,' he said. 'The brother of the man you killed.'

The woman at the hospital had explained the aftermath of Galya's actions to her in a soft sad voice. At the time it had seemed like a story, a tale about some other girl who had been brought to a strange city to be bought and sold.

'I didn't want to kill that man,' Galya said. 'I didn't want these things to happen.'

'I know you didn't,' Lennon said. 'But I don't think that matters to him.'

He turned left onto a roundabout, then exited to a long straight road. The car slowed as they approached a cluster of buildings surrounded by a high wall. Floodlights cut through the fog that covered the site. Next to a closed pair of gates were emblazoned the words LADAS DRIVE STATION, POLICE SERVICE OF NORTHERN IRELAND.

The car halted. Lennon shut the engine off. He stared at the building.

'Is this where you're taking me?' Galya asked.

'Yes,' Lennon said. 'It was, anyway.'

'Was?'

He sat silent for a moment, his forearms resting on the steering wheel, thinking, his breath misting the car's windscreen.

'Please, what is wrong?'

He did not answer.

'Out here, on the streets, it is not safe,' Galya said. 'We should go in that place.'

'No,' Lennon said.

'Why?' Galya asked.

He took a mobile phone from his pocket and searched for a number.

81

The telephone jarred Strazdas from his bloodied dreams. He sat upright on the bed, still naked, still sweating and shivering. His heart hammered in his chest as his lungs tried to catch up. A splintering spear of pain shot from the centre of his forehead to the base of his skull to dissipate through his neck and shoulders. He pressed the heel of his hand to his brow.

The phone rang again. Strazdas checked the clock: almost eleven. He had slept for less than an hour. That made no more than three hours out of the previous seventy-two.

He reached for the phone before it could tear at his nerves again with its shrill voice.

'Yes?'

'Good evening, Mr Strazdas, reception calling. I have a Mr Lennon on the line. Shall I put him through?'

Strazdas swallowed. 'Yes.'

'Go ahead,' the receptionist said.

'You should hire some better help,' Lennon said.

'I don't know what you mean,' Strazdas said.

'I mean whoever you sent to do your dirty work, they fucked it up.'

'I don't know what you refer to.'

'We got away, the girl and me.'

'Which girl?'

'I've been thinking, though.'

'Mr Lennon, perhaps you should talk to my—'

'How would he know I'd been called back to the station?' Lennon asked.

'You should talk to my lawyer, the gentleman you met—'

'And how would he know what route I'd take?'

'Mr Lennon, I am going to hang up now.'

'Is it Dan Hewitt? Is that who you've got inside? He sold me out before, and he'd do it ag—'

Strazdas returned the handset to its cradle and cursed the soul of his brother for getting himself killed in this wretched place.

82

Lennon returned the phone to his coat pocket. As he did so, he felt the passport tucked in there. He withdrew it and opened it to the data page, the image of a girl looking back at him through the laminate. A girl who did not sit next to him in the Audi's passenger seat. But she had those blue eyes, the almost unnaturally fine features, the high cheekbones, the yellow hair.

He turned his gaze to Galya, held the passport up close to her face so he could see them together.

'What do you look at?' she asked.

'It might be enough,' he said.

'What is enough?'

'That I'm a fucking idiot,' he said as he put the car into gear and drove past the gates of the police station, leaving it behind until the fog swallowed it.

Lennon took the Crumlin Road, then the Ligoniel Road, heading west into the countryside instead of north towards the motorway, stopping only once to use a cashpoint. The damaged car would attract traffic cops on the lookout for Christmas drunk drivers and he couldn't risk being pulled over.

The motorway would have been faster, better lit with less ice, but the back roads carried less traffic. He kept his speed down, watched for ice, and studied road signs. Even on these roads, the journey should have been no more than forty to forty-five minutes, but the conditions meant they'd been travelling that long with no sign of their destination when Lennon's mobile rang.

He checked the display. Sergeant Connolly's number.

Why was he calling? He should have been at home with his family, enjoying Christmas like any other normal human.

'What's up?' Lennon asked.

'Where are you?' Connolly asked.

'Driving,' Lennon said. He kept one hand on the wheel, his eyes on the fog-shrouded road.

'I called Ladas Drive – they said you were due there.'

'I didn't make it that far yet,' Lennon said, avoiding the truth. 'The weather.'

'Well, something's come up,' Connolly said. 'I got a call from a mate, a constable I was paired with when I came out of Garnerville. He was one of the boys watching Paynter at the hospital. I thought you'd want to know what he said.'

'Go on,' Lennon said.

'Paynter committed suicide.'

Lennon eased the Audi to the side of the road, slowed to a halt, flicked his hazard lights on.

'How?' he asked.

'He faked a seizure,' Connolly said. 'In the commotion he managed to grab an officer's Glock. There was a stand-off for a minute or two – at least, that's what I was told – and they thought he was going to make a break for it.'

'But he didn't,' Lennon said.

'No,' Connolly said. 'He announced that he'd killed eight women, and had no regrets about it. Then he put the gun in his mouth and blew his brains out.'

'Christ,' Lennon said.

'Anyway, I thought you'd want to know straight away.'

'Yeah, thanks,' Lennon said. 'Here, listen.'

'Yeah?'

'I might be off work for a few days. Maybe longer.'

'What, now? But there's—'

'You'll know all about it tomorrow. Just do me a favour, all right?'

'What's that?'

'Watch your back,' Lennon said. 'Things could get tricky over this case. Just be careful what you say and who you say it to. Especially if anyone from Special Branch comes calling.'

'C3?' Connolly asked. 'What's Paynter got to do with them?'

'It's complicated,' Lennon said. 'Just keep your head down, all right?'

'All right,' Connolly said. 'Listen, Inspector, are you okay? You've been good to me, so, you know, if there's anything I can do for you, I will.'

'I'm fine,' Lennon said. 'Don't worry about me. Just look out for yourself.'

He hung up and dropped the phone into the car's cup holder. Galya stirred in the seat next to him. She'd fallen asleep before the city had faded from around them. Now she watched him with confused and heavy eyes.

'Something has happened?' she asked.

He considered keeping it from her, but knew there was no point. She faced enough dangers. Knowing one of them had died couldn't hurt her.

'Edwin Paynter,' he said. 'The man who kept you in that house. He's dead. He killed himself.'

She made the sign of the cross and stared straight ahead, no emotion on her face.

'He deserved to die,' Lennon said. 'For what he did to you. And maybe some others.'

'No,' she said. 'Only God makes to die. It's not your thing to say. Not his thing. Only God's.'

Lennon hadn't the will to argue the point, so he put the Audi into gear and released the hand brake. Ten, fifteen minutes, he thought, and they'd be at the guest house. He set off into the fog, wishing he believed in her childish dream of justice.

83

Galya spent the rest of the journey in thought. The man who had held her captive had called himself a pastor, a Christian, but she wondered if he even had a soul. If he did, where had it gone when he took his own life?

How did she feel about his death? Relief? Satisfaction? Pity? All of those things, but if she looked deep into her heart she also felt anger. Anger that he would not face her and know that she had got the better of him.

She scolded herself for gloating, even if it was only in her own mind. Mama had not raised her to be spiteful. But she had survived, and she could at least be proud. Galya let her mind wander, imagined she had died back there in that cellar and this grey world was her afterlife, journeying for ever in darkness and mist. The urge to cry came upon her, and she closed her eyes against it.

When she opened them again, they had pulled into a courtyard overlooked by a grand country house. Lennon parked the car in the farthest corner, beneath the boughs of a winter-stripped tree.

'We're here,' he said.

He climbed out, closed his door, and walked around the car. Galya allowed him to take her hand and help her to her feet. The horizon glowed with a mass of lights, iridescent in the fog.

'What is over there?' she asked.

'The airport,' Lennon said.

'Where is this?' she asked.

'It's a guest house,' he said. 'Like a hotel. We're staying here tonight. Come on, let's get out of the cold.'

He closed the car, locked it, and guided Galya towards the house. Lights burned behind closed curtains on the ground floor. Lennon pressed a doorbell. A few moments later a curtain peeled back at one of the windows, and a lady of senior years peered out.

The curtain fell back into place before a light came on in the hall, visible through the rippled glass of the door. The lady's silhouette appeared on the other side. She slid a security chain into place and opened the door by a few inches, worry written plain on her face.

'Can I help you?' she asked.

'We need a room,' Lennon said.

'At this time?' she asked, her eyebrows arching upwards. 'On Christmas night?'

'I know it's last-minute,' Lennon said. He placed his arm around Galya's shoulder. 'My girlfriend's mother, back in Latvia. She's taken ill. We've a flight first thing in the morning.'

She looked at each of them in turn. 'Well, seeing as I've no stable or manger for you, I'd better let you in. Should I be expecting three wise men?'

84

Lennon thanked God that Galya had the sense to hold her questions until they got to the room. Once inside, she ignored the flowery curtains and stale-cabbage smell of the place and sat on the end of the bed.

'Where will we fly to?' she asked.

'Not we,' Lennon said. 'Just you.'

'Where will *I* fly to?'

'I don't know,' he said, pacing in front of her. 'The earliest flight I can get you. As close to your home as I can get you.'

'Why? Because of that man in the car?'

'Yes,' Lennon said. 'Strazdas has someone on the inside. It's the only way anyone could have known to come after us when we drove to the station. And I've a good idea who it is.'

'Who?' she asked.

He opened his mouth to tell her it was DCI Dan Hewitt of C3 Intelligence Branch, but realised the knowledge could bring her greater danger than she already faced.

'Just someone,' he said.

'A bad man?'

'Yes,' Lennon said. 'He used to be a friend of mine. He's dirty.'

'Dirty?'

'He takes bribes, money, from bad people.'

'Will you arrest him?' she asked. 'Put him in prison?'

Lennon laughed in spite of himself. 'It's not as easy as that. And he has a grudge against me.'

'You mean he doesn't like you?' She smirked. 'I think you don't like him.'

'No, I don't,' Lennon said. 'But if I'm right, then no police station is safe for you. It means you have to get out of here. Go home.'

She nodded. 'Home. I want to go home and see my brother. But you will be in trouble.'

'Maybe,' Lennon said. 'Probably. But I'm getting you on a plane anyway.'

The landlady showed Lennon to the computer in the guest-house lounge. It was an old machine, and the internet connection crawled, but within a few minutes he had established that the only flight that could do Galya any good was a seven a.m. plane to Kraków. He knew nothing about public transport in Eastern Europe, but he had to hope she could get a train from there to Kiev, and from there to whatever village she came from.

But the price. He had a moment of panic as he tried to remember how much credit he had left on his MasterCard. Not much, but maybe enough. He wouldn't know until he tried, when the website would either accept or reject his payment.

Relief came as he entered the card number and he was presented with the confirmation page, and a link for online check-in. It seemed to take an age for the ancient printer to spit out a fuzzy bar code on an A4 page.

The landlady watched from the doorway as he worked. 'All done?' she asked when he stood up.

'Yes, thank you,' he said. 'Sorry to have disturbed your Christmas.'

'Don't worry,' she said. She brushed his arm as he passed. 'She seems like a nice girl. I hope you can sort out whatever trouble you're in.'

Lennon almost argued, almost said there was no trouble other than the ill mother he'd told her about when they arrived. Instead, he said, 'So do I.'

Lennon climbed the two flights of stairs to the room and paused outside the door. Susan would be waiting for him. He'd promised he would join her on the sofa when he returned, drink some wine with her while their respective little girls slept. With a sigh, he took his phone from his pocket. She answered on the first ring.

'Something's come up,' he said.

'Doesn't it always?' she asked, and disconnected.

'Fuck,' he said to himself.

Galya lay sound asleep when he entered the room. He took a seat by the window, facing the door. He placed his Glock on the table next to him and set the alarm on his phone for six.

Five and a half hours' sleep, if he was lucky. But he had never been lucky.

85

After an hour of phone calls, and another hour of self-punishment, Arturas Strazdas began to pull himself together. He had been through the process before, reassembling himself from the pieces that had scattered over the previous hours and days.

He always began with a period of silence and contemplation. Sitting quite still, counting every wound he had inflicted on himself, remembering that he was a sane man and sane men did not harm themselves like this. Sane men channelled their rage, used it to fuel their lives, not destroy them.

The contact had said the girl's elimination was now a matter of when, not if. Strazdas had no reason to stay in this city a minute longer than necessary. He should be in the taxi provided for him, the contact said, and on his way to the airport by ten in the morning. If not, a police car would come for him instead. And that would take him to a station for questioning.

One or the other, the contact said, simple as that.

So Strazdas took him at his word and set about his own reconstruction.

Once he felt sufficiently balanced in his mind, he shaved and showered before dressing himself in a fresh shirt and his good travel suit. His stomach gurgled, and he checked the bedside clock.

Almost five in the morning.

Would they provide room service at this time? Some toast, perhaps, and a boiled egg?

He would try. A sane man has to eat. And Arturas Strazdas was, most definitely, a sane man.

86

Fog still lay heavy on the courtyard when Lennon helped Galya to the car, dawn two hours away yet. Ten minutes to the airport, he said, then she had half an hour to get through security and onto the plane. He pressed the documents into her hand. She had to go into the terminal herself, he said, and walk straight to security. All she had to do was show them the printed boarding pass and her passport.

Simple, he said.

Galya did not believe him.

She remained silent as Lennon drove. The car's headlights barely penetrated the fog, and the hot water he'd poured on the windows to defrost them had frozen, making the darkened world seem to ripple and distort.

The vague form of the airport emerged ahead, revealed only by the glowing haze of its lights. Lennon steered into a car park facing the terminal. Galya could barely make out the shape of the building, and could see no one walking to or from it, but she knew they were there, hidden by the grey.

Lennon shut off the engine. He reached into his pocket and handed her a paper bundle. When she felt the coarseness and weight of it, she knew it was money.

'Three hundred and fifty,' he said. 'It's all I had. You should be able to change it in Kraków and get a train to Kiev. Once you get home, take your brother and leave. Don't stay there. Strazdas will find you if you do.'

'Mama's farm,' she said. 'It's our home. Where will we live?'

'I don't know,' Lennon said. 'You'll figure it out. You're smart and you're strong. You'll know what to do when you get there.'

Galya thought about it and realised that yes, she would. Back home, the man who Mama owed so much money to, he could take the farm. Galya and her brother would be free of him and his debt. She could live with that. She looked at Lennon's lined face, saw the scars beneath his skin.

'Your friend Susan,' she said.

Lennon paused, then asked, 'What about her?'

'You should make her happy,' Galya said. 'Then she will make you happy.'

Lennon smiled. 'Maybe,' he said.

'No maybe,' she said. 'Only yes.'

'Let's go,' Lennon said, reaching for the door handle. 'You need to get on that plane.'

He climbed out and walked around to the passenger side, opened the door, and helped her out.

'Remember,' he said as he closed the door. 'Don't talk to anyone if you don't have to. Go straight to security. They should be boarding by the time you get through. Go straight to the gate and get on the plane. That's all you have to do.'

'Thank you,' Galya said. She hesitated a moment, then wrapped her arms around his broad shoulders.

He resisted for a moment, then returned the hug.

'Make Susan happy,' she said.

'I'll try,' he said.

A few feet away, his voice deadened by the cold, someone said, 'Jack.'

87

Lennon looked for the source of the voice, moved between it and Galya, one hand already reaching for the holster attached to his belt.

The tall and slender shape of a man stood beyond the Audi. He limped forward, his left hand raised, a revolver gripped in it, his right arm held tight to his side as if it pained him. Dried blood drew deep red lines across his cheek, cuts and grazes criss-crossed his forehead and jawline, his hooded jacket torn.

'Connolly,' Lennon said.

He reached behind with one hand and shoved Galya away, his other freeing his Glock from its holster.

'I'm sorry, Jack,' Connolly said.

The first shot hit Lennon's left shoulder like a punch from a heavyweight, threw him against the Audi. He kept his legs under him as adrenalin hit his system ahead of the pain. By instinct, his right hand came up, his Glock aimed square on Connolly's chest. Before he could get a round off he felt a punch to his gut, then another, and his legs deserted him.

Lennon went down on his back, his right hand still raised. In the periphery of his vision, he saw Galya crouch over him, her mouth wide, but he heard no scream.

'Run,' he said.

Connolly entered his line of sight, his pistol aimed not at Lennon but somewhere over his head.

'Run,' Lennon said again. 'Now.'

He fired at Connolly's body, no idea if his aim was true or not. Connolly jerked and fell against the side of the van, his face twisted in pain.

Lennon took a breath, held it, steadied his right hand, the Glock's sight lined on Connolly's chest. Connolly brought his left hand up, the pistol looking back at Lennon. As a hard chill spread from Lennon's gut, he squeezed the trigger, saw Connolly's gun's muzzle flash, saw him go down, saw a deep cold blackness where the world had once been.

88

Galya ran at first, her mind closed to the pain, the money and documents clutched to her chest. She slowed to a walk as the building came into view. She crossed the road that cut in front of the terminal entrance. Airport policemen ran into the fog, following the sound of the gunfire. They did not notice her.

The doors swished aside and a flood of warmth washed over her. More policemen hurried to the exit, static chatter on their radios, concern on their faces. Still, they did not notice her.

She followed a sign saying *Departures*. The arrows led her through shops and restaurants, people drinking coffee, eating toast, cases stacked on trolleys. They did not know the world they lived in, the dangers that hid beyond their vision.

Galya did.

But she kept that knowledge buried, forced it down inside, in case it might show on her face as she approached the security man who waited ahead.

'Boarding pass, please,' he said.

Galya handed it over.

He looked at her clothing, a glimmer of distaste on his features. Galya read his thoughts. Just another migrant, another miserable parasite leaving its host now the money had burnt away.

She smiled for him when he scanned the pass and handed it back.

'Better get a shake on,' he said. 'It's probably boarding by now.'

'Thank you,' Galya said.

She joined the short queue for the security search, obediently placed the shoes and coat that Susan had given her in the trays provided, the bandages on her feet hidden by thick socks, and patiently waited until it was her turn to pass through the magnetic gate. On the other side she did not complain when the female security guard patted her down.

A short walk took her to the departure gate where a flight attendant gave her documents only the briefest of glances. Another walk across the tarmac to the aeroplane, and then she boarded. She found row twelve and sat down.

When the lady in the seat next to her asked if she was all right, Galya said yes, thank you, and wiped the tears from her cheeks with her sleeve.

Everyone believes in God when they fly, she thought.

She said a prayer for Jack Lennon's soul.

89

Strazdas sat in the hotel foyer, his suitcase at his feet. Eight forty-five, the contact had said. He checked his watch. Eight forty-seven.

His phone rang.

'The taxi is on its way,' the contact said. 'Get in it, get on the plane.'

'And the girl?'

'I suggest you give the driver a decent tip,' the contact said. 'It's Boxing Day, after all. He's done me many favours in the past.'

'What about the girl?' Strazdas asked.

Silence for a moment, then, 'She got away. It went wrong.'

Strazdas took his knuckle between his teeth and bit down hard, tasted salt. He breathed through his nose, a low groan resonating in his throat.

'It's done, and that's all there is to it. A good man died in the process. Just remember that. He wouldn't have had to but for your stupid bloody vendetta. Now let it go.'

Strazdas noticed the receptionist's attention on him. He forced himself to release his knuckle from his teeth. Something hot dripped on his chin. He wiped it away and smiled at her. She turned her gaze back to her paperwork.

'You hear me, Arturas?' the contact asked. 'It's over. There's nothing more can be done.'

'There is one thing,' Strazdas said. 'I will send a letter to your superiors. I will name you as Detective Chief Inspector Daniel Hewitt. I will enclose a record of all the payments you have received over the last eighteen months. Those payments will not be traceable to me or any of my companies, but they will cause your superiors to examine your bank accounts, your investments, your lifestyle.'

Strazdas saw the taxi pull up beyond the hotel's doors.

'Be careful, Arturas,' the contact said. 'Once these things are spoken, they can never be taken back.'

'Goodbye,' Strazdas said. 'I have a flight to catch.'

90

It all came at Lennon as flashes of light, images, tableaux, faces, smears of waking, all of it punctuated by the pain.

First the sky, lost in fog, but all the blacker for it. Then the policemen gathered around him, fingers in his mouth, his head moving through no will of his own. The need to cough, and the agony as it seemed to tear him in two.

Next, the inside of the ambulance, lights so bright they cut into his skull and burrowed into his brain. The paramedics busy around him, the oxygen mask that made him feel as if he were drowning.

Then the hospital, more lights, nurses and doctors, more probing, the urgent voices, the bloody swabs, a long needle that pierced his chest, whines and beeps, then a constant high tone, like a string made of cotton and noise that stretched on and on until it faded to black, and he thought of Ellen and how he wished he'd known her all her life, and Susan with her sad eyes and how he'd like to see them once more but the darkness was so warm like a bed on a cold morning and—

Then a lightning crack, and he was back with the pain and the bright punishing lights, then another mask, and he was gone again.

91

The driver did not speak when he took Strazdas's case, nor on the journey towards the airport. The vehicle looked like the cabs that worked the streets of London, but he had seen many of them in Belfast from the window of his hotel room. A perspex screen separated him from the squat man with the pimpled neck who gripped the steering wheel.

As they travelled, Strazdas pondered what he might say to his mother. The very thought made his scrotum shrivel within his trousers and his bladder ache. Most likely he would say nothing, yet. When he landed in Brussels he would immediately seek out a flight to some other destination. From there he would begin tracing records of the girl: who had supplied her to Aleksander, where she came from, her family, anything that might help him track her down.

If he was lucky she would return home, and there she would be vulnerable. And once her stain was wiped from his mind, he could return to his mother, an honourable son.

Daylight seemed to struggle for a way through the fog, but Strazdas could feel rather than see that the taxi had settled onto a long straight when the driver looked up at his mirror.

'Fuck,' he said.

Strazdas turned in his seat to look out of the rear window. He saw the flashing blue lights first, then the silhouette of the car solidifying in the murk. A siren whooped.

The driver flicked an indicator on and applied his foot to the brake.

'What are you doing?' Strazdas asked.

'I'm pulling in,' the driver said. 'What the fuck do you think I'm doing?'

'No,' Strazdas said. 'Keep going.'

'Your arse,' the driver said as the taxi mounted the hard shoulder and slowed to a halt.

The car eased up behind and its lights died. The driver's door opened and a suited man climbed out. As he limped up alongside the taxi, the driver wound his window down. The suited man looked along the road in one direction, then the other.

The driver asked, 'Jesus, Dan, what's going on? You scared me there. I thought I was getting a ticket. I can't afford any points on my—'

Hewitt pulled a pistol from his waistband, aimed at the driver's forehead, and pulled the trigger.

Strazdas moved before he heard the shot, grabbed the passenger-side door handle, and threw himself out of the taxi. He hit the ground shoulder first, hauled himself up on his feet, and lurched up the grass embankment, his feet slipping on the snow.

A gunshot cracked through the cold air, and something slammed Strazdas's leg from beneath him. He howled as he fell back and rolled down the slope towards the still-idling taxi. The icy tarmac of the hard shoulder scraped at his hands and knees before he came to rest by the taxi's rear wheel. He tried to squirm his way underneath the vehicle, but a hand grabbed his ankle and hauled him back.

Hewitt stood over Strazdas, the pistol staring at the point between the supine man's eyes.

'I won't send any letter,' Strazdas said. 'It was only talk. I won't, I swear on my mother's life.'

'Too late for that,' Hewitt said.

Strazdas screamed.

Two hammer blows to his chest, and he could no longer beg, could no longer scream, only watch as Hewitt stepped closer and leaned in. He felt the heat of the muzzle against his forehead, smelled the cordite, and cursed his mother to hell.

92

Susan waited by Lennon's bedside when he woke, Ellen in her lap.

'Welcome back,' she said.

'Where am I?' he asked.

'The Royal,' she said. 'They moved you here from Antrim hospital two days ago.'

'I don't remember,' he said, his voice cutting through his throat like sandpaper.

'I'm not surprised,' she said. 'They had you doped up to the eyeballs.'

'Were you there?'

'Yes,' she said. 'I held your hand in the ambulance. I've been with you every day.'

'How long?'

Susan smiled. 'Well, I wished myself a happy new year last night.'

'Thank you,' Lennon said.

She nodded.

Lennon looked at his daughter. He forced a smile for her. 'Hiya,' he said.

She kept her expression blank. 'Hiya.'

'You been a good girl?' he asked.

She smiled then, and said, 'Mm-hm.'

He reached his right hand out towards her. She gripped two of his fingers in hers. He went to say something, he was sure it was important, but sleep outran his words.

Two days later, CI Uprichard sat by Lennon's bed.

'The standard of visitors is going downhill very badly,' Lennon said.

'It's going to get worse,' Uprichard said. 'You get yourself into some messes.'

'How bad?' Lennon asked.

'Don't worry too much about it now,' Uprichard said. 'Just concentrate on getting better. That's the best you can do at the moment.'

'How bad?' Lennon asked again.

Uprichard sighed. 'Pretty bad. The way things look right now, I can't see a way out for you. Helping that girl flee the jurisdiction was probably enough to end your days as a police officer, but with young Connolly's death, even if it was self-defence . . . Well, you better have a hell of a case to present to the inquiry.'

'Has anyone looked into Connolly?' Lennon asked. 'Why was he there?'

'His wife gave a statement,' Uprichard said. 'And we got access to his bank accounts. They were in debt up to their eyeballs. Loans, credit cards, three months behind on their rent. Then two big deposits from an offshore account, one of them sent on Christmas Eve that didn't clear until after the holiday. His wife said they were close to being put out of their house, and then he told her he'd found a way to make the cash for a deposit on a place of their own. It looks like someone was paying him good money to go after you.'

'It was Dan Hewitt,' Lennon said.

Uprichard stood up. 'I didn't hear you say that.'

'It was Hewitt. He was working for Strazdas. He put Connolly up to it.'

'Proof, Jack,' Uprichard said, waving a finger in Lennon's direction. 'Evidence. Unless you've got plenty of it, don't you dare blacken a good officer's name.'

'It was him,' Lennon said. 'I'm going to get him. I'm going to bring him down.'

'Enough!' Uprichard's face reddened. 'Enough of that. I won't listen to it.'

He put his head down and bulled his way to the door. He paused, his shoulders rising and falling with his anger. Eventually, he allowed Lennon a backward glance.

'I almost forgot,' he said. 'I have something for you.'

Uprichard returned to the bed without looking Lennon in the eye. He dropped an envelope onto the sheets. Lennon picked it up, turned it in his hands. It was addressed to Police Man Jack Lennon, Ladas Drive Police Station, Belfast, Northern Ireland. The postmark said Kyyiv.

'I looked it up,' Uprichard said. 'It's Kiev. It came this morning. I thought you might want to see it.'

'Yes,' Lennon said. 'Thank you.'

Uprichard shuffled his feet. 'Well, I'll leave you to it, then. Get well, Jack. You'll need to be fit as you can to get out of this hole you've dug for yourself.'

When he was alone, Lennon examined the envelope, studied the neat girlish handwriting. He started to open it, but found his eyes too heavy to hold, too dry. He looked up at the clock opposite his bed.

Right on cue, a nurse entered the room ready to release a dose of painkiller into the IV drip that hooked into his hand. Once she did, he would fall into a fathomless dark sleep.

'What have you got there?' she asked.

'A letter from a friend,' he said.

'Do you want to read it before I hit you up and you go bye-byes?'

Lennon placed the letter on the bedside locker.

'For later,' he said.

Epilogue

Dear Jack Lennon,

I write this letter in a city south of my old home in Andriivka, near to Sumy. I will not write the name. Now this city is my home, and the home of my brother Maksim.

I hope that you are alive. I pray to God that you are alive. I think you are not, but I will write this letter anyway.

For to come home was five days. The train goes from Kraków to Warsaw. It goes from Warsaw to Kyyiv, and then another goes to Sumy. I sleep on the train. I have dreams about the man who took me in his house. I think I will always have dreams about him, but they will get better.

When I come home Maksim is happy. He was afraid for me, and now he is not. I do not tell him what happens in Belfast. I tell him I could find no job. I tell him I had a car accident.

I tell the man who lends money he can take Mama's farm. We leave there and come to this city on a bus. Today, I have a job in a cafe. I will have only small money, but I will pay for a room for us. Soon Maksim will have a job also, and he will go to school to learn English like me.

We will be safe. I will be safe.

Some time when I sleep I dream about you and Susan. I hope you are alive so you will make her happy and she will make you happy. Be kind with her and your small girls. You will be happy.

Thank you.

Galya Petrova.

Acknowledgements

Many thanks to all who have helped bring this book into existence:

As ever, my deepest gratitude goes to Nat Sobel, Judith Weber and all at Sobel Weber Associates for their support, guidance and friendship. I couldn't navigate these waters without you.

Caspian Dennis and all at the Abner Stein agency for everything they do for me.

Geoff Mulligan, Briony Everroad, Alison Hennessey, Kate Bland, Ruth Warburton, Vicki Watson and all at Harvill Secker and Vintage Books for their kindness and support.

Bronwen Hruska, Juliet Grames, Justin Hargett, Ailen Lujo and all at Soho Press for treating me so well and showing just what a passionate publisher can achieve.

Betsy Dornbusch for still being my friend even when I sometimes don't show that I appreciate it, and to Carlin, Alex and Gracie for helping me explore San Francisco.

My Soho Press touring buddies James Benn, Henry Chang and Jassy Mackenzie for making the road a much less lonely place.

David Torrans and all at No Alibis for keeping on keeping on.

All the indie bookstores across America who have made me welcome both in print and in person.

The online community of readers and writers who continue to fly the flag.

Hilary Knight for her friendship and hard work.

Sidney McKnight for letting me in on the secret of the buttermilk shandy. But no, I won't be trying one.

James and Louise Morrow for being there when it mattered.

My mother, and the rest of the clan, for just about everything.

Jim, Sally and all the Atkinson family for letting me steal their daughter.

And my beautiful wife Jo for making me happier than I ever deserved to be.

Finally, the book *Selling Olga* by Louisa Waugh (Phoenix) helped me enormously in researching this novel.